Angie Situation

(INNOCENCE)

Angela Sherice

KARMAIC PUBLISHING

Library of Congress Pre Assigned Control Number
LCCN 2010925624

p. cm.

by Angela Sherice.

Sherice.

Angie Situation (INNOCENCE)

ISBN: 978-09709806-6-3 (KARMAPUB) Angela Sherice

KARMAIC PUBLISHING
UNITED STATES OF AMERICA

Cover art and design by Angela Sherice
Author photo by Angela Sherice
Written and edited by Angela Sherice
Printed in the U.S.A

ACKNOWLEDGEMENTS

Grateful acknowledgement goes out to everyone who inspires me, encourages me, ennobles me and truly wish me well, because that would mean at some point; I either, have or I continuously do the same for you. That is how kinetic energy and kindred spirits work.

It is only by way of my Creator, and you, that the pulse of my beating and bleeding heart makes it way to my pen.

You keep me supplied with inspiration, love, light, the reason, and something to write about.

With love and because of yours,
Angela Sherice.

I graciously thank you all.

CONTENTS

PREFACE

"It served no comfort to her and turned out to be the biggest slap in the face of her life as a mother when (a whole century later) we were watching the news one evening at her house. A close relative of "Attic Man's" was on the news for molesting his girlfriend's daughter. My mom turned to me and said: "That's [Attic Man's] brother, did you know that?"

I replied: "I was going to ask you that-considering the fact that they have the same unusual last name."

"Yeah, I think that runs in their family though," she replied, feeling proud that she dodged that bullet, feeling confident that as close as Attic Man was to her child (me)-that sure as hell did not go down.

She then began to run down what seemed like a list of legendary and hereditary molestation accounts she had known and heard tales of throughout the years about Attic Man's male relatives such. Reminiscently, I turned to her and said: "You know what Ma? That must be true because [Attic Man] used to do that to me all the time when I was a little girl!"

I said it merely thinking that she would say: "What? You're kidding!" But instead, her eyes got big and like a deer in headlights, she turned to look at my face quickly then averted her eyes; suddenly embarrassed to look me in the face. She swung her arms in a rebuking manner and continued to scold me out of the corners of her eyes, repeatedly yelling out my name as if that was something I should have kept to myself after all these years. I had no idea that she was going to take it so hard because it was so long ago. She shook her head "no" non-stop, as if I was still a child and someone else delivered this news to her *about* her child. But instead, it was me-an adult-telling her mom, far too many years later, *about* what happened (with me) back when I *was* a child.

She was befuddled. She didn't want to know the details, and at this point I dared not go into detail and tell her everything. It was the most awkward moment and emotion that I had never seen my very own mother show. My mother normally had an answer and a comeback for everything-always. This time however, she was speechless. She felt so sodomized, so victimized and so traumatized, that she kept throwing her hand at me in what seemed like complete and utter disgust:

"Angie! We've had so many conversations when you were a little girl about anybody touching you or saying something to you that made you feel uncomfortable-all of that! Don't you remember me talking to you about these things! And I mean all the time! E-v-e-r-y-day Angie-damn! How could you do this to me! Oh shit!" she snapped back and yelled at me like it literally burned her. She was so disgusted by the news. She yelled like she was trying to convince herself into remembering having these talks with me, as if-she could have, she would have dug her hand into my brain to pull out the recollection of me storing the talk into the palm of her hand, just so she could say: "here's the proof right here!" That wasn't going to happen, because I didn't remember the talks.

What I did remember were her constant words: "You see a muthafucka fuckin' with her-just kill him and save me the trouble!" That was something I constantly heard my mother say aloud when she would have friends over or if we were out somewhere. Whomever we would be standing around would look me up and down then whisper something in her ear. Like clockwork, she would always respond aloud: "That's okay. You see a muthafucka fuckin' with her-just kill him and save me the trouble!"

It wasn't until later in years, I learned that the whispers in her ear would be: "Look at her little shapely body and that child's face-what are you going to do with her?" that made her respond with: "You see a muthafucka fuckin' with her-just kill him and save me the trouble!"

My mother always had a way with words and one hell of a mouth.

She was one of a kind with them both.

She could just spit, on cue-a master wordsmith.

She was always very entertaining and the type that would tell you: "fucking with me would be like running through a lion's den with a pork chop suit on."

She seemed to almost have a new one every day.

It was nothing for her to tell you: "I've been around the world twice while you are working your way around the tea-cup still looking for the handle."

If you got in her way too much, she would kindly tell you: "let me fuck this cat, if she has any kittens-I'll give you one."

Translation: Mind your business-simple as that.

I couldn't wait to come home from school the day that I learned the word for her vernacular was called: "idioms." So the next time someone looked me up and down and whispered in her ear and she responded: "That's okay. You see a muthafucka fuckin' with her just kill him and save me the trouble," I nudged her and said: "momma, that's called an idiom!" Yet this time, this moment, this wordsmith-some twenty (plus) years later, she was sitting in front of me: speechless, wordless, "idiom-less" feeling more like an idiot and that it was she who was put in the lion's den with a pork chop suit on while I was the one who had been around the world twice while she was working her way around the tea-cup...still looking for the handle. Somebody had already fucked with her kitten over twenty years ago, and I was just now giving her one: the one and only conversation about it-finally.

She behaved as if I was the adult that delivered this news to her about her little girl-yet it was me, her grown little girl, sitting there telling her something that nearly set her back almost twenty (plus) years.

It felt weird to me to see my mother like this. Tears filled her eyes as she sat there-speechless-shaking her leg while sitting at the kitchen table as if it was me who had raped her of twenty (plus) years of good housekeeping and motherhood right there in a five-minute instant.

I was numb sitting there, just like I had been numb for years. My emotion was misplaced. I hadn't a *clue* as to why she was so mad. It confused me-badly. I didn't feel traumatized then or in the moment of me telling her, so her shock and awe threw me off. My emotion about it was so misplaced-just like it had been-for years.

My mother sitting there in front of me with tears in her eyes is what felt "uncomfortable" to me.

Don't cry for me, cry for my mother-for that was the night she died.

Don't cry for me, I never did. I never felt like I should, or had a reason to.

Even when I say: "happened to me," and "did that to me," it feels weird. It feels weird because even though Attic Man was the start of me chasing sensations of [what I would call] my "pee coming," throughout my busy little childhood life, thoughts played out in my head of me sitting there seducing him and approving everything he was doing to me. I would take his giant face in my tiny hands and kissing it all over as he kneeled in front of me; enjoying it and moaning with pleasure-like two consenting adults would.

The most "uncomfortable" any and all of it got to me was the day he tried to penetrate me. I quickly sat right up to slap his face so hard-with my tiny hands that I know he saw birds and stars: "That hurt! Don't you dare do that again!" I yelled and pointed my tiny finger into his big face-facing my little face as he kneeled in front of me and repeatedly apologized in that pathetic child-molester-like whisper that I can still hear so clearly. But he was so apologetic and near tears when I disapproved that I was "uncomfortable" no more.

For far too long, I had grown to like and receive him wiping [what I would call] his "mushroom," and his lips on [what I would call] my "flower"-repeatedly. When he tried to go in, that was when it didn't feel right-it didn't feel comfortable-because it was painful. All else felt pleasurable and was therefore "right," because it didn't hurt. So in my mind, everything was okay-nothing was wrong therefore, there was nothing to tell my mom that was "uncomfortable" going on with me. In my mind, I merely had an older boyfriend who looked like Marvin Gaye, and "secrets." An adult can't reach a kid by telling them to report what feels uncomfortable or what's hurt them (in that way-in that place), because it just might feel comfortable and right. Once it's done right-it feels right and then becomes a "secret."

Kids love "secrets." In hindsight and looking at my mom's hurting face, twenty (plus) years later, I figured it all out: If you tell a kid that secrets are for grown-ups and not for kids; then a kid would have secrets no more. I probably would have understood that, and told all my "secrets" to her. When I was a kid, I had just as many secrets as I've had many conversations about many things with her. She too, would have probably been in the know about all my "secrets" had she (this wordsmith) known the right words to say-to *me*: her child. Unfortunately, the people who I had secrets with, whispered in *my* ear: all the right words. And my mom was the one who didn't have the clue or cue…

My emotion and thoughts about it were misplaced because it all went so smoothly that it didn't seem like anything more than a secret. The "pleasure" for my body was way before my mind could understand it, and because there was no pain or trauma; I grew older to question whether or not it was really "molestation" (because of my willing participation). As a full-grown adult (now), and by standard definition-it was. But because I did not feel traumatized at the time and for years thereafter; I grew to convince myself that it was something else. Because of my confusion, I never felt like a "victim" and I never felt "molested" by standard definition any more than I was "virgin" by standard definition-the night I lost my virginity with Santana.

For years, the best way I could make sense of it all was that I experienced some things that I should not have at an early age. As a result-later in life-I just grew older to like to fuck: my oral and phallic stages stuck with me and were much a part of who I was, just as sure as I needed my fingers to feel and my feet to walk.

Even as a child, it seemed like all day my body was tingling inside and my flower was on a non-stop throb. At seven years-old, I learned what to do to control the tingles at the most inconvenient time: at latchkey-afterschool, while napping when the lights went out. That was the day that I learned that balling up my hand to hunch on top of it, would remedy the tingles. The sound of the teaching assistant yelling out at me in a somewhat loud and surprised whisper: "Angie! Don't be doing that! Quit that!" rang in my head as I lay there frozen; easing my hands from beneath me and lying flat onto my stomach with my chin dug into the blue and white mat-my arms and legs stretched out in position as if I was about to make a snow angel. Outside of the latchkey assistant's yell, I didn't feel traumatized or "uncomfortable" at all.

But later in life, I think as a result of it all-it caused a kind of numbness; the kind that may have presented itself in other ways that carried on throughout my life until I understood and made sense of it all. Making sense of it all was all a matter of getting to that point in life where I had to train my mind to catch up with my body, because my mind wasn't ready for what my body was experiencing.

Unfortunately, breakthroughs and answers won't come from a deep one-on-one conversation from just the "right" people. And often times, those conversations are much needed from those same people who are breaking you in. They are usually the "just the right people"-only they know, because they are the ones sharing secret private moments with you-that shouldn't be. They won't talk to you and have that one-on-one with you. They won't tell it on you, because they are very much a part of it and don't want to get in trouble themselves. There will be no secret note slips, or messages in a bottle sent to your parents, because when it's done spinning, the nose of the bottle will point back to them. So, "just the right people" won't tell on you (for you). "Just the right people," won't tell on themselves (for you).

Other times, the "just the right people" are your peers. They won't tell on you because they are your boyfriend(s), and to them-the two of you are merely sharing private moments. They do not have the capacity to decipher what's really going on with highly sexualized teen girls in the bedroom with them. These teen boys can't talk to you, re-direct you, or go tell your parents on you.

Santana, a sixteen year-old boy, was merely enjoying himself with a highly sexualized and fully developed fourteen year-old girl. The most any sixteen year-old boy can conjure up in the form of *any* questions to initiate *any* kind of dialogue is: "were you really a virgin?" (if the highly sexualized girl was a virgin). And if she wasn't a virgin (but was merely highly sexualized), to him-he just happened to be having sexual relations with the type of girl who gave and received pleasure in ways that his other peer girls (who hadn't been messed with), didn't have it in them to give and receive.

For the girl who had been messed with-her delivery and receipt of pleasure is two and three times over the girl who hasn't been. Their "sexual spirit" is different even if they did no more in the bedroom than the girl who wasn't messed with. Because of their "sexual spirit," their delivery and how they receive pleasure thickens the sexual experience, whereas the girl who was not messed with-hers is "thin" and diluted (in comparison).

The most I could get in the form of any breakthrough with a sixteen year-old boy with just as many raging hormones as I had tingles was: "were you really a virgin?"

At age fourteen, I did not have the capacity to share with him-what seemed "natural" to me for seven whole years before him. To catch a seven year-old *girl* masturbating is not normal-it's not "natural." One thing about little girl's clitoris' in comparison to a little boys penis, is that-that lil' button can be left alone to mind its own business until that *very* moment that it has been *stimulated*. A girl can manipulate it (naturally) from merely washing or wiping-day in and day out, but from the moment it is actually *stimulated*, that little girl's clitoris is never the same again. And if she starts to masturbate at far to an early age, that's a problem-that's not normal. She's tingling in ways that a seven year old girl has no business tingling.

The "just the right person" would come in the form of that instructor telling it to my mother. Did she ever? That is a question I never knew the answer to. Some parents get to the bottom of it, other's ignore it as something "natural." For boys-maybe, for girls-never. I will never know if my mother knew because she was good at talking a bunch of shit and entertaining people with her vernacular, but when shit hit the fan, she would ignore or wipe the problem away; far-far away from her. I remembered that about her, even while looking at her shockedness of finding out some twenty (plus) years later.

Now that...I muthafuckin' *didn't* forget.

Surely, a grown man like Tim *had* to think (at least a time or two): "why is this little girl enjoying these moments like this in such a way? It's not normal." Yet, he wasn't going to go pay my mother a visit and tell her what I was doing, and liking, while huddled up and tucked away with him. He got his pleasure-and it was over with. He most probably wiped his brows at the thought and relief that I was enjoying it and was a willing participant, simple as that. Despite the fact he knew it was wrong.

Sure, I almost got my breakthrough good and into my later teen years-from an older "boyfriend" I was seeing. Though I wasn't a child, I was still too young for him. We had been fucking so regularly until one day he snapped. Grunting like a crazy man, he pulled right out of me, got up, lit a cigarette and walked over to the wet bar at the other end of basement bedroom where we lay, many-a-days. He stared at me lying there. It spooked me the hell out. He poured himself a drink while his hands began to shake. I insisted on slipping my clothes on and getting the hell out of there before that glass was half-full. When he looked up, I was dressed and at the door, on route up the steps and out of that house. I had never seen him in this state of mind. He pointed that cigarette at me and took a sip of his champagne:

"You stay right there."

I was startled but I stood still.

He went in: "You've got just as much chance in life as any these motherfuckers up here living in "Woodmond" or "Bensonhurst" (two ffluent parts of town where no one but the rich and/or famous lived).

I listened on.

"You're just as smart, just as talented, just as beautiful, just as worthy as any of those motherfuckers living up there! But you-you've got to quit fucking and put your attention on only the right things to get you there!"

I was utterly confused, feeling many ways awkward.

"You say that like I've been with a lot of men. I don't have casual sex. I've only had two boyfriends in my entire life," I defended.

"I know-we've talked about that. That's not what I'm talking about. A woman can have a hundred men and not be ready, but can have the same hundred men and be ready! You are not ready-with two or twenty! Only in bed, and that's not good for a man who wouldn't mean you well. Your mind's not ready to know the difference." ...he asserted: "You...you...need to stop fucking altogether. These motherfuckers out here would love you for that. Take care of your business," he said-like he was any different, and totally drew a blank at the fact that I had been too young for him since the day he started fucking me.

He scolded me in ways that began to sound like he cared, but was talking in riddles because he knew that the same person he was warning me about happened to be him, too.

I was confused, so I responded with what I felt was really happening inside of him:

"Are you saying all that because you're older than me and now all of a sudden you're getting a conscious about it?"

He shook his head and wiped his face with his shaky fingers: "You're not ready-*here* for the type of shit that goes on: *here*," he pointed at my head-first, then the bed-second. The conversation ended up going nowhere, just a little further than the typical. Because "just the right person," got a conscious about it but then, subconscious as well-and didn't want to look like a hypocrite. He knew that my mind was ready to comprehend that much.

I kinda-sorta understood what he was saying, but didn't quite understand what I could do about what was already in effect-having yet not coming to terms with the cause. I would merely say: "Nothing's wrong with me-I just got started at an earlier age."

I never had a one-night stand any more than I'd ever been "easy." And the fact that I didn't go on in life to desire and molest kids, didn't do drugs and alcohol, get caught up into prostitution, or wasn't plagued with chronic pornography fetishes and other various sexual deviancies and abnormalities; *really* forced me to think that since I wasn't the typical case, I had no right or reason to call it what it was.

It's just that later in life, during trying to make sense of it all, my emotions for some things were misplaced, others-nonexistent. My attraction to and for other things were simply lopsided and I equated "real love" with "making love" as a prerequisite for anything solid and worth committing to, and in doing so-it brought me a lot of pain and a whole lot of pleasure.

I felt like my stagnant phallic and oral stages of loving to rap on the mic and put my needle to a record or two until a muthafucka stuttered and sang opera was never a problem or issue-but rather, an art form. Each and every time, it felt "right" and new. It was something that I treasured, dissected and perfected-then churned it for whomever I felt I was solid with, earned it, and committed to. I couldn't help myself, and I would lose control of myself while in the middle of it like some outer-body, slash, out of mind experience. Everything was right about it in my body-to calm my tingles. I just wanted the feeling, and to lose my head at the edge of the bed. Pleasure, love, being in love, thinking I was in love, on my way to being in love, falling out of love, falling back in love-it was all the same to me, as long as I could calm my tingles in between-even despite the hurt and tears that came with it, whether the tears and hurt was mine or theirs.

Truth be told to myself, going through life, I knew I had *some* issues. Sometimes I'd bleed blood and other times I bleed metal-either way, deep down inside; the only "uncomfortable" I felt was cut-open, hollow and numb during those "trying to make sense of it all" times in my life.

I have issues that I am fighting, and have fought with all my life. Some, I have won-others I still battle.

Life has not allowed me the time to dwell on my past, play the victim or claim victim, but instead-forced me to deal with the hand I was dealt: pokerfaced. During trying to make some sense of it all, behind my humor, the jokes I'd tell and the sun in my smile and eyes; I had both-tingles and tears going on inside of me.

I know full well who I am just as much as I know throughout my adult life, the problem has been what I feel, and as result; what it is I liked to do.

Yes, I had been broken down, broken apart, come undone and massively hit rock bottom at various times in my life. That being said, just rock with me while grow up, throw up and get to the breakthrough, the bottom, or the end of the situation…"

1

THE ROOTS of PICKED FRUIT

One thing was for certain: Santana was all mine. Rather than losing my virginity *to* him, I lost my virginity *with* him-we lost our virginity together. So to us, we were kismet. I loved him because he made me feel so very special every single day of the six months before this night, and I felt as though he earned this night about as much as I had learned and yearned it.

It was the 14th of March, the night that Dr. Huxtable gave Rudy and all her friend's rides on his leg as fat boy Peter hung on for dear life.

Santana and I became even more inseparable than we were the six months before, and even then, we were sickeningly conjoined at the hip like we were Siamese twins.

We made a pact and had already been in the habit of writing letters to one another every day.

That whiny baby-talk he would hand to me [wanting me to read while in front of him; filled with constant wanna-be rap alter egos, slang, grammatical errors and misspellings that he knew I hated oh-so badly] was indicative of the immature teen-aged boy with raging hormones that he was, in comparison to my young, mature self-but with raging hormones that could lay his dormant in a heartbeat.

With a whole new chapter in our relationship, and more to write about-now-because of it, the very next morning after this March 14th night, his letters began to read like this:

"Hi Angie.

Hi ya doin baby?

First let me start out by saying I love you. I really do. Baby last night was so special to me because I lost my virginity to very special young lady in my life (you might know her). But I pray that you aren't pregnant. I mean you're so young and innocent and still mama's baby.

I don't want that to change baby. Baby I'm scared. But happy. I love you so much. But apparently I might not. Don't get me wrong, I mean, if you were, I'd stay wit' cha and we'd be a happy family. But I want our child to be born on purpose, not because of carelessness. I don't want our child to be a mistake. I love you.

P.S What are you going to do after school?

Go take the test or home so we can fuck some more?

Love,

Santana

P.S.S My next letter will reminisce

P.S.S.S No mistakes… Nyaa!"

March 16th:

"My Darling Angie.

Thinking about last night. Every time I do, my nature jumps. Baby I love you so much and living without you is impossible. Angie, the things that turned me on most was holding you in my arms, the female scent you possessed, calling my name and most of all, when you were saying that you were all mine and do you what you want. And when I said I wish you were my wife and you said "I am," that really made me feel like fucking you to the extent where you would just collapse. And what really-really turned me on was when I asked you did you want to stay on top and then you said no and that you wanted me to fuck you!

I hope I satisfied you.

It made me see clearer than clear that I had finally found a young lady whom I love (and I mean love) for the rest of my life and when you started crying, that made matters the best they could ever be.

Letting me know just how you felt about me.

I wanted to sleep with you all night and wake up and smell that pussy. That would have been nice.

Baby my love for you will never fail 'cause it's too deep to be filled with someone else's love.

And you know it's true.

But, umm…there's something that is bothering me a lot. It's really dumb, but it's trippin' me out. Maybe it's normal, maybe it's not. I wasn't going to say anything but I just realized it yesterday, but I'll get back. Just ask me about it. I love you so much."

It had finally hit him.

Those first two days, we had been so busy exploring one another, that all he could think of was how good he was feeling; the sensations and newness his virgin body was experiencing. With all that we were doing filling his head with so much, when he finally got a chance to process it all, it hit him and he finally popped the sixty-four thousand dollar question: "Angie, were you *really* a virgin?"

But, umm…well, it's like this:

I was a "kinda" virgin but far from virgin (by definition).

All I could think of was *chasing* sensations that my body had longed for-having experienced those sensations before. I needed to finally get this thing off of my chest and to alleviate the tingles going on inside my body. I grew to love him, I grew to trust him. We were so close and talked about everything, but this night I didn't want his conversation. I didn't want to hear any words at all. I just wanted him to follow my lead: back to the bedroom where his mouth, hands and body were to follow wherever I wanted them to be. I couldn't help myself. He was perfect-but most importantly, he was perfect for me.

I unbuttoned his pants-I couldn't wait to feel it. I absolutely positively could not wait. Almost like an animal, I yelled out: "ahhhhh," plunged-then devoured him. My lips were speaking a language all their own while my tongue was dancing and spiraling with him trapped alongside my jaw as if it and my mouth were wrestling. I couldn't help it. I needed it badly. The more he screamed out, the better I gave it to him-every which way I could. I was tingling and throbbing everywhere.

I grabbed his wrists tightly while I pulled him downward to sit on the edge of my bed-where I'd always fantasize about getting it. Trying to convey with my body, a feeling to him like I had done this before; I stood above him with his head in my breasts, and with the most unsophisticated embrace. I clutched his face and head shoving it right between them while trying to decide where I wanted to start on his body first. I had so much going on inside of me and inside of my mind that I damn near growled out in frustration while kissing him passionately. The heavy breathing from the excitement he was feeling was turning me on even more.

I sank my teeth gently into his neck while massaging his shoulders then sat down on my knees and began to unbutton his shirt while caressing his chest. He started breathing harder while moaning a long winded: "ooooh," repeatedly, as if the present he had been waiting on was coming towards him. The harder he breathed and moaned, the more intoxicated I got. My synapses were firing like crazy.

It felt like I was assembling this moment about as good as the dirty little thorough premeditated acts that carried on in my head. They were precise and exact like a set of instructions necessary to fix something that needed to be fixed a while ago. I had been so ready and waiting for this moment, along with every paint-by-numbered thing that was going to be required of Santana this March 14th day-like a list that was checked twice-all naughty, no nice.

I unbuttoned his pants with the eagerness of opening a present on Christmas Day. My tongue nearly fell to the floor. I couldn't wait to see it, taste it and feel it. I yelled out desperately like it was delicacy that had been withheld from me, then I devoured him with my slobbery and shaky lips that were speaking a language all their own. My tongue danced and spiraled with him trapped alongside my jaw as if it and me were fighting and tussling like crazy.

I couldn't help it. I needed it badly. The more he screamed out, the better I sucked him, working hard not to get my teeth in the way by balling my lips up to cover my teeth while my tongue did a dance up and down the shaft of his penis. I was throbbing. He was brick.

I pulled my entire mouth from him, smacking as I pulled from the head of it. I then held his penis in my hand with the tips of all five of my right hands fingers while my strong, wet tongue started from the top of him, and began whipping across his thick and pronounced shaft. I began teasing it with my mouth like I was playing the flute, while my tongue continued to spiral him up and down.

I needed him to be distracted some, so that I could go where I wanted to go-where the crevices of my mind and within my diary's lines had gone time and time again. So I spiraled up to the top of his shaft and devoured the head and moved my head n circles as I flicked the tip of my tongue round and round, in and out of his opening. My lips hungrily chanted on the head as if I was chewing a big wad of bubblegum.

I took his knees and pushed him back some, then made my way down lower. I pressed my tongue between his loosened sack to press on that "space" I had read about that was so supposed to be sensitive to a man that if you caressed it right; could send sensations through his body unexplainable. I wanted to do it right. I arrived there, intent on doing it *just* right. The louder he moaned my name, the more I knew I was doing it right. I was passing my very own tests.

I got cocky and felt more powerful. I didn't realize it would be this easy. Our magic and our moment made me feel like I was a magician. I wanted to try it again. So while caressing the head with my thumb, I went beneath his sack and French kissed that space as if it was a pussy with no clit. With my brows frowned and my tongue feeling diesel, I began to tease, tickle, lick and suck it so good that it felt like it was swelling in my mouth.

I was so wet. I got cockier and placed my face in his sack and yelled out-I was so aroused. I went for the left one-the right one-then the left one; juggling them both in my mouth while my lips, mouth and tongue were doing some kind of dance in this juggling game.

His testicles were just the right size to allow me to play games with them: making sure my tongue and each one was chasing each other while in my mouth. It was so fun in my head-right where these things were all very well-rehearsed even before he lay there and I lay a hand on him. His excitement would not let me stop playing this game of kissing catchers in my mouth.

I then revisited his space just beneath his sack again, and oh boy did I love listening to him continuously gasping, moaning and riffing-he didn't know what to do with himself. It was magical. I didn't read how explosive it would be-they left out that part.

I began to undress quickly while treating his head like a spiral staircase; devouring him while he screamed screams I never knew were possible coming from a human being. I came up for air to tell him what it was I needed:

"I need to be at the edge of the bed. I need to be right at the edge-please," I said-desperately.

"I love you. Okay. I love you. Okay," were the only words he could quickly utter in between his gasps and moans. He was intent on following my lead from the very start. All he knew to do-was anything and anywhere I wanted to do and go-no matter what it was. I wanted to submit, not now-but later.

He was so excited at the sight of my body. He grabbed and held onto me tightly, like he did not want to let me go. He kept trying to sink his teeth into any part of me where my skin would show from beneath his tight grasp-hovering all over me.

"Wait, please wait," I said to him.

I sat there at the edge of the bed and put him in front of me-on his knees. He began mimicking every touch that I had just given him while repeatedly confessing how much he loved me so. I was throbbing and wet-so busy trying to get this feeling off of my chest while he caressed my breasts. He was so masculine and it turned me on. Oh boy did it turn me on. I didn't expect that-the magic in it this moment. He seemed to become even more perfect to me and for me than he ever was before.

I laid back and rested the heels of my feet on the bed rails, opened my legs to see what, if anything, he would do about it while his face was right in front of it. "He had better pass this part of the test," I said in my head. Then he did it. He did that thing…that thing…ahhhh that thing…He did it. Yes!

Almost assembled:

When he spread my legs open-sparks started to fly. It tingled, snapped, crackled and popped like Fourth of July. "Ahhh I love you!" I exhaled loudly because he gave to me-that exact sensation I had wanted. It's something about spreading my legs wide open that drives me up a wall-he could never understand. And then that thing…ah, man. He could never understand that thing: the fascination I had with the clitoris and the magic that happens while at it.

He began to French me-fluently while all down in my pussy. He had his tongue and lips right where I wanted them to be-yet, I wanted more. I finally had a body at, and on my body in a way that felt totally right, so I wanted it all-as if this would be the first and the last time. I used him up this March 14th night.

I needed his mouth on it-his entire mouth. He began to chant all over my clit the way I did over his head when he had his turn. He, his tongue, and lips where I wanted them to be.

More assembly was required:

I wanted more-rougher, more aggressive, so I begged him to lock in on it and just pull it mercilessly:

"Pull it hard!" I repeated over and over-not caring anymore about what he thought of me or what he was doing at this point. I screamed helplessly into the air while he made sounds beneath me-probably freaking out at feel of me growing inside of his mouth after what he'd just done for me. I loved it. Many times in my diary and mind I fantasized about having it this way-my way.

He fixed that.

I was on my elbows, head back and about to bite my bottom lip off. Oh my goodness I was so ready to finally get my fuck on, but I still needed more. I needed him to put it on me-no, not that kind of put it on me. I needed him to thump me with the head, and spread my now blossomed flower while he watched it and told me how beautiful it was. That turned me on, and I had been alone with that moment in my mind over a thousand times. As I lay there with my legs open, enjoying the feeling of him caressing my clit with the tip of his dick, I needed to know that he loved the anatomy of how I was built and that it too, was driving him just as crazy as this moment was satisfying me: "Tell me you love it-tell me that you like what you see-and what you are doing," I whispered.

"I love it! I love it!" he groaned and repeated-while trying to push it into me. He was eager.

I squeezed my legs around him tighter while bending my knees inward; begging him to keep doing what I was instructing him to do to my clitoris with the tip of his penis: "Go round and round. Separate my inners-push up on it, push into it, thump it, and wiggle back and forth on it."

He was on cue, busy, and aroused. He then began to aggressively wiggle it from left to right as if he was erasing it; watching it pop back and forth right along with him. I could tell that he was growing more and more eager to get inside of me, but little did he know, that aggressive wiggling was just what I needed him to do. That was the sensation I had been used to and was eager to feel again.

He was so perfect and worthy. He just was. With him, I had no inhibitions or fears whatsoever. I knew he could handle me and my every requested desire with ease because I knew that he loved me and worked hard to keep me happy and loving him. We were very close, but he had no idea what my mind and body had been going through for so long, and I took it all out on worthy-him. So to let him know that he was even more worthy of this moment, I finally let him inside. Upon entering me, watching his eyes and his body shake was the most exhilarating thing I had never imagined. His lips were quivering so badly while I lay there watching him have his way with me. I was taking every inch of him while holding my breath and gasping-more shocked that it was finally happening, than I was able to comfortably enjoy this part of the moment. He was busy grunting and groaning-and shocked that he was finally inside of me while trying to control himself to last longer. I certainly did not want it to end as yet, so I made him pull out of me.

He was in so much agony-looking as if he was about to cry.

I wasn't done with him-I needed it all that night.

I treated this moment like a coach thinking of his next play for the team, as I stood there naked with my hand on my hip, frowned brow-thinking of what I could instruct him to do next, completely technical and premeditated as if to say: "No fouls please! Let's go!"

I walked over to the corner of the room while holding his hand. I then slid down in the corner of the wall with my legs wide open like a butterfly. I needed him to just give it to me mercilessly. I insisted on having my night as close to what had plagued my mind for so long. He fell to his knees with nothing to support him but my knees clutching him and the wall in front of his face. I loved that. I needed him as frustrated as I was repressed and frustrated from needing to get all of these sensations and tingles out of my body…

He got inside of me and began pounding away; this time-screaming out and riffing like he was really singing a song. I was there, me: my person and my body, but it began to feel almost like I wasn't a part of his pleasure anymore-just he and my pussy going at it. That began to turn me on even more.

He balanced himself by holding my inner thighs open and began to pound into me like a mad-man.

All I could hear going through my head were his screams and pleads, while my thoughts replayed a movie scene I had seen where, while giving it to his girlfriend mercilessly, the man yelled: "*Birth is pain! Death is pain! Beauty is pain!*" I often masturbated with that movie's scene going through my head-fantasizing what it must be like to get tore down like that. I was finally getting it-just like that.

My night was perfect and I was done. Everything that I had ever written down, every sensation that I had been chasing, and everything my mind had fantasized about; I got-that night. I was tired and full. After rolling on top of him for a while, I was ready to fully submit to him. I finally allowed him to have me the virgin way: "man on top."

Unscrewed. Unplugged. Assembled and fixed...

I felt good that I made a perfect choice, because for such an overwhelming amount of time, I had it played out in my mind what I would do with "him," whoever "he" would be. All I needed was the right person. I knew what I wanted to do, and what type of person he would have to be. I knew that he would have to fit the idea of what I felt a boyfriend should be-for me. Santana ended up being that "he."

So when he finally popped the sixty-four thousand dollar question: "Angie, were you *really* a virgin?" If what it means to be virgin is to be: "pure, initial, first; and not altered by human activity," well then I definitely was not a virgin by any stretch (of reality).

At age fourteen, I did not have the capacity nor did it even cross my mind to tell him how I already knew of those sensations. My experiences early-on had taught me that was what a body was for: to give and receive pleasure. But instead, I could only reply by telling him that I had spent a lot of my (fourteen year-old) life reading books and studying any and all things having to do with erogenous zones, physical and sexual anatomy, and making love. That was true, but it wasn't all.

At age fourteen, I did not have the capacity to understand (much less communicate to Santana) that my first time having sexual intercourse may very well have been special because-of, but for me, I was a chasing a sensation-a feeling: first-in search of a "him" that I could use to bring me that feeling I had been chasing: that feeling of my pee coming.

At age fourteen, I did not have the capacity to communicate to Santana that at age seven it was probably not-so-normal to have had countless sexual experiences already, two of them-oral: one me on her (a neighbor and someone my mother knew who was two/three times my seven year old age) and the other: him on me (he too, was two/three times my seven year old age). I called him "Attic Man" because that's where it would take place-he was the "first." In addition to having me lie on the edge of his bed and spread my little legs open; exposing my (then) little flower to him, he would masturbate his head onto me and then rub it round and round and thump and rub it back and forth onto my clitoris. I grew to like it from the very first time he did it. It happened so many times, and I would look forward to visiting him-just to feel that sensation. It would tickle from start to finish.

Don't judge me, I was seven years old-I didn't know any better...

At fourteen, I did not have the capacity to communicate to Santana, that I had already known what it felt like to climb on top of a male penis and grind senselessly until it felt like my pee was coming.

I would take my "experience" with me while visiting my mother's best friend's house-she had a son the same age as me. While his mom and my mom would be on one end of the house, he and I would be tucked away in his bedroom with me straddled all over that poor boy, grinding him senselessly until my pee came. I loved that kind of pleasure so much that I would be yelling out to him: "I want to have your baby!" while pecking and kissing his face-holding his big head like I really knew what I was doing. All I knew was that it felt good. I had that feeling before and couldn't stop chasing it. So with a willing participant who I felt comfortable around, I had to have it.

Don't judge me, I was seven years old-I didn't know any better...

At fourteen, I did not have the capacity to communicate to Santana that at age eleven, it was probably not normal that I had a constant grinding partner-twice my age-tucked away around the corner from where I lived. He lived next door to one of my peers, so I was easy access.

By permission, I would leave home to go over to my friend's house. She, her mom and sister's had lots of friends, so her house was always crowded with people coming in and out the front and back doors. While there, I would manage to slip away to Tim's house-next door.

I would walk up the dim stairway and up the steps, into his dimly lit third floor bedroom then right into his bed. There, I would be straddled and grinding him for what seemed like hours at a time until I would be dripping sweat everywhere-soaked at the seat of my shorts while walking home. I loved grinding him better than the boy my age, so I was over there a lot. Tim and me hardly ever talked. It was probably more comfortable for him to look at my developing body than it was to hear my pre-teen voice and rhetoric; reminding him of something he'd rather ignore was actually happening with a girl my age.

I was conditioned not to talk to him. He would lay there and I would just crawl up on the bed and get on top of him. He would then wrap his arms around me tightly-like he loved me. In return, I would wrap my arms tightly around his body then dig my face into his chest and from there-start to grinding with him until the momentum would increase and I'd begin screaming like a banshee. He would allow me to go crazy on top of him, and my flower would just pop over and over and over. The way we were tucked away in his house; I was free to scream and grunt and be as wild as I wanted to without ever being in my usual hurries that I would be in-during these kinds of moments. It was a good thing that he didn't want to end my life, because he could have certainly gotten away with it. No one ever knew I would be right next door, tucked away-far off and up into some part of this man's house where I couldn't even hear the goings on right next door at my friend's house. By the time I reached his bedroom, we were completely shut off from everything. I loved every minute of it. I didn't think there was anything wrong with what we were doing. I had a thing for people older than me and I merely thought I had yet-another older boyfriend, and that we too, had a big secret. Simple as that.

So much taboo and secrecy had already been a part of my life and my (young) person that even at age fourteen, I did not have the capacity to see any of it as a "problem" or something that should not have happened. I think at age fourteen, I merely saw my life-seven years back-as secrets and private experiences; natural things that were supposed to happen in order to prepare me for womanhood and life.

At age fourteen, certainly, I probably knew that a seven year-old girl should not be having relations of any kind with anyone, much less someone two and three *times* her senior. All I knew about these secret things is that they were obviously supposed to be just that: secret. Why? Because each and every time they would happen, I would walk inside of rooms and the doors would shut behind me. I would hide behind couches-so no one could see me. I would be enclosed in closets-occasionally cracking it open for air, but shutting it back after inhaling and exhaling doses of oxygen and ecstasy. That's why.

At fourteen, I did not have the capacity to communicate to Santana that by age twelve, I had developed an almost uncontrollable and insatiable appetite for oral sex with older women, most probably as a result of my experience with Valencia-a deep, raspy-voiced athletic girl that was two/three times my seven year-old age. That was the very first time I had ever seen [what I would refer to as an] "upside down triangle" filled with hair, smack dead in my face, me-kissing it, and liking it. It made me so fascinated with pussy that I thought about it every day, ever since. I couldn't help myself. I was already curious about my own after learning the sensations that happen to it, that I was curious about everyone else's too: what it looked like, what it smelled like. Was it like Valencia's? Was it like mine? Those questions and those visuals plagued my mind.

Although Valencia, Attic Man, and Tim were two and three times my senior; I remembered enjoying myself-very much so, even to the point of sitting up from the edge of my bed and kissing Attic Man's face and telling him repeatedly how much I loved him and seducing him with my little childlike hollow pecks for kisses. I merely thought I was being "sexy." I was "acting sexy-" the way a little girl would try to "act sexy" in a way that if her mother caught her in that kind of an act (even with a little boy her own age), she would be so shocked that she'd just and whip her ass or redirect her because of it. While "acting sexy," he would sit on his knees in front of me: moaning and groaning, baby-talking me and calling out my name. I would be holding his giant face and head in my tiny little hands while he close his eyes and exhale as if he was really receiving [my] caress from a full-grown woman. I never forgot his gentle demeanor, his delicate and sensitive "way"-like he was really in love with me-they way a man would be shamelessly in love with a woman during that "honeymoon" phase in a relationship. And that's what I thought it was.

At age fourteen, I did not have the capacity to communicate to Santana that at age thirteen; I had already been shaking it up with a girl my age, whom I met in third-grade. I (theoretically) lost my virginity to her. I say theoretically because our third grade relationship began with kissing and grinding one other until our pee came and our pubic bones were sore from the grinding. We kissed and grinded any which way possible: in every closet, on all three floors of her house or behind the couch of my house from third grade until eighth grade. As we got older, we knew there had to be more to moaning, kissing and grinding one another, so we graduated to her perfecting the art of caressing [what was by now] my full B-cup breasts. She would caress them in ways that would nearly bring me to piss and tears. She not only grew up with me, she grew with my developing body, which by age ten;

[what was by now] my full B-cup breasts. She would caress them in ways that would nearly bring me to piss and tears. She not only grew up with me, she grew with my developing body, which by age ten; would give my mother's grown-woman friends (and any grown woman) a run for her money. My third grade girlfriend was there through it all: on me and with me, while I blossomed like a sprouting tree and she picked at every branch and leaf-eventually discovering that there was a secret garden at the bottom...

Together, we discovered what magical things could happen when she slid her fingers right into it.

So technically, she entered me first-then came: Santana.

So with all that having happened before age fourteen, I did not have the capacity to communicate to Santana that by the time he met me, I had already lost [not just theoretically my virginity], but I had already lost anything remotely close to being: "pure, initial, first; and unaltered by human activity" (as defined: "virgin"). If: "pure," "initial," "first" and "unaltered by human activity" was the definition of the makings of what "virgin" is, then by age fourteen when Santana and I met, I was already seven years genetically altered. And on that March 14th night, though a part of me belonged to him; much of what happened between us, I had already felt before. I just need a "him" to fulfill the one and only feeling I had never experienced: an actual penis inside of me. Every other sensation I had already experienced for seven whole years before age fourteen. So, I could understand his questioning whether or not I was really a virgin-because I "kinda-sorta" was not. March 14th was not the night I really lost my virginity (by definition) because I lost any innocence and "virginity" at age seven starting with being in that attic and seven whole years after that. "He" (who ended up being Santana) just got [lucky?], got farther and got in: "first..."

2

THE PRECOCIOUS RIPENING

I was just: "different." All my life I've been "different," I felt "different."

If it wasn't for the fact that I have a picture of me at age seven holding a baby doll in my hand, I would swear that I never even played with toys because I didn't. Of all the things I can remember, playing with that doll was not one of them-that's for sure. The girls my age would have Barbie Doll parties, where they would bring all their Barbie's different outfits and such. I never once went to any of their Barbie parties-because it just did not interest me. For me, it was such a lame and childish waste of time. I didn't understand it. I didn't see the fun in it. I would rather read a book, watch a movie, practice singing, dancing or close the door to my bedroom and entertain myself doing those things-if no one else was around or available to do them with.

I was sweet and talkative. I liked talking to people-constantly. I was a people watcher: adults-mainly.

I was very curious about how they lived, and things they would say in conversation with one another as compared to how they would talk to us kids. The funny thing about me is that I wasn't a mouthy, cursing, smart-mouthed lil' girl. I spoke when asked to speak and conversed when the invitation was extended. I could hold a conversation with an adult then come down to conversing with kids my own age.

That earned me "power" when I was a little girl. I was always the delegated one by my friends and as well; my friends' mother's-they all loved me. They much preferred their kids to be around me over most any of our other friends, because all their parents knew that I was smart, talented and wanted to be somebody when I grew up. It was as if they felt like some of "me"-my personality-would rub off on their kids in some way that would eventually make them proud parents of "Little Miss Personality."

I lived a double-life at a very young age. As compared to the average child that experienced such things from ages seven to thirteen, with the goings on in my lil' life, I showed no signs of what the typical child would probably show. The kids I hung out with probably would have folded in two-to have lived the life I had lived up to that very point. My friend's parents, like my mother, had no idea the things I had already experienced. My curiosity about adults and ability to hold their attention and interest was because of far more than they could never imagine. I would often hear adults whisper to my mother: "girl that child's been here before." That was all they could say from observing me.

I was just: "different."

Rather than feeling terrorized, wetting the bed at night, having nightmares, feeling withdrawn and acting out; I thought I was living a normal life, but that I had "secrets" nothing more.

Secrets like mine don't always manifest themselves in ways that you most commonly hear about. I was never threatened with threats like: "you'd better not tell anyone or else!" I was never threatened with any bodily harm or claims they would hurt me or my mom if I told someone. I wasn't manipulated with candy and toys or led like a lamb being led to slaughter so, to me, all was well-as-was. I wasn't maladjusted with any personality disorders or having behavioral problems at school.

I was involved. I was active. I was eager. I was always interested and insistent on learning to do things on my own.

I insisted on being trusted to wash every dish in the house, demanding that my mother remove all the knives and sharp objects to let me stand in that chair and have at that dishpan with the bubbles in it!

I insisted that my mother's friends bringing their red buckets of funky chitterlings and allowing me to stand at the kitchen sink from sun up to sun down every Thanksgiving through New years; cleaning the skin off until you could almost see through each wrinkled grey piece. I loved hearing grown-ups praise me for doing things for myself and around the house that grown-ups could do, and that I could do better than the average kid (my age). I loved to feel dutiful, useful, worthy and good for something.

I was quite spoiled-a very free-spirited child who rarely was told "no" to anything.

At age six, outside of getting my ass whipped in the middle of a department store for screaming, kicking, and insisting on getting the pair of black patent leather shoes I wanted, I was never told "no" or got spankings and such. Even to observe such a scene outside of it being me, seemed immature and childish to me-like that kid was "acting like a child" and probably deserved that spanking.

I was independent-and trusted.

By age six, I was able to comb and style my own hair.

It was picture day and I was insistent on wearing my hair like Chaka Khan, but my mom had other plans for my hair. I began kicking and screaming; fighting her off and away from me with the hair sheen in one hand, and the hairbrush in the other-refusing to let go of either. Outside of that-I was never a problem child.

At age five, outside of getting caught with one leg out of the window of our third-floor bedroom (pillow case in hand) thinking that my clothes stuffed in it would fly me away to: freedom, the sky, and the great outdoors, I never did anything bizarre or crass. My middle brother could manipulate me into doing anything (or his dirty work).

After our being punished and made to sit in the back room for the day, he had to come up with the remedy for us to escape, so he sent me to test the elements first. After that spanking, I never put myself in positions that would cause me to get spankings-ever again. That didn't feel good to me.

Outside of those typical kinds of things-I had no problems or issues.

Any freedoms or liberties I took-I earned.

I pretty much deserved most everything I asked for-and mom and dad made sure of it.

I deserved anything I wanted to do, and anyplace I wanted to go.

I was an easy child to raise. My mom and dad never worried about me or had to constantly discipline me. I received lots of attention and praise for my talents and academics. My dad made it a tradition to make sure he spent at least twice a week with me: full daddy-daughter days-taking me to dinner, shopping, to the movies or riding around in his car for hours of conversation, yet I never felt compelled to tell him what was going on in my secret life. It was private life. My mom and dad had no idea that something like this, for all those years, could have ever happened under her nose, care and watchful eye.

I was a very happy child. Precocious little me can remember being entrusted with a lot of "little responsibility" at seven years old. I was busy: school and church on Sundays and Wednesdays. I fought tooth and nail making sure my mom and dad bought my pink, yellow and mint green night-gown for me to get baptized in at age six. I attended Vacation Bible-School and camp every summer. I had friend, family, dad outings and constant neighborhood fun with friends. You name it-I was doing it. My schedule was full.

Like any other normal well adjusted kid where I lived-I kicked ass and got my ass kicked by other kids on occasion. Third graders, we were. The little mean bitch made her way around the corner to me and up on my porch and wailed on my ass so quick and fast that she had me in total shock and awe. All I could do was cover my face with one hand and grab onto her t-shirt with the other hand then scream with the force of a thousand punches: "If you stop punching me-I'll let go of your collar!" I never lived that beat-down, down, in a household filled with brothers who for years, used that as leverage against me. I had just got done living in the shadows of the notorious "Landon Harris Ghost of Classroom Past" smack-down, and no thanks to Collar Girl, I was right back into an "If-You-Stop-Punching-Me-I'll-Let-Go-Of-Your-Collar!" notch under all my brother's belts. They loved to re-enact those two ass-whippings I received whenever I would behave like the spoiled little brat of a sister that I was to them at times.

Landon Harris was a cute boy and classmate of mine. One day, when our teacher gave us all a demonstration on how things that sank or swam. After some time, she felt like we should know which objects would sink or swim. She began dropping objects into the water then asking each of us which objects sank and which objects swam. Everyone in the circle did well until we got to Landon; he missed practically every object. All the kids laughed at him after each time he failed, and on the only one-that I (almost) joined the laughter on, I barely got a chance to crack a smile before he reached over and knocked starch out of me. All I remembered was my little tortoise shell glasses flying one way and my face flying the other. For nearly two school years I was branded with a new name at school: "Landon-Smacked-Her So-Hard-That-Her-Glasses-Went-Flying-To-The Left-And-Her Face-Went-Flying-To-The-Right!"

That was okay though, Landon merely had a raging crush on me. It merely killed him to see that I (almost) laughed at him. But I bet you by the time I got off that floor from searching for my glasses, I looked up and put two of those four eyes on him-it was on and poppin' from there! All hell in his heart broke loose and from that point on, life as he knew it was never the same. I swear that boy followed me around ever since that day; clinging to me like laundry static.

So outside of being beat-branded by Collar Girl, smacked by Landon, and in later years; bum rushed and nearly ganged-raped at Leroy's store by "Cable-Boy" and his boys; that was about as traumatic as childhood got for me.

My secret life was merely a pleasure to me-it didn't cause me any pain or problems. I wasn't exposed to porn or sex of any kind on television. I wasn't exposed to drugs, a drug lifestyle, or a dysfunctional household with absent parents and bad examples of the same. I can very well warn and proclaim: "Daddy's guard your daughters! Watch their every move! Keep up constant dialogue with them! Know where they are at all times!"

…but that would merely be a public service announcement and something that was true for even-me, yet and still-under their nose, care and watchful eyes, they saw and knew nothing. I kept conversation going with my mom and dad-at all times. My mom and dad did guard me, nurture me, protect me and watch my every move. I was where I was supposed to be at all times. It's just that sometimes I slipped away next door, upstairs, in the attic, around the corner, across the street, in the closet, or behind the couch. But I was never too far from hearing my mom call out to me: "Angie!"

Yet and still…

3

RIPE & READY. GANGS, BANGS & PANGS.

Ah man. I had my day all planned out until Aunt Dot and Mother Nature started gossiping.

Ten years-old on a hot summer day and I got my period. Typically, I would wear cut off jean shorts-but this particular day, I searched high and low for a full pair of jeans.

Every summer, I would cut every pair of jeans that I wore in the fall, winter and spring, so that I could have tons of jean short choices in the summertime. My mother *hated* that. By the time school came back around for the fall, she would be screaming at me for having no jeans for school. This particular day-I know how she felt, because I was out of my head from trying to find a pair; knowing that I most probably had none. By some stroke of luck, I found a long pair and wore them with a pink and mint green polo t-shirt and a pair of sneakers. I did not want any part of my skin exposed at all. If I could have-I would have covered up to my neck that day.

I had gotten up early that morning-my mom was gone to work. I went to the bathroom and there "she" was when I wiped. I sat on the toilet seat and smiled; ready-and in complete preparation for what I was supposed to do next. Obviously, since I had been reading any and everything I could about sex, what to do when I became a woman, was too, something of interest to me. I had no recollection of having my mom tell me exactly what to do when that day was to happen-I only read about it.

There were no sanitary napkins in the linen closet, medicine cabinet, under the bathroom sink or in my mom's room-just tampons. I called her at work to tell her the news. She giggled and whispered through the phone: "Oh my baby's a woman now-bless her heart."

With a half-frown and a smile on my face I said to her: "But mom, there are no pads here-only tampons. I don't want to be sticking nothing in me like that," I said to her-reminiscing how (during my reading) I skimmed past "how to use tampons." The cartoon-like picture of this woman with her head back, mouth open and one foot up on the toilet did not appeal to me. The whole page and picture played in my head while I was talking to mom. "Pads would suffice-thank you," I said-cutting her off-not hearing a word she was saying while I reminisced about the corny tampon lady.

"I'm going to have [your friend Dana's mother] bring over a few pads for you until I can bring you some-home when I get off from work," she explained.

"Hold on," she paused, putting me on hold to place the call six doors up from me.

She returned back to the line: "Ms. Andrea should be ringing the bell any minute to bring you a few pads over, and I'll see you when I get home."

"Okay," I replied-while I sat on the chair of my third-floor bedroom: pigeon toed and eager; waiting for my doorbell to ring.

Dana's mother finally made it to deliver my essentials.

The doorbell rang: she held onto it as if she was singing and giggling my name before removing her finger to release it.

"Here I come!" I yelled, repeatedly out of the third floor window-down to her.

I ran down to the second floor and peeked in to one of my brother's rooms and he wasn't in there.

I continued to run down the steps to the first floor, and there my twin brother lay; watching television on the couch.

"Here I come!" I yelled down the steps leading to the front door.

I heard my brother yell while throwing a pillow at me:

"Uhd! You're nasty!"

I figured I had blood on my light-blue night gown and it grossed him out. I didn't care, I kept running down the steps to get to the bottom to open the door for Mrs. Andrea who stood there with a big smile on her face-she too was "so proud of me."

She looked me up and down, rolled her neck back-giggled-then gave me a hug so tightly; echoing the same thing my mom said: "Oh Angie's a woman now. Bless your heart baby," she said.

I gave her a side smile-not knowing whether I was supposed to say "thanks," throw my thumb up and say: "yeah-check me out," or what.

"Now do you know what to do with these?" she hurriedly asked me; ready to educate me.

I replied, "Yes, I do. I know what to do." I laughed assuredly; finding it so funny that these two old battle axes acted like I was supposed to be asking them a ton of questions when little did they both know [I thought] I was damned near ready for the world and all that was to come with it by age ten. My period, like anything else was something I had been planning for and read about-ready for the moment it was to happen. I just wasn't ready for was what happened in Old Man Leroy's candy store some nine hours later.

From the moment I got those sanitary napkins, I had done everything right.

I took my time as if the world had to wait on me that day. Aunt Dot and Mother Nature was the boss of me, but I was the boss of Father

Time that day. I took my bath different and slowly that day. I combed my hair intently and differently that day. I prepared and handled myself like a complete "woman" that day, but I had been preparing for that day to arrive like a wife prepares for her wedding day to arrive.

I was so dramatic. When I went to visit my friend Dana and other friends, I was quiet and reserved, feeling like I was now on some different level than all of my friends, because they hadn't got their periods yet. That day, I felt very secretive and protective of myself, as if-beginning this day, I had to do things a little different than the day before because I was now a "woman."

By the time I got dressed to begin my day; I noticed that my brothers talked to me slowly and intently. We hadn't fought all day like we used to do while my mom would be at work. In awe, they stared me all up in my face as if they were going to see something different in it that they didn't see the day before. I could tell that my mother told them over the phone not to piss me off, because they were on their best behavior, and anything I said-went (that day). So for about nine hours into my womanhood, I was able to have it all my way until running into "Cable Boy" and his buddies in the middle of Leroy's candy store. Well, something like that…it was the other way around.

Totally fucked up my big day.

All I did was go to the candy store to grab a bag of Crunchy Cheese Doodles, A Little Hug fruit punch and a pack of watermelon Now & Laters hard candy. That short trip turned into a situation at a distance unforeseen. When I walked in, no one was in there but me.

Behind me was a Galaga arcade game to the left, and a Pac-Man arcade game-to the right. I was leaning to the right side with my elbows on the counter. My knuckles were dug into my right cheek as Leroy (the store's owner) began to brown bag my goodies. The front door of the store swung open to one of the six boys who smiled at me as I turned around with my right hand above my brow; squinting from the glare of the bright outdoors-shining in my face and through the dimly lit hole in the wall neighborhood store.

The one boy looked at me and smirked then ran back outside as the door shut quickly behind him. By the time I reached for my brown bag from Leroy, the door swung back open, and like a swarm of bees, all six guys came running in and around me while one of them pressed upon me with his hands grabbing my waist; humping and thrusting into me like animals in the wild.

I reached my hands into the eleven by fourteen serving window's ledge for support. I tried bucking back and kicking like a wild horse because I was so afraid that he was going to try to wrestle me to the dirty floor of the store. I held onto that window for dear life, I must have looked like Carol Ann hanging on while getting pulled by the Poltergeist.

I started screaming bloody murder when each boy took turns grabbing me from behind while holding on to my waist and humping me like wild animals. I was **so** angry and disgusted. I let go of the window while trying to turn around and keep my balance, but they had me pinned and bent over. All of them were taking turns hunching on me while grabbing my one fully developed breast-the other stuffed with toilet paper. (I was one of those girls-who for almost a year-had one fully developed A-cup left breast while the right one remained swollen and looking like a little bud that, at any moment was going to pop out and catch up with the other one).

I tried hard to keep my balance and not fall to that filth because I knew that it would be a bad situation if they got me down on that floor, but before I knew it-my back was flat to that filthy floor-I couldn't over power them at all.

They all hovered over me, as I screamed for Leroy's help. I could hear him faintly from beneath the chest of one of the musty boys lying on top of me hunching and pumping me wildly while I screamed and cried my heart out. This three-minute catastrophe was so barbaric and painful that it seemed like I lay there for hours. I was so tired and worn out that it felt to me, what it must feel like for football players running into one another on the football field.

Old Man Leroy had the door to his store and counter's entry and exit wall so booby-trapped (from being afraid that this kind of thing would happen to his cash register rather than a person) that it took him forever to get from behind that damned counter. Knowing Leroy, he probably was struggling to decide how he was going to watch his cash register while trying to help me fight off the pack of wolves.

I never recalled Leroy's candy store ever getting robbed, so all of that self-made booby trapped wiring he did to lock himself in (while servicing the neighborhood through that stingy eleven by fourteen window), ended up backfiring on poor little me-laying there getting treated like a piece of meat that had been tossed into that lion's den.

By the time Leroy made his way out to them (with his rolled up newspaper in one hand and a full forty ounce bottle of beer in the other-as weapons) they had all scattered about; busting their way out of the beat up wired self-made front door.

Leroy kneeled down to me as I lay there in fetal position, crying my heart out. He began apologizing to me while running all their names off to me. I held my hand up to quiet him as I shook my head and said: "No, no need for that. I already knew who they are."

They all hung out together-every single day. None of them lived on our street. Each one lived a couple of streets over and the ringleader lived in a different neighborhood altogether. They had friends on my street that they would visit, so everybody knew who they were from being known as big-time troublemakers. Each one of them had double names like: Tom-Tom, Bay-Bay, Day-Day, Ray-Ray and Kay-Kay. The ringleader was the only one with a single syllable acronym name (one that he earned, courtesy of a cable tv channel-because it was rumored that he was the original inventor of stealing cable television). That earned him massive street-cred and the moniker of an entire cable channel's acronym in place of his own (real) name.

"Go get your brother's baby, go on and get your brother's!" Leroy said to me as I began to peel my tired little body off of his filthy sticky floor. I felt *so* icky.

"Say no more," I gestured and said to Leroy. I was so agitated and disgusted.

I then peeled myself off of his filthy floor-still holding on to my brown bag full of goodies.

The first day I got my period, and feeling ever so violated; I stood up and placed my hands to my knees, bowed my head and cried and little puddle of tears that fell straight from my eyes down to the sticky floor without even rolling down my cheeks. "Does anybody have any reason why these two should not be joined together in holy matrimony? Speak now or forever hold your peace." ...In an instant; my big day was squashed; squashed like a woman's wedding getting interrupted by an objection unforeseen. I felt so robbed of my special day-all lost to these saps who had no idea what they were in for, when I made my way out past Leroy's beat up store door that he was standing there holding open while yelling at Cable Boy and his boys outside:

"Stupid little twerps down there humping on that lil' girl! You lil' nasty fuckers! Get 'way off from in front of my store! Get 'way from here! Don't come back 'round here no more! I'm getting my gun! I'ma get it! I'll get'cha's!" he threatened; still swinging that forty ounce of beer and rolled up newspaper as if he was going to do some serious damage with them both. Those weapons of choice he had in his hands did not convince these thugs that he had anything remotely close to a real gun near or on him. They proceeded to curse and laugh at Leroy as if he was merely cracking jokes with them.

My walk home from Leroy's was all but two minutes away. From my porch, I could step right down and peek around the corner to see if Leroy was open-on any given day.

When I got to the corner of my building and in front of my porch, I turned to make sure those heathens were all still standing there arguing with Leroy. They had no care or concern that I was gasping and crying hysterically. They had no idea that I had just became a "woman" some nine hours earlier that day, and in an instant-they made me and it feel icky like Leroy's sticky floor that they plastered me to.

By the time I placed my right foot onto the first step of my porch, it was like an alarm had gone off in the neighborhood: my mom was just getting out of the car from work. People were running up to her trying to tell her what Old Man Leroy had told them. All the while, you could still hear Cable Boy and his boys laying into Leroy with laughter, watching him fight with words and a forty ounce.

"Are you okay Angie! Are you okay baby?" my mother kept asking me over and over-while in between her care and concern; calling upstairs to Twin so that he could get downstairs to kill the muthafuckas and save her the trouble...

"What's wrong with Angie!" Twin yelled from the first floor window-repeatedly-all the way down the steps while slipping on his sneakers at the same time. He busted through the front door:

"What's wrong with Angie? What's wrong with Angie?" he continued asking. All the while getting prepared to kick *some*body's ass for every teardrop he was watching fall down my face-that's all he knew.

All I had to do was stand back away from the porch, get close to the curb, and point down to the sight of Leroy still trying to swat Cable Boy and his boys 'way off from in front of his store. Twin could sum up what happened from there. Say no more, because he commenced to saving my mother the muthafuckin' trouble by charging across the street like a lightning bolt; going in on all six of those fools with the speed and force of a rolling bowling ball knocking down a full set of pins. He was knocking and socking three of the boys at one time, while they were falling into Leroy's wooden and wired barely there door. They were so caught off-guard; yelling and screaming for dear life-while catching quick, swift savage beat downs from one fiercely angry boy who loved his twin sister despite how much he picked on her.

The other three sat from across the street watching in horror, still knowing they did not stand a chance even if they tried to do a six-on-one. My brother was a madman that day-like a bull in a China shop. Those boys had no idea how hard my brothers worked to treat me like a little princess and refrain from taunting me with the daily: "stop-punching-me-I'll-let-go-of-your-collar" jokes for the day, and now this? Oh hell no.

In what seemed like the blink of an eye, and a scene out of a movie; my now crazed twin brother made his way across the street to the other three boys. Cable Boy was the first to shoot off running up the back way of our street. The two remaining boys got smashed together like a set of bowling ball pins entrapped in my brother's hands. One fell to the ground, as my brother held on to the other one. With the one under his foot, and the other in a full-nelson; Twin was hungry for that ringleader. He yelled out to the onlookers: "Where did [Cable Boy] go? Where did he go? Where did he go? Where did he go? Where did he go?"

We all knew (if you weren't from the neighborhood) the uphill direction that Cable Boy ran-was the only way off of the street. And from the very bottom (where we were); getting to the top of it was quite a long ways to go-even if you ran rather than walked. The unfortunate part about not actually living on our street was that, like snitching, we had a "code" of our personal street. Nobody was to ever know or go through the quick secret back way to get *off* of the street if you didn't live on the street. Cable Boy and his boys didn't know that if you did not make that dash to the right, and through the wooded back alley down past Old Man Leroy's store; your only way off our street was that long haul up hill. No matter how cool you were with the boys on our street, that secret back exit to get off the street was privileged information that only the boys in the neighborhood shared amongst one another-just in case they ever needed to use it for a quick getaway. Cable Boy and his boys weren't privy to that information, so Cable Boy had no choice but to run the wrong and long way.

The APB was put out on him, and all my brother's friends headed up the back side and front sides of the street to make sure he would be cornered from wherever they met him on the hill, which ended up being about mid-ways before he was off the street. When they cornered him; they backed him down towards the front side of the street where my brother walked slowly up on him like the grim reaper. You could practically hear theme music playing. I don't know if Cable-Boy was opening his mouth to apologize, plead his case, talk shit or all three, but before he could utter a full sentence, my brother had his hands around his throat; lifting him off the ground as if he was a killer in a horror movie. Cable-Boy tried his best to fight back but he could not, he was in complete shock. Twin then released him so that he could allow Cable-Boy to go toe-to-toe with him, but instead, Cable Boy threw what looked like a terribly rehearsed drop-kick that he had rehearsed one too many times with his lil' brother and cousin's. That puny little leg got caught up in my brother's hands like a fly trap-it seemed to annoy Twin even further.

He then lifted Cable-Boy up and tossed his body on top of the banister railing that hang six-feet high over the cement-walled basement apartment where my third-grade girlfriend lived with her dad, brother and sister. In what was looking like a murder about to be committed; my third-grade girlfriend and her dad stepped outside their door only to see poor Cable-Boy hanging from their basement apartment railing looking like a piglet being roasted while trying hard to catch his breath.

Twin was merciless as he pushed, punched, bent and bitch-slapped Cable-Boy like a slab of lard while hanging him over the railing as if he wanted his body to break in two. My third-grade girlfriend walked up the steps to me and began to rub my hair and forehead, then asked:

"Are you okay Boo? Are you okay?"

"Yes," I nodded back to her.

As a nickname of endearment, she always called me "Boo," way before it was a popular term of endearment.

Twin was busy handling his functions for his sister-torturing that poor boy. My TGGF's father was finally able to convince him to unwrap Cable-Boy from hanging six-feet over and above the cement floor of his basement apartment:

"Come on my man, let him go, he 'got your point-he don't want no more. Let him live young-blood, calm down. Your sister's alright now my man. This lil' knucklehead punk's not worth it-let him go. Look at him crying. Let him down man, he's not worth it," pleaded my TGGF's father. My brother then unwrapped Cable from the railing and lifted him back safely over and onto the ground.

He was so weak and crying at this point that he had no more energy to try that cornball ass drop-kick he pulled at first. Unlike the loudmouth he was earlier; he limped back toward the top of the hill to freedom as if he was just released from a cage. It was he-who know had his hand over his brow, looking to the light for God to lead his ass up and away from Twin, and out of my neighborhood-where he had no business carrying on like they way he did in territory uncharted by knowledge he was not privy to…

~~~~~~~~

Life eventually returned back to normal, and I was back to having fun with my friends again.

We liked to get together and take turns singing our favorite songs to each other and using one another for each other's audience. The fun in it (for a few) was giggling at my TGGF-she sang the worse out of everyone and couldn't hold a note if her life depended on it-lord knows she tried. For about two years already, she and I had been secret kissing buddies, so I secretly had her back-no matter her shortcomings, awkward ways or in spite of the fact that she did not fit in with my other friends; just me-outside of them...

In addition to taking turns singing, a life that was good and normal also included whipping out the tetherball and rope, then heading to the bottom of the street to wrap it around the pole and go at it for hours at a time. All who wanted to play, knew the rules: just take a seat at the end of the wall and wait your turn to step up to (me) the tetherball champ; whose forearms stayed red, swollen and welted so much that the pain eventually turned numb.

The only time I would get a break and some sit down time at the end of that line on the cement wall, was when big-corn fed Jasmine would bring her bodacious presence to the set. Her apartment was way up the street towards the top of the hill, all she had to do was step outside and look down the hill for a crowd, screams, laughter and commotion. She knew that we were huddled there and it was game-on. It was like she could sense the excitement in her body, so she would head down that hill to prepare us for her reign of terror. We would know when she was coming because we could practically feel the earth move under her feet. When she would arrive down to the bottom of that hill, she would change the energy of the whole game. It was one thing to be beating my friends in the game-it was challenging, but fun. We spent a lot of time laughing at everybody stepping up with their "A" game having told themselves that this time, they were going to sit *me* down. But when Jasmine would sit at the end of the wall, I would get annoyed from having to use up all my endurance; knocking that ball back and forth from playing with my mediocre-skilled friends, knowing full-well that I was going to need all the endurance I could muster up in order play Jasmine's big corn-fed ass. Because of the tension, our laughter and fun of the sport would turn serious and quiet. All our brows would be frowned up, and we seemed to be fighting one another with the ball in between us-instigating the fight.

It was one thing for me to be kicking butt in tetherball, but she gave kicking butt in tetherball a whole new meaning. It was like, when she would hit the ball, if you weren't quick and careful; she could wrap you around the pole with the rope *and* the ball. The tetherball had its own sound when she would hit that bitch. It sounded as though she would bust a whole in the ball each time she hit it. If you played her too hard, and she was forced to use both hands, we would pray that the rope was tied to the pole and the ball tight enough, because we remembered all too well, both flying off the pole and headed uphill a time or two or three.

Part of me hated Jasmine's presence on the set because she didn't have that kind of "respect-fear:" that fear of being defeated-not even possibly. It was almost like she knew she was going to beat everyone twice over but wanted to come down and interrupt the game just to stroke her own ego. I would sometimes hold the ball and rope in my hand, then glance over and scowl at her. I would fantasize about the rope being long enough to toss the ball out to swing toward her face, so I could say: "oops, 'scuse me," just so she could look me in my face before giving me a run for my money and sitting me down. The way she would sit there eating her barbeque potato chips and orange Jungle Juice, smacking all loud and paying no attention to other people's game-totally annoyed me. She wouldn't turn her head away out of fear or shyness, bur rather, sheer disregard-as if in her mind, she was saying: "I can beat you with my eyes closed." She even disregarded her champion opponent at the pole-always. She didn't give a damn who won, because she knew her big heavy handed ass was going to clear the set real quick after a round or maybe two, because nobody wanted to play against her with the exception of me and "If-You-Stop-Punching-Me-I'll-Let-Go-Of-Your-Collar" [girl].

Watching big Jasmine and Collar Girl go at that tetherball would be like letting two beasts in the wild go at it in a game of survival of the fittest. It was always a treat and a long entertaining match to watch. Sometimes it would go so long that you would either forget which one won or you would be so tired from vertigo, and your head bouncing from left to right: Jasmine (then Collar Girl). Jasmine (then Collar Girl). Jasmine (then Collar Girl). Jasmine (then Collar Girl)…by the time the game was over, we really didn't care who won.

Listening to the sound of both of them hit the ball was an experience in and of itself. Each punch sounded as if the air was trying to escape both their abuse, or like the ball itself, wanted to take legs and run. I could only relive the pain my head was going through while Collar Girl made her way up my steps and beat the crap out of me that one day-three years earlier. I wanted out of that ass-whipping: stat! It seemed like she had so much fun at my screaming and poppin' her collar; that ever since that day, she only felt half alive if she wasn't teaming up and starting trouble with another shit-starter nicknamed "T-Rubble." Her nickname was fitting, because all she did was stir up riff-raff and trouble. The both of them would be doing their best to terrorize me, but I was a defiant little something. **Nobody** was going to bully me comfortably and easily. I had been there-done that in my little life-time years before this and refused to allow it to blossom and manifest ever again.

No matter how many times I sat outside on my porch, from four doors up where Collar Girl and T-Rubble would be sitting, a rock would always come flying down-hitting me upside the head. Even after screaming and nearly stomping a hole in my porch's cement steps, and yelling at them both with the force of a good tetherball beating; you best believe I was coming *right* back outside to sit *right* back on *my* porch. Sometimes I would get fed up enough with the rock throwing, that I would run off the porch to go and fight back. And each time, I would run into Collar Girl's fist.

No matter *how* many black eyes she gave me, I *refused* to let her scare me away to oblivion. I was not going to be forced in to staying in the house because of these girls. I had no shame, and besides, I was lived there first! I wasn't going anywhere! Trying to bully me was a full-time job. I insisted it be.

Bully me? Oh hell no!

At eleven years old, I had way too much eleven year old clout: The love and adoration from of every parent of my eleven year-old peers, all the way down to the love and respect from our church and Sunday school teachers. I was the lead in every church play and provided spontaneous entertainment many-a-day, for the adults and older teenage girls who would stop me from playing with my friends just to ask: "Angie, do me an acting scene where the girl is in love with someone!" "Angie, do me an acting scene where the girl is fed up with her cheating husband and she's going to leave him!" "Angie, do me an acting scene where the girl just got attacked!"

I nearly had to take orders for the requests I was given.

Innocent, kind and totally shameless without a shy bone in my body-whatever you would ask me-without any thought, or contemplation-spontaneously; I would deliver. I was happy, athletic, humorous, animated, theatric, artistic and dramatic. From age nine, I attended a school where I was being groomed for art, drama and dance; so the adults and the older teenage girls where I lived always wanted me to exhibit what it was I was learning five days a week/eight hours a day while away from home.

I would burst into character for them, and then laugh afterwards while they would all clap and hug me with words of encouragement:

"You see? That baby's going to be somebody-watch and see!" The people of the streets where I was raised, made me feel so special. They had no idea about my secrets and the life I had been living up through that very day. They were so helpful for my self-esteem and self-worth and I didn't even know it at the time. I had no idea that I so badly needed their words of encouragement that later-ended up meaning more to me than they would have ever known...

Other times the adults and older teens would put singing requests in: "Sing something for me Angie!" they would say. I loved to pretend to be exhausted and overwhelmed by all their requests and surprising them by bursting out impromptu classics like: Natalie Cole: "Keeping a Light," Deniece Williams': "Gonna Take a Miracle," "Silly," or "Too Much Too Little Too Late." It would be shocking to them because it was uncommon for a girl my age who (little did they know) had been studying and teaching myself just *how* to sing just like whomever I would be singing. I was an expert at imitating the Natalie Cole's and the Deniece Williams' with the emotion of heartbreak, shame and despair, as if I had experienced everything that I was singing about. Other times, I would be singing Natalie Cole's: "Our Love" or Deniece Williams': "Free"-gesturing and performing for them while standing on the steps in front of our brownstone-like apartments; singing about love and freedom from the type of relationship that I still had yet to experience, and was light-years away from being able to identify with- but singing and them as if somehow, I too (at eleven years old) had experienced every lyric.

While every sinister, secret and wrong thing was going on; everything else was going right. Because I didn't see the sinister and the secrets as wrong, but rather: "right"-right along with all that going my way.

From my eleven year-old point of life's view, the only sinister and wrong worth reporting to my mom was a first-grade bully named Cindy and the pre-teen blues that Cable Boy and his boys, Collar Girl and T-Rubble all gave me. All else felt good, because I knew what felt bad: getting beat-up, black-eyes, gang-grinded, and bullied did not feel good. In my life up through this point, *that* is what "made me feel uncomfortable."

So, bully me? Oh hell no!

At eleven years old, I had too much clout as well as a mentor at that time, and much earlier in my eleven year old life as well. Life could have started off badly and with me having my spirit broken had it been up to Mrs. Cavanaugh. She was a fat meanie of a teacher who spent most of my kindergarten school year disciplining, yelling and placing our noses into chalk drawn circles on the blackboard.

She would have us stand there for the entire class on most days, occasionally switching us off by placing us underneath her desk and stuffed between her fat legs and stinky feet.

She spent practically my entire kindergarten year doing this to all of us kids, putting these acts in heavy rotation as if this was part of the school curriculum. It didn't seem to bother me once I got home any more than it did when I got free from under her desk while at school.

Life at home for me was so busy. I was always at church with the Lord and the Mormons, who set up worship down in the basement apartment at the back end of my building.

I divided the other half of my time with the Lord and Reverend Knight of the Baptist church.

Both churches were on the opposite ends of the city just like they were the antithesis of one another-in the way that they fellowshipped and the way that they looked. Reverend Knight's church was a complete hole in the wall with drapes that varied in design and color. You could tell they were hung for blocking shade rather than vanity. His pews were a few, but where the pews stopped, the metal chairs held us comfortably and safely. It was there where I learned my first black gospel song: "I'm Goin' Up To Yonder." I was serious-business about singing that song from the bottom of my lil' heart. At least once a month the church would sing it and allow me to start it off until the chorus part of the song would begin, and then the choir would take over from there. I loved them for that. I fell more in love with the church and the Lord, so much so that at six years-old I orchestrated my own baptism down to the night gown that I wanted my mom to buy for me, to wear for it: "Pastel Easter colors"- I insisted and made happen.

My other part-time with the Mormons was special to me too. I would be prepared-with my hair in ponytails, those black patent leather shoes (thank ya' much), white stockings, and full length slip already on. In the basement of the apartment building that I lived in, located three windows beneath my bedroom window; the moment I would hear those Mormons crack the door open, I would hurriedly put on one of my many ruffled dresses that I had laying out-ready to wear. I was serious-business about dressing and being prepared for church and you had better disturb my groove: "Here I come! Here I come!" I would yell out my window-bright and early; bidding my mom farewell in a hurry, then dashing down to the little neat and tidy basement church with rows of wooden pews to spare, matching curtains and no metal chairs. Over in the corner would be what I often thought about and loved so much: those pretty golden bells. I would slip my little fingers into the black handles and grab me one, and then we would be off to the neighborhood to paint it golden: me and the Mormons-ringing our church bells and collecting as many people as we could magnetically attract, to follow us back to the little basement church.

They didn't discriminate. I didn't discriminate. Everybody from 8 to 80, blind, young, crippled or crazy would have service with us. I welcomed them all because that was my church home, too.

Before service would begin (which consisted of quietly reading the scripture and modestly singing from hard cover hymnals); I would make sure all of our pretty golden bells were placed back in the corner of the church in their righteous place for the next time we would wake up the neighborhood for followers and fellowship. Those bells to me-were like diamonds. I polished them so good that they never had a scratch on them. I guarded those things with my life.

Both churches welcomed me with open arms. I was so inspired and happy that I cared nothing about my kindergarten teacher Mrs. Cavanaugh or my kindergarten through first grade bully: Cindy.

She knew my routine and would frequently hear me say that I had to hurry home to pee so that I could come right back outside to play. I was always in a tight and a rush to get home. Cindy took it upon herself to follow me home one day and forced me to pee in a corner by my building's basement back door, rather than allowing me to get up to our third floor apartment to pee in the toilet. When she passed that test, she figured she could make me do other things that I did not want to do-like harass my best friend Rhonda, all because she refused to reveal to Cindy; the Halloween costume that she was wearing in the school's Halloween parade.

Rhonda was defiant and would stand up to Cindy. Myself and everyone else gave in and showed our costumes, but Rhonda stood her ground. She insisted that hers be a surprise and indeed, it was. She was so pretty and so happy in her red tights, blue body suit, a big gold belt, her mother's big gold bracelets and black wig; feeling like Wonder Woman for a day at our school parade.

To test Rhonda's super powers, afterschool, Cindy made me follow behind Rhonda on her route home-forcing little ole' me to try and intimidate Rhonda-for her. I felt so badly for my friend that in between my kicks and yells that I was told to give her, I kept apologizing. Rhonda already knew I had long been caught in the rapaciousness of Cindy's rage and ridiculousness, and there was nothing my little self could do about it.

After watching me kick and hit Rhonda too lightly, Cindy would get up in my face like a drill sergeant and yell some more-forcing me to hit Rhonda harder. She would not let up until she saw that I put Rhonda through some kind of torment.

Growing tired of Cindy's yells and needing to hurry home to pee, I caught Rhonda off-guard and hurriedly pushed her to the ground, then proceeded to run home, hoping I could beat Cindy there.

I did. I made it to my building, past the back basement door and up to my third floor-with my key around my neck and into safety.

While at church with the Mormons part-time, and at Reverend Knight's church the other part-time; I would pray to my Lord that eventually my dear friend Rhonda would forgive me, and that I would never have to put up with anyone like Cindy ever again. I was defiant, serious-business and hell-bent about not being bullied. So for a whole five years since then, the Lord had been making good on his promises to me up to and through Collar Girl. And she thought she was just going to bully me easily?

Bully me? Oh hell no!

My first grade teacher Mrs. Tolliver would have just as soon as broken her box of chalk to know that years later and after all her love, encouragement and grabbing me by the cheeks; forehead-to-forehead, grunting in my face and poking into my chest: "don't you **ever** let anyone tell you: Angie-that you can't do **anything**, because you can! You can do anything, and I know this!" she would assure me-daily. She would probably turn over in her grave to know that her passion for teaching and my ease at learning did not pay off, but instead, some bully who beats up tetherballs and got inspired by my poppin' her collar, was now bullying me in ways that could have easily broken my spirit. Mrs. Tolliver was so impressed with the fact that at six years old, I knew how to spell words like "giraffe," and countless other words that were spelled unlike they sounded, that she kept me and a couple of other 'special" kids at a desk close by hers-away from other kids. There was no way in hell she would accept anything not right or like, seep into or get next to her golden-child.

Bully me? Oh hell no!

My second grade teacher Mrs. Belland, would have just as soon as broken her box of number 2 pencils to know that years later and after all her love attention, and affection; some bully who beats up tetherballs and got inspired by my poppin' her collar, was now bullying me in ways that could have ruined my self-esteem. Mrs. Belland was from Maryland; a shy, timid lily-white lil' lady with a mushroom hair-do and bright blue eyes. You could tell that she had never been around one single non-white kid for this length of time in all her life. I was the only one with enough personality to bring her out of her shell to make her comfortable enough to run the class. I would sing-talk to her and end whatever I was sing-talking with the words: "Miss Belland from Mare-landddd." She would spend the majority of the class teaching and squeezing me so tightly; rocking me back and forth like she never wanted to let me go. She needed me around-to give her the momentum she needed in order to do her job. She was interested in being there, but she was as scared as she was timid as she was interested, but needed me to balance it all for her. I was her diamond-child.

Bully me? Oh hell no!

My third-grade teacher Mrs. Jasper, would have just as soon as let that pretty red apple on her desk rot to know that years later and after all her attention, adoration and encouragement; some bully who beats up tetherballs and got inspired by my poppin' her collar, was now bullying me in ways that would normally cause a child to withdraw from the world. Mrs. Jasper was the wife of one of the members in a classic singing group, so she loved to acknowledge and separate her singing talented kids from the ones who weren't. She treated the fifteen minute talent portion of her class as if it were a part of her curriculum. Mrs. Jasper was old-school and around my mother's age. Little did she know, my mother and older brother would play a lot of old-school classics around the house every Saturday morning that I would be cleaning up-and that's how I learned the songs I would sing. When Mrs. Jasper learned that I knew and could sing songs she could relate to, that at my age, I should have known nothing about; that won her over. I was her star-child.

Bully me? Oh hell no!

I had too much clout as well as a mentor: Mrs. Tipton from fourth grade through seventh-grade, who spent a tremendous amount of time: loving me, tending to me, adoring me, encouraging me *and* wishing I was her child. All my mother had to do was say she didn't want me and Mrs. Tipton would have been glad to hand her the walking papers. To know that some bully who beats up tetherballs, and got inspired by my poppin' her collar, was now bullying me in ways that would normally cause a child to have massive irreconcilable behavioral problems; she would have had a conniption fit. Anything that Mrs. Tolliver, Mrs. Belland and Mrs. Jasper felt, Mrs. Tipton felt it one better. Every single thing they felt I could do-Mrs. Tipton felt I could do it better. I was her baby "everything," let her tell it.

Bully me? Oh hell no! I had way too many people who looked after me and was growing up to be way to much of a lady for that kind of child's play.

My right boob was making its way to catching up the fully blossomed left boob I'll have you know. There was no way in hell Collar Girl or anyone was ever going to sit me down with a rock, a couple of threats, a black eye, and a finger in my face. I was blossoming, growing up, coming up and busting out in places that girls my age could only dream of, and I was slowing becoming more and more a little queen bee by the days. There was no way in hell, some girl was going to bully me and think she was going to have a pleasant life in my neighborhood-one that she arrived to well after I did.

I ruled with kindness, and interest in care about me. I was a happy child, with lots of personality-the queen bee of all of my peers and their parents. By the time the social dichotomy of how everything was forming, Collar Girl had to try and beat me in a major way that she could not: *earn* her own clout. Either that, or she had to make up her mind to put her fists and rocks down to try and join me (provided that I let her in). I had no enemies, so I was not going to keep putting up with that bullshit. She however, was just as defiant and insistent on bullying me and my other friends as I was insistent on not being bullied. I had no idea where she came from with all this fight and fire inside of her, but I was a lover-not a fighter. I loved everyone and everyone loved me. That pushed she and T-Rubble out and away. I was untouchable, guarded and protected, and by this time, had no interest in letting either one of them in. I was running shit.

My friends and me would have "umbrella parties" and I was the head of them. Like a gang would have you "jumped" in, to hang-you would have to "dump" in. By invite, in order to be a part of my umbrella party you had to chip in by stocking up on penny candy, watermelon Now & Laters hard candy, Crunchy Cheese Doodles and Little Hug juice drinks. From there, you would have to step into our private little huddle (if I liked you and you liked my friends). I was such a female king and elitist from having being taught and experiencing that different things had their place-even if that included people, so, not too many invites had been given out because my little club was exclusive and you couldn't jump-in empty handed.

When you would get behind those two big umbrellas to block the view from the outside of the porch, you had to place your brown bag-front and center and then dump your penny candy, watermelon Now & Laters hard candy, Crunchy Cheese Doodles and Little Hug juice drinks. Low and behold if you came in with a couple of Snickers or Payday candy bars, you got extra love and special consideration during initiation. I was the gatekeeper of that covert operation and if I heard footsteps coming anywhere near our huddle, I would slide that umbrella over to the side and peek from behind it; squinting my eyes and daring anyone to try and infiltrate.

One thing about me was that I was nice and fair to everybody. But if you were mean to me-I'd never fuck with you, and you'd feel and regret it in the worse way. The tug-of-war and eleven year-old social clout of mine forced Collar Girl and T-Rubble to be closer to one another than each of them really preferred to. By the time I was through with those bitches, they had no one but each other to hang out with. They didn't have to see too much of each other however, because if it wasn't for Collar Girl's aunt and uncle, and T-Rubble's older brother putting them on punishment four out of the seven days of the week; they barely made it outside to see one another anyways. They just conducted the majority of their shenanigans, bull crap and shit-starting from their bedroom windows, while me and my peers went swimming, attended church, camps, Sunday school, karaoke and played tetherball, all-with a special kind of peace.

In between the talks about "life," with my dad, observing my mom (who lived life and whose thought process was the total antithesis of my dad), life at the school I was attending, the secrets, and the way I was living my life up through this point; I was slowly learning about secrecy, compartmentalization, cliques and elitism. My queen bee wings were growing by the day.

At home, everything was right, comfortable and going my way.

I was a growing little lady and knew all too well that I was a growing little lady, without fully understanding (at the time) just how I got like that-my body, my ways and my mind.

However, now was the time to make everybody take notice, and to be treated like the queen bee that I had blossomed into. So save the narrative.

Anybody got a problem with that had to speak (now) or forever hold their peace...

4

THE QUEEN BEE in ME

"Playtime" was nearing an end, when my right boob woke up for good and finally said hello to the world. The completely developed left one had been around for about a year. That right one had finally caught up with it. Both had now arisen: perky and straight-forward like they were kissing the wind.

I was *so* happy to rid myself of having to stuff the right side of my right bra with tissue. It was such a task trying to demi-plie' and arabesque my way through dance class with Mrs. Eckhardt constantly pirouetting up and down past all of us-patting and positioning our body parts.

Like clock-work it seemed to happen. Right at the moment where I'd stand facing the bar in first position: heel-to-heel, then turning with one hand on the bar-arm extended; frappe'ing forward then backwards. That seemed to always be the moment she would move in. She used that as her chance to run by and hold us by the front of our chests to straighten our backs, then she would look down and smack our asses-checking for any jiggle whatsoever. If she caught any jiggle she would yell out loud: "jelly booty-no jelly booty!" I had been so tired of trying to guard my right titty tissue while trying to keep my ass tight in dance class for Mrs. Eckhardt's approval. Thanks to her, it had been no problem bouncing quarters off of it-all praises due to her pressure and scrutiny.

The summer of that school year, I turned twelve years-old and playtime was definitely over back home with the girls and me under those umbrellas: "*Playtime is over bitches! This aint no muthafuckin' sit-in! I'm twelve years-old now and a full-grown queen bee, with cultured, polished and celebrated queen bee ways. It is now time to show and prove. I got my titty in full bloom-sitting up on perk, my ass tight and on perk and a fully blossomed flower with lots of grass on it. These lil'girl games are beginning to be a bit passe' to me-the kissing and grinding games are getting tired. It's time to try something different bitches!"* I may as well had said, but rather-demonstrated.

I decided that if they were going to hang out with me any longer, we were going to have to switch it up-and I meant pronto! I was already into other secretive "bigger and better things" and harboring secrets that their little minds could not comprehend, but still, it was now time for these girls to put up or get shut the fuck out. Putting up penny candy and bad food was not what I had in mind, nor was it an option:

"Save the drama for your mama and the goodies for your footies bitches! I'm on a diet anyways and I've got Mrs. Eckhardt on my ass-literally. So penny candy, watermelon Now & Laters, Crunchy Cheese Doodles, Little Hug juice drinks, Snickers,' and Payday candy bars aint cutting the mustard anymore," I may as well had said, but rather-demonstrated.

My umbrella parties soon turned into secret parties where everyone could still bring goodies (for each other-not me). Seeing some goodies was what I needed. I was growing and blossoming in ways that astonished me. I didn't know if it was with the help of my "older boyfriends," or what. I was just amazed and obsessed with why and how I was sprouting in ways that I was. I wanted to know why all my friends my age were still looking how they were looking: like six-o'clock. I wondering if my body was "giving me away-" telling my secrets about what I had been doing for the past six-years of my little young life: next doors, up stairs, in attics, around corners, across streets, in closets, behind the couches and such. I needed to know if everybody had what I had underneath their clothes. I needed to know if everybody's flower had grass and blossomed like mine did. So one day in the middle of my salivating at all of their junk-food goodies that because of dance, I wasn't allowed to have; I said to them all:

"Let's take turns going around one by one. Roll your pants downward so I can see what you got-if you got something down there, like some hair-like I do. I got a whole lot! Wanna see?"

Their eyes got big: "Oooooooooohh you do?" they asked, mesmerized at the thought of that possibly being true, considering the fact that I was always much more physically developed than they were.

Mother-nature played some tricks on me. In my mirror, I was like a freak of nature. About the only things we had alike as we grew together from eight to twelve years-old, were our baby faces, skinny arms and skinny legs. I left them behind when my one-then both boobs grew, my little booty grew (tight-no jelly), and my straight little hips developed a little curvature in them that you could see if you stared long enough. With that serving as visible proof, they all knew I most probably was not lying when I told them my flower had fully blossomed into a garden.

Everyone was sitting there looking at each other all stupid-trying to figure out who was going to go first.

I adjusted the umbrellas so that we could get some light inside our private little circle. I stretched my legs out from Indian-style position, watching their faces glued to my crotch and eating their Crunchy Cheese Doodles intently. Vulgarly and with a smirk on my face, I then sat back on my left arm and thrust forward so that they could get a full view of my pretty and fully blossomed flower. I flipped my shorts down some and showed it to them.

Like the juveniles they were, they all stretched their eyes open and squealed out and covered their mouths saying: "Ah!" as if I was in some kind of trouble. They were giggling and sitting there in complete girly shock. I let them stare for another couple of minutes as I looked at the astonishment in each and every one of their faces. Like dominoes, they all began tugging at their own shorts in a hurry, trying to expose themselves, but more curious to look down at themselves to see if anything different had grown on them through this moment that wasn't there as of early that morning. They were merely checking rather than exposing. The moment each of them could gather up enough sparse hair, they were up on their knees; mooning each other with their bald and barely haired little purses that had no comparison to my full pocketbook.

I sat there and turned my nose and face up-thinking in my head, how much I couldn't understand how we were either the same age or one to two years apart, but they hadn't blossomed like I had. That confused me so. I was so preoccupied with finding my physical equal for some sort of validation that I wasn't a complete freak of nature like in the back of my mind I thought I was. The comments my mom's friends would make to her, rang in my head: "Oooh what are you going to do with her?" and to me: "Ooh Angie you'd better keep those boys away from you!" while mom would chime in with her usual: "That's alright. You see a muthafucka fuckin' with her, kill him and save me the trouble!"

This preoccupation I had with finding my physical equal was about to cause nobody but me the trouble when Rita (my friend from school) had moved onto my street and a few doors up from me. We had been the best of friends at school for the entire school year, but when she moved on my street, if she was going to be my friend (*there*) she had to be trustworthy enough and willing to join in our raingear games. At school, I was one person-and played by the rules. But at home, I was another person-I made the rules: and anybody my umbrella shared everything from our candy to our kisses and now: a peek into our purses.

Things seemed to be going well under that umbrella when we all let Rita join in, and while it was cool and all; she was yet another purse bitch-that annoyed me. I wanted to see a grown bitch, or at least someone older that was my physical equal-even if she was my age.

It was her older sister Charlene who piqued my interest because she was about three or four years older than all of us and twice and a half my size. I could look right at her body and tell that she had what I wanted to see. Though she was older and much bigger than all of us, she liked being around us because the other older girls (who I would sing for) didn't quite mesh with her because she was slightly tomboyish. They were set in their ways and were well-past that initiation type of cliquey stage (where we all were). They just didn't give a damn. One thing about our street is that we were one big happy family. It was like life began there for all of us, we all grew up and developed there-in every way. Our groups and associations were formed since we were all tots there. The leaders were the leaders-forever, and the followers were the followers-forever. You got your place, you learned of your place and you remained in that place-comfortably. Of those of us who closely associated (the kids, us pre-teens as well as the older teenagers); none of our families seemed to ever move out and away from the neighborhood, so, if you moved in-you stuck out like a sore thumb. And if you stuck out like a sore thumb, you had to find your way.

Charlene couldn't find her way, and I had my eye on her.

I knew she was cornered and had nowhere else to fit in because if she wasn't in the house by herself, she would come around me and my buddies-trying to see if we would accept her. After enough subtle torture and apprehension, I finally accepted her-slowly. And well, since I did-they all did.

I would stare at her for long periods of time-undressing her with my mind and eyes-merely curious about her because not only was she twice and a half my size; I could tell that she most probably had gotten her period by observing the size of her breasts. But I was dying to take a peek at what I could almost bet was a pocketbook like mine. So after some time of feeling her out; enticing and making her feel welcome behind our umbrella with her sister (who I would have loved to trade for her), I decided to test her.

I knew it would take some time because she didn't seem as pliable as my buddies who were my age; we all seemed to melt into what we would do-as one. But with Charlene, I could tell that she would have to be tested-not molded. That annoyed me, because I had no time to play around trying to mold a bitch-my curiosity was getting the best of me.

So the day I decided that I would let my friend Rita *and* her sister Charlene get behind the umbrella on a 2 for 1 brown bag candy special, I was hoping that Charlene would ingratiate herself to me by letting me see her goodies. I had to think of a way to get Rita out from under the umbrella to run my test on Charlene to see if she would be down. The goal was for me to switch Rita out for Charlene, permanently-if this all worked out:

"Rita, head around to Leroy's to get your candy bag and then run over to the Dixie Cup Lady and grab me and Nina a raspberry Dixie Cup will you?"

"Okay," she replied, as I handed her the money.

I moved over and released her from under the umbrella and quickly turned back around-watching Charlene sitting in our circle eating up the goodies as if she was enjoying free lunch at school. With no time to waste I got straight to the point-the only way I always knew how: "Charlene, are you a grown lady yet?" I challenged her.

"Yeah I'm grown!" she yelled and smiled, feeling the sugar high from the junk food of my labor that I so graciously let her enjoy-free of charge, for now…

"That's not what I'm talking about though," I said, while cracking open my sunflower seeds, sitting Indian-style and looking into Charlene's eyes-seductively.

"Did you grow anything down there yet is what I'm asking. 'Cause I'm grown too-I got a lot down there."

Nina and the rest of the girls gulped down Little-Hugs and waited attentively on Charlene's next move.

"I got a lot too-probably more than your lil' pipsqueak tail!" Charlene laughed and asserted-thinking this was something that was going to be merely said then over with. But no, I was serious.

I moved in for the kill-looking at her with a serious face:

"Let me see then-show it to me!"

Nina and the girls laughed out.

Shocked and laughing, Charlene rolled her face back into her neck and responded: "Hell no. I ain't letting you see my stuff!"

I yelled at her:

"Well either you prove it or quit eating OUR stuff. And get out!" I snatched her goodie bag from her hand. I emphasized the word: "our" hoping that my buddies would assert themselves with me-but they were scared. Charlene was kind of solid-bodied, and I was secretly hoping that I would not have to threaten to let go of any collars on my porch again.

Charlene stood up and yelled: "Y'all are some nasty lil' things!"

"Nasty how? You are the one who said that you had grown lady stuff!" I flipped it on her.

Nina and the girls laughed loudly as Charlene looked really confused-remembering that she did say that.

So before she could flip it back on me, I looked at Nina and the girls and began to yell: "Charlene is a liar but Rita is truth! Charlene is a liar, but Rita is the truth!" repeatedly while Nina and the girls began to chime in.

Before Charlene knew it, she couldn't remember who asked who first. All she could do was cover her ears and do her best to yell over me and four other girls screaming: "Charlene is a liar, but Rita is the truth!" ... like a broken record-in every soprano octave unimaginable.

We were surrounding her like we were the hood version of "Children of the Corn."

I didn't care if her head popped off, all I wanted out of it was my secret to roll from out of its crevices.From over the umbrella, I saw her sister (my friend) Rita, approaching the porch with her goodie bag and the two Dixie cups for Nina and me.

I rushed in: "Rita your sister is a liar!" I yelled, as the rest of the crops lowered their voices while Charlene took her hands from her ears and yelled to her sister:

"They are nasty! They are nasty!"

That pissed me off even more because now I really felt that our secrets from behind that umbrella were going to get out, so I had to give it to her hard:

"CHARLENE IS A LIAR (BUT RITA IS THE TRUTH)! CHARLENE IS A LIAR (BUT RITA IS THE TRUTH)! CHARLENE IS A LIAR (BUT RITA IS THE TRUTH)!"

I reached for mine and Nina's Dixie cups and snatched the goodie bag from my friend Rita, who in my eyes at that moment, turned into the same infiltrator I felt her sister Charlene was at that moment-simply because they lived in the same house.

We sang and repeated that song nonstop while Charlene continued to cover her ears. I could tell that our screams and that song rang in her head like those loud gold bells that I used to ring as a little girl for the Mormons.

I didn't give a care if she heard our screams in her sleep that night. All I wanted was for our secret to be kept about what goes on behind our umbrellas. I was serious-business about secrets being kept out of the hands of any outsider.

With that, and as far as I was concerned, Rita and me could keep our friendship for and during the school year-outside of umbrella play, for she was no longer invited-because her sister was an outsider.

For me, it just didn't feel right to let her hang out with us in that way anymore. Quite frankly after that incident, I didn't too much care for the crop and me congregating under the umbrella anymore.

I came to terms with the fact that the girl I wanted to see was not going to want to hang out under umbrellas with silly little girls built like six-o'clock.

It worked out well for me to leave them to their Barbie Doll and dollhouse play while my TGGF and I hung out at her house in closets, or at my house behind the couch playing our own version of playhouse.

Rita and I would still hang out occasionally, whenever I would be over her house.

I would do my best to meet Charlene eye-to-eye-needing her to submit, wondering what, if anything she remembered that would put my umbrella secrets out and onto the street. It seemed like every time she would look back at me, in my head-all I could hear her say was: "your lil' pip-squeak tail!"

My squinted-eyed gaze had no affect on her whatsoever.

She knew that she could take me if she had to, and I knew she could too-so I didn't want any trouble.

I just wanted my secret back from her.

All she had to do was repeat her words: "ole nasty thing!" And I would have known for sure that what happened that day-stuck with her enough to repeat it to someone else.

As long as she didn't utter those words, regardless if she would submit or no, that was *almost*, just *partly*, submission enough for me. I refused to flat out ask her had she told anybody, because then-she would have thought she had me by the balls. I wasn't going to give her that kind of power, knowing that with no one to hang out with, she sure as hell needed some kind of leverage. I wasn't going to be up under her foot.

No matter how many times I made it over to my friend Rita's house, Charlene would not back down from my stare. All I could do to try and subdue her was come get Rita to join me and the girls in a game of tetherball at the bottom of the hill, or for swimming at one of the two local pools that we frequented. Charlene's obvious summer boredom and the loneliness in her face proved to be much more apparent as each hot summer day passed.

I felt bad for her and wanted her to hang out with us but I just needed her to submit at least one time-eye to eye. That was the only security I could have and know for sure that she would keep my secret safe.

My TGGF was possessive. I did not want it to get out to her or the lil' thirteen year old boy who was crushing on me. He lived further up the street from us and he too, would hang out at the local swimming pools where we'd be. So until she fully submitted, she was not going to get a spot on that cement wall waiting to play tetherball, splash and fun at the local swimming pools with us, or anything remotely close to what her sister was having the pleasure of enjoying.

Eventually the loneliness wore her down, my gaze finally worked:

Squint. Stare. Squint.

Head turned to the left somewhat.

Squint.

Result: Under her breath and with her lips folded, Charlene laughed a little bit with a look on her face as if to say: "This lil' pipsqueak think she's tough. Let me let this lil' girl have her way before I have to lift her off of her feet by her fuckin' neck!" She took a deep sigh and smiled (really laughing at me).

I didn't want any trouble. Hell, I was over wanting to check her out. I really felt sorry for her and how badly her summer was going and sincerely wanted her to be included with our summer fun. So, I was happy that we got past this issue. I smiled back and gracefully asked (in a curtsy kind of way):

"So…Would you like to go to Wilson's Pool with us?"

"Yeah!" she replied-happily.

She then ran up the steps to catch up to Rita, grabbing her towel and swim bag.

To Wilson's Pool, I liked to wear my yellow swimsuit and to Ginwood Pool, I liked to wear the silk, one-shouldered white swimsuit with the big purple and pink flower covering the front and back of it. My dad bought it for me and my mom had a rip-roaring fit when he brought me back from shopping the day she pulled it out of the bag. Outside of wearing makeup before age sixteen, my dad was one of those fathers who had no concept whatsoever about what was and was not appropriate for an underage girl. I can't recall how the conversation between my mom and dad ended-regarding the sexy white swimsuit, but all I know is that it was up in my room, in my drawer then on my body when I would go to Ginwood Pool.

Little did they both know, the basic yellow swimsuit happened to be my favorite because when I would get out of the pool, if you stared long enough-you too, could see that I was a "a growing lady," which to me, was perfect for trying to be cute for the boy who had a crush on me. Despite his crushing on me, I never sat around at the pool with him for more than five minutes at a time. I was always too busy walking up on the diving board; threatening to dive but never would.

I was so fascinated and found it to be amazing that kids my age had no fear of diving off the diving board into waters deeper than five feet. Watching that would be the highlight of my swim fun.

Well of course Rita's sister's Charlene took full advantage of my astonishment and admiration of the few females at the pool who would dare to dive and jump; that was all she seemed to do-over and over. She would stand in line with the boys and a handful of girls between every fifth boy waiting their turn, feeling like she earned her keep with us after learning that I, the leader, was awe struck at watching her flossing like a dolphin. I was so jealous. I thought it was *amazing*. I could only fantasize about doing something like that.

The closest that me, Nina and the girls would come to seeing the bottom of twelve feet of water, was when one of the older boys would take turns holding us in his arms while we would wrap ourselves around him like vines to a brick wall; and viola! He'd take us under-destination: bottom. Return: shooting to the top of the water like a missile. While under, I would be eyes wide-open like a guppy; trying to capture that deep, wide-bottom mass that I feared so badly. It was so wonderful for us-getting our experience of seeing what it was like on the bottom floor of twelve feet of water versus the five-feet that we swam in, dog-peddled in and had splash-fights in. I longed to jump off that diving board down into the bottom of it.

All the while, Charlene and the rest of the whales lined up like packs of sardines and dived in like amusement park show-dolphins. Those show-off bitches. I was star struck about as much as I would roll my eyes. Charlene got a kick out of that-the fact that she knew I scared to dive into the deep water, but when the church we attended shipped us off to camp that summer she had to park her tuna in the same can we all did: four feet maximum waters and no diving board: "Flossing like a dolphin and playing like Orca is over bitch!" I wanted to say, but rather, thought in my head.

She didn't feel too lonely at camp however, because the church had open slots for other neighborhood kids to come along as well-even if they did not attend church with us. That left room open for Lena: a big-tall, pigeon-toed girl who used to comb her hair to the front of her head like Gary Coleman. She was a major tomboy and neighborhood loner who would join us in tetherball, other times she spent her time playing basketball with the boys. Amongst one another, we called her Big Basketball Lena.

She and Charlene kept each other company at camp during the times Lena would peel herself away from me and my yellow swimsuit that she too, must've liked just about as much as I did. She never paid me that much attention back at home, but that yellow swimsuit must have had her thinking about me in a whole new way. No matter where she would be around the camp, she would always seem to magically appear whenever I'd be getting out of the swimming pool. Lena stuck to me like a bad habit for as long as she could until my TGGF would show up and pick at the seams of her tomboy dreams-she was not having that bullshit.

My TGGF and all her awkward ways. She wouldn't say anything, she would just give me a look and I knew what it meant. Whomever was around, I would have to leave them right where we stood.

At camp, she would give me that same look when Lena would come around me, but followed by: "ugh," with her face turned up. Her face turned up with a lot more "ugh's" after that Wednesday when the camp held a church concert and I took to the mic to sing "Going Up To Yonder," after all these years-all by myself: the entire song.

While everybody was playing around laughing and singing

remixed and adlibbed versions of church songs they could piece together, nobody had any idea how serious I took singing "Going Up To Yonder." I brought church to camp in a way that shocked everybody and made Lena flock to me for more of a reason than just my yellow swimsuit.

That Thursday and Friday, besides the cockling of the real rooster yodeling in the mornings to wake us, swimming in the afternoon and roasting marshmallows at night; the only thing I remember about the last two days of camp was hearing my TGGF turning her face up and yelling out: "ugh" countless times-because Lena wouldn't let me be.

When we returned home from camp, Lena still stuck to me like white on rice. The weirdest thing about it is that she never said much to me-not even at camp, she would just come around and up close to me-maybe say something corny and unrelated to anything in particular. I really did not know how to take her or what kind of conversation to have with her because all she would do is smile when she would come around. But she turned "coming around" up a notch and got bold one day. Caught me by surprise when she rang my doorbell while I was in the house. My TGGF was sitting right outside on the porch next door unbeknownst to me at the time.

When the doorbell rang, from the first floor window I looked out: "Who is it?" I yelled.

Lena then stepped from my porch awning and looked up at me without saying a word-her usual.

Resting my hands up on my window's ledge, my eyes stretched really big as I looked over at my TGGF sitting the next porch over with some other friends of ours. She twisted and tooted her lips up and began to nod her head up and down-slowly; looking right at me up in the window and looking back at Lena on my porch as if to say: "you're busted!"

I stepped away from the window and stood in the kitchen, hoping that Lena would just go away and the next time I looked out of the window, my TGGF would be gone too-but instead, the doorbell rang again.

I ran down the steps, opened the door and there stood Lena: bouncing her basketball back and forth from my porch's brick wall.

"What's up girl?" she asked-perplexed.

"Nothing, just in the house," I replied, with my foot in the door. She then pushed the door open and began to walk up the steps as if my words were: "Come on in Lena, right this way."

I closed the door slowly-thinking that my TGGF would come busting it open but no, instead, the door slowly closed, and there Lena stood at the top of my steps saying: "come on upstairs Angie."

I walked up the steps slowly-looking up at Lena standing there like a groom waiting on his bride. When I reached the top, I hurriedly walked past her and headed straight for the refrigerator to pour me something to drink. With the kind of smirk on her face as if she thought it was funny that she finally had me sequestered and kidnapped, Lena asked: "Well, can I have something to drink too?"

"Sure," I replied.

Feeling like a serving winch, I poured her something to drink as well. The moment I handed the glass to Lena, I heard my name being called:

"Angie! Angie! Angie!"

I looked out my window sill-resting on both my hands and looking down to my TGGF whisper-yelling: "Ugh! What the hell is she doing up there?"

I turned my head back to look at Lena sitting at the kitchen table-so as to let my TGGF know that she was near.

"You'd better get her OUT of there!" she grunted.

I nodded my head really fast, turned right around to Lena like serious business, shut my window then said: "Well Lena, I have to be getting out of here-we are about to go to the store. I will be back later though."

She stood there with that same playful look on her face and replied with a bunch of nothing relevant to anything in particular as she began to walk down the steps. When she got to the bottom, she looked up at me standing there and began to speak with some relevancy: "Ok, Angie well can I come back later?"

"I will have to see when I get back because my mother will be home from work. She's tired when she gets home. I will talk to you later though okay?"

"Okay," she replied then opened the door and walked to the other side of it.

I stood there and breathed a deep sigh of relief. A few minutes later, I ran down the steps to run outside to see where my TGGF was. When I opened the door, she was sitting right outside on the porch steps:

"What time does your mom get home Angie?" she asked.

"She'll be here about six?" I replied.

"Hmm," she said-thinking about something.

I quickly interjected:

"Um, Kenya's mom got us some tickets for Kingsman Amusement Park that we have to use before the end of the summer. We're going one Saturday afternoon very soon. She's going to drop us off and let us hang out all afternoon then come back to get us. I got an extra ticket if you want to come," I lied and offered as an apology.

"Ooh you do?" she replied-not really caring about that.

"Yeah I'll go," she agreed.

We stood there quietly while she put her thinking cap back on and then looked at me:

"Let's go to my house, okay?" she said.

"Sure," I replied.

Off we went to her house where there were three floors of space and a total of about ten closets.

I followed her lead as we went from room to room while she tried to find the perfect closet for us for the next hour or two. We settled on the third floor television room, where she turned the television up for the television to listen to us and watch the door...

5

ANOTHER LEVEL. BLOSSOMING. BEAUTIFUL.

Summer was nearing an end and all of my friends and me were preparing for the school year to start.

I was feeling good. Got plenty of exercise: lots of swimming and tetherball, no junk food, and sweating it out in countless closets with my TGGF for extra cardio. Mrs. Eckhardt's sure to be proud of me when I return to school-still-no jelly booty and actually quite a few pounds lighter than she last saw me a few months ago.

The trip to Kingsman Amusement Park was something I was looking forward to because I liked to hang out with Kenya. She was my informant on a little mission I had been working on for almost a whole year. I was intent on making good on it before summer's end.

Mission details:

Her older sister had a friend named Ms. Paula-they were thick as thieves.

Ms. Paula had a daughter named Pam-she was around all of our ages, but she got on my nerves so badly because she was very immature and whined if she so much as dropped a pencil. But I had to be nice and put up with her because not only was she Kenya's friend, but her mother was so unbelievably beautiful-I loved to look at her and *she* was my mission. She must've been in her mid to late twenties, well-dressed, sexy eyes, medium height and a medium build. Hair hairline was the closest to her eyebrows that I had ever seen on anybody in my life, but her pretty eyes could distract you from staring at that for too long.

She was so nice to me and tended to favor me over all of us that would hang out at Kenya's mom's house where she and her older sister lived. She was actually kind of mean and seemed to be annoyed when Kenya's friends would come over while she would be visiting. She'd go into one of the many rooms and take naps or talk on the phone. Her usual was to slam the door when she heard all of us, but when she would see me, she would smile then feel the need to act courteous. That would be the only time she seemed to smile, and when she would, she would say to me: "Hey gorgeous." (What the hell did she do that for? Because that word was always in my mind about her whenever I'd see her)...

My comeback:

"Hey Ms. Beautiful," I gave her a nickname.

I was crushing on her hard for a long time. I sure as hell was going to make possible-a mission out of what seemed impossible, as if my life depended on it. I was much too methodical and had a way with and to anything that I wanted. Despite her being older than me, she was no exception to my harmless deception that I had brewing for almost that whole year where she was concerned (but knew nothing about).

I was growing up and was no longer the victim of "being selected," I was doing the choosing.

Though I had been pretty steady with my TGGF since third-grade, the fact still remained, we were still the same age. I just had a thing for older men and women that I just couldn't shake from out the crevices of my mind. And because she was older, she could keep a secret-this I knew for sure.

As for Ms. Beautiful and my mission, part of the ingredient had to include her annoying daughter, who, as much I hated admitting it; was like the annoying little sister I never had. I love-hated her. For many months and Sundays, I had been finding it tough to put up with Pam, but every time I would see her mother's beautiful face and smile-it would make putting up with her a whole lot easier. So putting up with her being around Kenya and me was literally a labor of love (in the greater scheme of things and according to my plans).

Pam accompanied us all one Saturday afternoon for a lunch date that Kenya's mom set up for us. Kenya and me sat in the back of her mother's van and doing what we would normally do every time we got together: have her dish all on Ms. Beautiful for me. Every Sunday in the church pew, we would spend the entire two hours passing notes and whispering about Ms. Beautiful, while I would be probing Kenya to tell me all that she knew about Ms. Beautiful's boyfriends, her dates, what kind of person she was, how she behaved, things she'd do and say. Anything Kenya could offer-I listened.

Kenya always seemed to enjoy running her mouth like a water faucet, and I loved to take it all in like a sinkhole. It would be funny watching her sudden bursts of mimicry to better describe anything that Ms. Beautiful would do or say-about anything. I didn't care what she would tell me, I just wanted to know any and everything I could, trying to see how I was going to work my hand around her "way."

With Ms. Beautiful's daughter, Pam, sitting two rows in front of us (whining about something to Kenya's younger sisters), Kenya and me sat in the back of the van doing our same thing we were going to be doing in the pews the very next day: talking about how Ms. Beautiful's Friday or Saturday night went and what, if any men she went out with.

My mission was finally put into action when I set it up so that I could stay the weekend at Ms. Beautiful's house, under the guise that I was sleeping over from finally taking Pam up on one of her many invites to annoy me on her own turf. She wanted attention from me and secretly admired me like a big sister and God knows I'd try, but I figured after I could gather enough information about Ms. Beautiful, I would redeem my rain check with Pam to make the mission go as planned.

Executed.

Ms. Beautiful and my mom talked on the phone and worked things out on a Friday night. That next day, Saturday evening, Ms. Beautiful rang the bell with Painful Pam standing next to her. I could hear Pam's mouth from behind the closed door-getting closer and louder as my mother opened it.

"Oh goodness, how am I going to make it through this weekend with her?" I asked myself as I stood at the top of the steps with my fists upside my head. But when I looked down the steps-there stood Ms. Beautiful, and I nearly heard angelic theme music. If it is true that your pupils dilate when you look at something pleasing to your senses, then mine must have had a thousand swirly circles in them.

"Hello Painful Pamela and Ms. Beautiful," I wanted to say, but instead, because my mother was down the steps with them, I politely said, (curtsy-like): "Hello Pam. Hello Ms. Paula. I'll be down in a second."

I quickly grabbed my packed bag and joined them at the front door...

"I guess me and the girls will do some cooking when we get to the house, then watch some movies until they talk themselves to sleep-right girls? I know this one will!" she laughed and pointed at Pam.

She softened her laugh and gave me a hug then said: "This one'll probably talk me to sleep won't you Ms. Angie? She can go!" smiled Ms. Beautiful, laughing with my mother.

I kissed my mom, then Pam and I began to head out the door while she and Ms. Beautiful were small-talking at the door.

"I'm getting in the front!" I yelled at Painful.

I rolled my eyes at her.

"Oh, I guess I'll let you get in the front since you are a GUEST in MY car and at MY house!" she yelled back at me, playfully.

I rolled my eyes again.

Beautiful finally made her way to the car and when she got inside, she turned on her inside light and smiled: "Well hello Ms. Angie, how are you doing gorgeous?"

I smiled and looked back over to my left and replied, (curtsy like):

"I'm good. Well hello Ms. Beautiful, how are you doing?"

Ms. Beautiful replied:

"I'm good. I'm happy that you'll be staying the weekend with us-it'll be fun."

"Uhd, all this beautiful-gorgeous stuff and both of y'all ugly," echoed Painful Pam's from the back seat.

Ms. Beautiful rolled her eyes, shook her head, looked to the right and smiled back at me as if to say:

"She is such a child isn't she?"

I shook my head and looked back at Ms. Beautiful as if to say: "Yep."

We began to pull off to head over to Ms. Beautiful's humble abode. I sat back comfortably in my seat, feeling good about how my almost one year mission had come into fruition and we were finally on our way to being alone-well, almost-after I could find a way to alleviate my Pain.

While riding, Ms. Beautiful kept playing a song that I was nodding my head and snapping my fingers to: Stevie Wonder's: "That Girl." More and more (little did she know) it was an almost surreal lyrical moment that had art imitating life: right in my head, plus the moment, divided by my mission.

Painful Pam was in the back seat rolling and restive; annoying me-still, but relevant nonetheless. After all, she got me where I wanted to be: right in that front seat, rolling with Ms. Beautiful on route to complete my mission.

Rapture...

We arrived.

We got into the house while Pam grabbed my hand before I could even sit my bag down, so that she could show me her room and all the spoiled little things in it.

"Hold on Pam, let me gather my bag and stuff, girl!" I said to her.

Ms. Paula was laughing and shaking her head-all to used to Pam's behavior.

"Where's your son?"

I asked, knowing he wouldn't have been there-because most times when she and Painful would visit Kenya's big sister, he would be away with his dad (whom I heard he lived with-says Kenya).

"He's with his dad as usual," replied Ms. Beautiful.

"Oh okay," cool, I said-nodding my head.

We spent the duration of the evening and into the night watching movies, playing board games and pigging out on the mini-feast Ms. Beautiful had cooked for us already. I hung out with Painful all throughout the house: everywhere from the son's bedroom, her bedroom, the living room and the kitchen. All the while, I attentively listened to her run her mouth a mile a minute, but was desperate for her to talk herself sleepy before she could talk me to the point of nodding off. She almost had me-a few times in this.

A short time later, we all retired upstairs for the night while Ms. Beautiful went to her room, and Pain and I went to her room. I listened for the loud door slam that I was so used to hearing Ms. Beautiful do when she would be over Kenya's house but instead, she left the door open. When she got comfortable, a few minutes later, she yelled my name: "Angie! Angie baby come here for a second please!"

I smiled and looked over at Painful laying there with her back on the floor and her hands rested upon her chubby belly-winding down and relaxing. I was so happy.

I entered:

"Hey doll. Do me a favor. With your pretty handwriting...that one thing you do-the special kind of cursive...can you write something with that kind of Old English style of handwriting for me?" she asked. "Oh...you mean calligraphy?" I confirmed.

"Yeah, I want you to write something in this blank card that I have. I have another card with a message in it, but with your handwriting, I'd love it if you would handwrite that message in the blank card for me-will you?" she asked.

To make her laugh I replied:

"Oh, so you're asking me to plagiarize the words from one card, and handwrite it into another as if they were your words huh?" I had a serious but cynical look on my face on top of the laughter beneath it.

She looked a combination of both embarrassed but startled and replied with an ashamed giggle:

"Well, I mean...I just..."

I burst into a giggle then pinched her cheek and replied:

"I was just playing! I don't care, I'll do it for you!"

She then placed her hand on her chest and let go of the rest of her laugh to harmonize with mine.

To quiet her down so that Painful wouldn't roll onto her stomach then up on her feet and in to join us, I whispered to Mrs. Beautiful:

"Sure, but when I was at Kenya's doing it for them, I had special pens for that Ms. Paula-seriously. Those pens are what give it that 3-D look. Those sharp corners enable you to turn the pen and give it that look you are looking for. A basic ink pen won't give it the 3-D look but I could still write it kind of Old English style for you. It would look a step above nice cursive handwriting," I explained.

I proceeded to show her how it would look on a blank piece of paper and then translated the words she stole from the one card on to the blank card: *"We fit together just right, your warmth spreads through me like the sun."* When I was done, she gave it a big gracious smile and me-a tight hug:

"Thank you baby, it's so pretty, so nice! I'm so happy!" she extended.

"You're welcome," I replied and smiled.

"Anything for you," I said-flirtatiously.

So as to not wake up Painful, I tip-toed my way back into her bedroom and there she was: asleep on the bed-all sprawled out. I headed back to Ms. Beautiful's room happy as a lark, but my entry read distraught: "Hey Ms. Paula, Pam is asleep sprawled all across the bed and she was supposed to sleep in her brother's room. I don't want to wake her, so after my shower-may I sleep in here with you, if you don't mind?" I asked, sounding like a lonely kid kicking rocks.

"Of course you can sweetie. We all could fit in this king-sized monster if we had to, so there is definitely room for me and just you!" she laughed.

"Good!" I replied-enthusiastically.

After my shower, while in the bathroom, I dried off. I lotioned my body down and slipped on my drawstring pajama pants with a tank-shirt that I already had in the bathroom waiting for me along with my towel, bar soap, washing-cloths, deodorant, toothpaste, toothbrush and cap.

I climbed up into the king-sized monster and got comfortable.

We lay there for a while with the television on. She sat up with her back against the headboard while flipping through the pages of a magazine, sipping on her drink, and looking back and forth at the television and occasionally-at me.

I was lying over on the opposite end of the bed with my head on the pillow. Instead of watching the television, I watched her until she began to nod and fight sleep.

Sleep won, Ms. Beautiful lost, and the monster summoned.

She lay the magazine down on the nightstand to her right and slid further under the covers. She then looked over at me, patted my cheek and slurred the words: "I thought you were over there dozing off.

Goodnight baby, I can't hang," she chuckled.

I lay there stiff as a board feeling scared as hell because there she was-my mission's destination accomplished and laying right beside me. My curiosity runneth over. Climbing under those covers was nothing like how we would get under the umbrella, and I could probe my home girls into showing me what they got. I had *no* idea how to go about asking Ms. Beautiful a damned thing. Not even a drink of water if I needed it. My approach definitely couldn't be the way I was used to cutting to the chase with my peers.

All this time, I felt like I had the perfect plan and now, here I lay:

frozen stiff like a board-glancing back and forth at her but planning to pretend I was looking at the television should she look up and bust me staring, planning and scanning.

I went for it, cutting to the chase like only I knew how to do:

"Hey, Paula," I whispered-seductively, dropping the: "Ms."-purposely-hoping I would sound mature and "her-age" receptive.

She lazily replied back: "Yes baby?"

It caught me off guard and scared me:

"Uh, Ms. Paula…nothing." I whispered again, feeling called out and busted.

I couldn't do it-I couldn't ask her. My mind and my thoughts began to race:

"Should I reach over and touch her? Touch her shoulder? I can't reach over to kiss her-that would probably freak her out! Should I reach over and touch her there and act like it was a mistake? Yeah-maybe I should do that! No-that wouldn't work. I don't know how she would take that. She might tell Kenya's big sister and mom! Ah shucks-none of that is going to work. What in the hell am I going to do? I'm all tingly inside. Why am I shaking like this? What's going on? Why can't I shut my mind off? Oh my goodness. My legs are shaking! I'm breathing all hard. I have to calm down. How can I calm down? What in the world is going on?"

Stiff as a board, I was feeling like I had better climb out of the monsters clutch, but it had a tight hold on me. I was practically glued there.

Ravenous…

I lay there, squeezing my legs tightly with my eyes rolling back in my head trying hard not to breathe so loud. The dirty thoughts played in my mind-rehearsing all that I could not reach over and do: touch her, clutch her breasts, caress her breasts, sink my teeth into her neck, kiss her gently, trace my tongue down her stomach while sinking my teeth into her skin, and then finally-push her knees upwards and open to see what I had imagined: a real-live true to life pocketbook that I'd just bury my face in while I hanging on to that beautiful flower's bud like her pleasure plus my life equally depended on it.

My mind delivered sensations to my body as if I was *really* French-kissing it, pulling it tightly, pulling it lightly, sucking it, chewing it, pulling off of it, teasing it with the tip of my tongue, teasing it with my whole tongue then devouring my mouth all over it-pulling it-whipping my tongue across it from left to right-vigorously: washing, rinsing, spinning and repeating.

I couldn't help myself. I had rehearsed it in my mind over a thousand times, and now I lay right next to her and it finally came to life-in my mind-yet, her body slumbered right next to mine.

I lay there shaking like I was cold and damp-except I was hot and damp. The more I replayed the thought in my mind, the tighter my hands gripped the sides of my thighs-fighting hard not to grab my pussy and embarrass myself right next to Ms. Beautiful. I'm older now-no longer a latchkey kid. The results of getting caught this time would be something I was sure I could not live down.

I kept breathing harder and gripping my thighs tightly asking God to help my mind to stop the thoughts inside of it: "Oh God, please stop these thoughts in my mind: "please stop 'em please stop 'em please stop 'em!"

As well, God too, must've been asleep because He sure as hell did not stop my thoughts and calm my shaking body. It got worse as my eyes kept rolling farther back in my head, the more I kept envisioning French-kissing it, pulling it tightly, pulling it lightly, sucking it, chewing it, pulling off of it, teasing it with the tip of my tongue, teasing it with my whole tongue then devouring my mouth all over it-pulling it, whipping my tongue across it from left to right-vigorously-while like serious fucking business I: twisted and turned it in my mouth in circles until my mouth, tongue and lips ganged up on it and chased it as if was trying to run from my slippery tongue and magnetic mouth. I was bubbling over like a volcano about to erupt; dying to bury my face in her pussy. It was agonizing and driving me crazy. My body got more excited the more my mind began to race at the thought of sucking her pussy, tired, from the chase of my mouth having outlasted it, and her letting me at it in such a way-while she was weak as a lamb and gasping like she was up and down many hills, valleys and mountains.

At this point, I was so ready to bust that I could care less about the distraction of her laying there. My pussy was throbbing ten decibels and about to explode. My clit and entire body began to throb so hard I could almost hear it. My heart was pumping towards the front of my breast plate and it felt like it dropped right down to my pussy then landed behind my clit. In that instant-it just busted uncontrollably. By reflex, I lifted my stiff right arm to cover my mouth with my eyes rolling to the back of my head. I crossed my right leg over my left leg and squeezed my thighs together tightly and came so hard, that I thought that I pissed myself. I wanted to scream so loudly-the agony was the most excruciating thing I had never felt in my entire life.

Climax...

Sigh.

She reached over at me and said, lazily: "Are you okay babe?"

I gasped and whispered in a barely there whisper:

"Yes, I'm okay. I'm okay. Um hmm," I said-blinking my eyes really fast and trying to focus with my watery eyes. All was over and Ms. Beautiful fell back into her deep slumber. This was my moment to get up out of that monster of a bed, knowing Pam was in her room good and asleep and Ms. Paula's slumber wouldn't allow her to notice that I got up.

I was so hot at the seat of my pants but I was sure it wasn't piss even though my "pee came."

I had been masturbating all my life, but never did this kind of thing happen. I didn't know if I had brought my period down for the second time in that month or what. All I knew is that I had no idea how to explain my mess-regardless if it was clear or red.

I was dying to check my underwear but I needed Ms. Beautiful out of that bed first. It was still dark outside. I knew I had a few hours before morning would come, so I lay there, nervous, no sleep at all-waiting for the morning hour for Ms. Beautiful to wake up and hop out the monster so that I could no longer be scared.

Morning finally came.

My eyes were wide-shut.

I lay there stiff and on my back, playing possum, while I could hear Ms. Beautiful moving about as if she was about to raise up for the morning. She sat up on the bed on her elbows, looked me in the face, tapped my shoulder, and with a smile in her voice-said: "Angie, are you up?"

I imitated her-responding lazily: "Huh? Huh?" as if I couldn't understand what she was saying.

I heard every word and was wide awake-I was just dying to go and check and change my underwear.

"I'm about to get cleaned up to fix you and Pam something to eat for breakfast, I will call y'all down shortly," she replied.

"Hmm? Hmm?" I lazily replied-acting as if I still could not comprehend a word she said.

Eyes wide shut, I could tell that she put on a robe, slipped into some house slippers and walked a few steps to the bathroom. When the door closed and the water turned on, I quickly opened my eyes, pulled back the sheet and opened my legs to look down-just to make sure the color wasn't red. It wasn't. I lifted my butt up to feel all behind me and it was all heat-no piss-nothing left but the seat of my underwear wet from cumming so hard.

"Thank goodness!" I whispered loudly to myself, in my head.

I lay back down and couldn't wait for Ms. Beautiful to take that first step down those stairs so that I could commandeer that bathroom. The moment I heard the first squeak of her feet hitting the stairs, I hung my left leg off the edge of that king-sized monster. By the time she hit the bottom step and made that left turn through the living room and into the kitchen, I had gotten up and pulled the top sheet all the way back to let the bottom sheet air-dry.

I tiptoed and made off into that bathroom to take a shower, and to stuff the underwear and pants that I had on, in the back of my bag-which was where I also wanted to place the memory of the previous night: bagged and in the back of the crevices in my mind...

While I showered, I could hear Painful banging and kicking on the door, screaming and whining out about how badly she needed in just to pee. I rolled my eyes in my head, and that was the moment I knew that the morning and the day was truly back to normal.

Plateau...

We ate breakfast on the go: partially in house and mostly-in the car, while Ms. Paula was rushing to drop Pam and me off to church where we would meet up with Kenya, and I would go home from there. We missed Sunday school, so I dropped my overnight bag in the closet then headed directly up to service. Kenya and I did our usual (when Pam would visit and have to go to church with her): force her to sit with Kenya's younger sisters while we would pass notes back and forth about Ms. Paula.

This time however, I had nothing much in the form of curiosity to offer and probe Kenya about because the mission was accomplished and my curiosity was satisfied. Though Kenya was my age, she was much more immature than I was, so I never told her what I had been planning-and definitely not what happened.

I seemed to have grown up a little more overnight and all my thoughts, missions, doings and goings on seemed to be better suited written down in my little red diary that I kept, rather than [what now-to me] felt like silly little bothersome notes that Kenya and I passed back and forth.

I broke that part of my connection with Kenya and me about as quickly as I broke the umbrella secret's connection with Nina and the girls after being infiltrated and the secret was out. My curiosity was about as satisfied and over, as my secret was in danger of leaking out.

Kenya could sense my indifference at this point, so she wrote and passed this note instead:

"You know my mom is taking us to the Amusement Park today at 3p don't you? I don't know if she is taking us or my big sister is, but we *are* going today rather than next Saturday, because school is about to start. My mother doesn't want us going on the same weekend that school starts that Monday."

"Oh really?" I wrote back-thinking of my TGGF; remembering that I promised she could get in on the trip-lying about having a ticket that I knew I never had, just so she wouldn't be mad at me about Lena.

"Okay, cool, that should be okay with my mom. I will meet you at your house about 2/2:30 then," I wrote back.

2:30pm came later that day and I showed up at Kenya's-walking in to Painful running her mouth and trying to decide what to wear from Kenya's closet.

"Hey Pam," I spoke, seriously-in no mood for her immaturity and playfulness.

"Uhd didn't I just see you!" she replied.

I rolled my eyes in my head, but didn't reply back.

"Your mom here?" I asked, with a curious eye, frowned brow and slight smile.

"No, she's still at home, probably asleep!" laughed Painful.

"Oh, oh okay. Cool." I replied.

We all gathered in the kitchen and the living room to prepare for the ride up to the Amusement Park. Rather than Kenya's mom, her big sister was driving us there and would be picking us up at 7:45 that evening. She stood in between the kitchen and the living room yelling out the rules, and where to meet at 7:30, along with: what not to do, where not to go, who not to talk to, what side of the park not to go to, how not to split apart, and who to continuously report anything to, (I'll let you guess): Me.

Off to the park we headed.

I could have very well told my TGGF about it right after church but I decided against it. My mind was so preoccupied with all that had happened last night, that I wasn't quite ready to face her just yet. Besides, with the few neighborhood kids and Kenya plus Painful; it was much more than I could deal with at the time. I just wanted to have a good time with nothing to think about, nothing to be in my head or in my way.

Kenya and me stuck together like glue, and rode the park's biggest and most popular rollercoaster ride a total of seventeen times in counting. We were so excited. We felt indomitable that day-like nothing in the world could touch us. We had the best time ever.

Kenya's big sister came to pick us up at 7:30p as promised-and without report of incident. Everyone had a good time and was pretty worn out from the evening.

I didn't wake up that next day until about 1pm. When I raised up from my bed, I looked down at my breasts and my newest fully blossomed boob had swollen up in the craziest-looking way; like a boob with a light-bulb attached to it.

I yelled out in complete and utter shock: "Maaaaa! Maaaa!"

My mom was already gone and off to work-probably having lunch by this time. My brothers were not in the house either. I called her at work with the kind of panic that she expected me to have the same day that I got my period but I was calm and in control-then. *This* time, I panicked: "Maaaa! Maaaaa!

My right boob is swollen real bad Ma. It's swollen real bad Ma! And it's lop-sided Ma! What's wrong with it Ma?"

"What?!" my mom responded.

"Is it hurting?" she yelled into the phone.

"No Ma. It's just very red and swollen-it looks funny Ma, I'm scared!"

I yelled, in tears-thinking that I was going to have to get it cut off or at the very least, it was going to shrink back down to nothing again and I would have to deal with having one breast for another long while or forever. I couldn't bear the thought of going through stuffing my bra again. I was getting *so* tired of feeling like I was a complete freak of nature-my emotions were going through enough already, from the weekend.

"Angie let me get off from here and get you over to the hospital, I'm on my way," said my concerned mom.

Lucky for me, per the ex-rays and the doctor, the swelling was most probably the result of riding the roller coaster ride back-to-back too many number of times. There was no benign or malignant mass to be worried about, but the doctor told my mom and me that the swelling should go down on its own, and all should be well "soon."

"Soon" didn't come soon enough because into Tuesday morning, my new boob was still swollen-though there was no pain.

Later into the afternoon, me and Nina, one of my umbrella girls, stepped out for the day to head to the store and to get some air and exercise.

Dee and Taryn, two of the few older teen-aged girls who I would sing for, were sitting at the top of the street-on a porch of another apartment building; snacking on some goodies and drinking some soft drinks. With her eyes pinned down and her hands carefully tending to something in her lap with her tongue hanging out; wiping it across a thin-white piece of paper, Dee asked: "Where 'you on your way to Ms. Angie?"

"Down to the strip mall, just getting out-getting our walk on," I replied.

"I heard what happened to ya' lil' titty from the park the other day!" laughed Dee, while Taryn and my friend Nina burst into laughter.

"That's not funny, my boob is still swollen-I'm scared!" I yelled.

"Come here Ms. Angie," Dee said, then looked over at Taryn-sneakily.

I looked at them both-apprehensively, because they looked like they were up to something.

"What are you scared of? Let me give you something to make it better-some natural herbs…

This is going to put your lil' titty right back to where it's supposed to be. Watch what I'm doing okay?" said Dee.

She began to place the tiny white cigarette up to her lips while I kneeled in front of her. She then asked:"have you ever smoked a cigarette Ms. Angie?"

"No, I-never," I replied.

"Good. 'Cause it's nothing like that," she explained.

"With cigarettes; you puff, inhale and exhale the smoke. Well, you do the same thing with this, except you inhale all the smoke and exhale as little as possible dammit 'cause this costs more money!"

Taryn and Nina laughed uncontrollably-clutching their stomachs.

Dee began taking a few puffs and slurping in through her teeth while quickly holding her head back and squinting her eyes. Barely, smoke came out of her mouth-if any.

My turn:

Puff. Inhale. Keep in. Hold smoke inside. Sift smoke in through teeth. No smoke exhaled. Success!

"Good!" said Dee.

"Now take a couple more puffs," she said.

She placed the tiny cigarette to my mouth again: Puff. Inhale. Keep in. Hold smoke inside. Sift smoke in through teeth. No smoke exhaled. Success!

Nina and Taryn watched intently at mine and Dee's back and forth exchange of the thin cigarette, as if we were taking turns fighting for it.

Dee yelled at me:

"Alright deep throat! You only left me with a bird-clips worth of herb left!"

She snatched what was left of the funny cigarette back from my mouth and smacked my forehead. We all laughed.

"Now here, take you a couple pieces of these Jolly Ranchers and take 'ya lil' tail on home and take a nap. You're going to get sleepy anyway-this is your first time. Y'all can go to store," she asserted.

"Angie you will feel better when you wake your butt up. I promise you that!" she assured me.

Taryn busted out laughing and Dee did as well.

I felt they loved me too much to give or tell me anything crazy, so Nina and I did just what they said.

We turned around and made a B-line right back towards home, where by the time I reached my house-I was a little more drained than usual.

Nina hung out on our street where we lived-sitting on the porch with mutual friends a couple doors over from mine. I went up into the house and lay down in my room-watching television until I dozed off to sleep.

Later that evening-around seven, I woke up. The first thing I grabbed for was my swollen breast. Much to my surprise, it was back to normal. The swelling was gone away, and it was as perky as its twin-all over again.

I followed my nose downstairs to the smell of my mother cooking in the kitchen and I stood on the bottom of the steps screaming with joy: "Maaa! Maaa! My swelling went down finally!"

"Okay… Calm down! The doctor said it would Angie, why are you so excited?"

"No, Ma, 'cause at first the swelling wasn't going down. Even through this morning when I woke up. Then I saw Dee and Taryn early this afternoon. It was something that Dee gave me that made the swelling go down!" I said, forcefully-rebuking anything the doctor said; discounting his credibility and expertise' altogether while trying to prove to my mother that whatever Dee had was: the remedy, the way, the right and the light.

"What'd she give you?" asked my mom, with a perplexed look on her face.

"Herbs, she gave me a few puffs of this real skinny white cigarette and told me to go straight home to take a nap and soon my swelling would go down. She said it was all NATURAL herbs!" I bragged-all too okay with anything healthy and holistic.

My mom frowned, twisted her lips up, then turned her head to the side and said:

"Wait'll I catch up with Dee. I'm not playing!"

She had a look on her face as if she wanted to burst out into a laugh but wanted to let me know that she was serious at the same time. I stared at her while looking in three directions: from left to right with my eyes darting back, forth and onto her (really fast). I wanted to burst into laughter from one of her many idioms that I could tell was on its way to the tip of her tongue:

"I'm gonna knock her into the middle of next week so she'll be looking at Sunday's from both ways!"

6
TGGF, MALE MODEL & ME

"Sooooo…how was the trip to Kingsman with Kenya and them?" asked my TGGF.

"Oh, it was cool. I thought we were going on an upcoming Saturday, but turns out-I learned while in church-we were going to be going a few hours after church let out. It was kind of spur of the moment," I explained.

She nodded.

"By the time church let out, and I ran home and got changed; Kenya's big sister was pretty much ready to take whomever was around and in the house. She was ready to leave as soon as possible," I interjected.

"It's cool. I wouldn't have been able to go anyways, so, it's cool," she said.

TGGF and me had a distant energy between us, splashed with a dash of her attitude with me, but we sat outside into the night on a vacant apartment's porch, just small-talking. Periodically one or two other people would sit on the porch with us (which helped ease the tension).

As a result of my ripping and running and trying to squeeze everything out of the remaining part of the summer, it had been a short while since I had seen her last. It didn't seem like she was particularly upset with me (per se') but it seemed like she could sense a wedge between us. I admit-it was, sort of.

She was kind of a loner anyways, so she was most probably bored without me around for as long as I had been away from her. It made it a lot easier for her to blend into the crowd with our other friends when we showed up together-other than that, she was cool with hanging out by herself, but I could tell she was lonely without me around.

Into the night, the tension in the air got even more strange when this guy that everyone was crushing on showed up.

Everybody liked him: all us pre-teen girls, Dee's group of older teen girls, the twenty-something's who were Kenya's oldest sister's age, and even the older ladies who were Kenya's mother's age.

Everyone talked about him-I never joined in with their talks of lust about him.

The guy was all but about twenty years-old, but every female from 8-80 couldn't help but lust him.

You name whomever, he held their attention. No one was exempt. He was a delicacy-new on the street and had moved into one of the vacant apartments a few months before summer. And when the weather changed, he would come outside without a shirt on and jog back and forth to Leroy's two, three and four times a day to get goodies, groceries and such-probably just for a little exercise with a little dash of an ego stroke-because he sure as hell was on everybody's menu.

A pleasure to look at, he occupied plenty of pages in my red diary and many a sessions in my mind when I'd masturbate, thinking of him. He had that nice v-shaped torso leading down to his shorts and when I would see that, it would excite me. It just spelled: "M.A.N" to me. He oozed sexiness through his pores.

I never spoke to him-not even so much as a mere: "hello." It would be a cold day in hell before I would ever give him any indication that he was more than a passing thought in my mind, because he *knew* he was the center of attention-but surprisingly, he kept his cool about it (falsely modestly so). I saw straight through it.

He was friendly with, and spoke to everyone. If he would spend any time small-talking, it would be only for a seconds. He'd be jogging in place as if in his mind, he was saying: "Make it snappy. I have to go-I'm just stickin' and movin.'" Outside of his male model good looks, that was the main thing that made him attractive: coming outside only to jog down to Leroy's, speak, and jog in place, throw his hands up to say hello, give high-fives to guys and jog right back home to his apartment is what made the women and girls wanting to chase and catch up with him-even more. It was funny to observe. He *never* deviated from that routine. He lived so close to the top of the hill, that his comings and goings could not be clocked. He could just leave his house, hang a left, walk a few steps, and be off of the street and on about his business-unseen. Leroy's was his only association and connection with the neighborhood-so it was a big deal when he'd come jogging down the hill.

Well, when nightfall came and my TGGF and I were still sitting out on the vacant apartment porch small-talking, he just so happened to have been making his run down to Leroy's. On his way back up the hill-he decided to stop jogging and make some conversation with the two of us. The night was perfect because no one was hardly outside. There were small groups of people scattered about on the street, but few and far between porches.

About three minutes into allowing him into our small talk; like the grim reaper, up from the basement steps-my TGGF's little brother started stomping and yelling: "Daddy said it's time for you to come in the house-Stupid!"

Right about that moment, those were near fighting words to my TGGF. We had already been uneasy with one another, but the porch visitors we had off and on throughout the evening, eased the tension in the air. The fact that Male Model was now joining us, and she had to leave him outside with me-only-pissed her off five times over. She secretly liked Male Model too.

Dumb, damp, dyke, deaf, disabled, definite hetero male or delusional; you couldn't help but stare at him. I mean, he looked as if someone drew him on a piece of paper, thumped it and said: "bring him to life!" and he come crawling off the paper and turned from a mere sketch to a man. He was gorgeous-regardless your flavor and taste in men (or no).

TGGF ignored Baby Bro and continued to sit there as if he was not calling out to anyone sitting on that porch.

"Daddy said get-your-butt-in-the-house, right now! You heard me! Don't make me go get him!" he repeated-yelling loudly and trying to be heard by their dad.

He then placed his hands around his mouth and whispered loud enough so that TGGF, Male Model and I could hear. But this time, not so loud-so Dad couldn't hear. As if he was re-enacting "Amityville Horror's" notorious "Get-Out!" line, he imitated: "Get-your-asssssss in-side!"

He then laughed like a demon-doll. She wanted to kill him dead.

I glanced over at her. She looked at me-giving me the evil eye-while Male Model stood in front of the porch drinking his soda and looking around as if he wasn't paying attention at all-so as to not embarrass her. Her anger wouldn't let her hold it back. She went for it and yelled at me: "SO WHAT TIME ARE YOU GOING HOME ANGIE?!" she demanded to know, not caring how she or it looked in front of Male Model. She was pissed.

"Uh, shortly," I replied-simply.

My eyes stretched wide-open, feeling put on the spot divided by caught by surprise.

"Iiiiiiiiiii hi. Hahahahaha, " he laughed.

"Time to tuck 'ya in lit-tle girl. Let's make it in the house! Come on! Come on!" laughed Baby Bro, feeling like Big Brother in charge-sent to break up her fun. He thought it was so funny to fan toward her the direction of the downward cement steps.

TGGF ran up on him and punched him in his back so hard. He jerked his shoulders up from the pain, but kept on teasing her all the way down the steps until the door slammed.

Show's over.

This fine specimen had no idea how many times in my mind that-as a token of appreciation for loving to look at him-I fantasized about sliding my mouth and tongue anywhere on his body I could guess he-himself loved.

Show time:

I continued to sit there, still observing [and happy] that no one was near Male Model and me to the left or to the right of us on any porch-all the way up to quite a few porches away.

Pretty much after Leroy would close his store, the lower half of the street and the tether ball corner where a lot of people would congregate, would clear out-no matter the season or the weather.

Male Model turned to me and sipped on his soda again:

"So how old are you?"

"A woman is not supposed to tell her age." I responded by rolling my eyes and in a way as if I said: "none of your business."

He laughed and rolled his eyes in his head and replied:

"Precisely! *Women* usually don't tell their age, but you are just a girl, a young woman. Girl!"

I knew that he thought that was going to get a rise out of me, but I ignored him by turning my head-just like the way he was all to used to me doing to him at every trip he made down and up the hill.

I always ignored and abhorred anybody or thing that didn't favor me or me-it, whatever or whomever I didn't like or didn't like me, just about as much as I would ignore or abhor what I could not have all to myself or my way. I made him feel really stupid-so he stopped asking.

He then began making small-talk and flicking his Bic cigarette lighter off and on while I stared at him through the blue, yellow and red flame. Before too long, we were into a full-on conversation about everything from school, to people, to where he lived before moving on our street-anything that came to his and my mind-we just kept it going. While in the middle of the conversation, he got bored with flicking the lighter into the air in between us. He then began to pretend to burn the strings on my cut-off jean shorts.

He looked so luscious standing right there in front of me.

His conversation got slower. His voice got lower: "Bring him to life!" …he slowly began to appear right out of the thoughts I would have of him from the pages of my red diary. I sat back on my hands and opened my legs some. I began to swinging them just enough that it wasn't too obvious, but in a way to confuse him and make him wonder if I swung my legs to make him stop burning my jean short's strands, or if I did it to try and seduce him. He was all too confused.

All I know is that my throbbing heart fell down to my pussy. If he could see me through my jean shorts he would have seen my heart all in the wrong place.

"You can finish burning them," I said-seductively. I wanted him to fuck me so bad-he had no idea just how much. I was secretly, *very* hot for him but absolutely, positively *refused* to blend my desire with the other people on the street who desired him too.

He looked down between my legs. I pushed myself forward while sitting at the edge of the steps-feeling so aroused by him and throbbing so hard. I wanted him to grab my crotch with his hands so badly. I couldn't help myself. He slowly brought the lighter down to the inner-thigh strands of my shorts rather than the strands on the top and outer thigh. I sighed out impatiently.

He flicked the lighter and slowly burned the strands with his left hand-then extinguished the mini-fire with his right-hand's fingers. Then the next strand, the next strand-the next strand-the next strand (repeatedly).

I thrust forward, slowly, while still leaning back on my hands.

"This is it. This is the night I'm going to finally do it," I sighed and said in my head. I had delegated him to be that one-over a thousand times in my diary and in my mind.

The more he stared into my crotch with the fire in his hands, the more aroused I became. The tough inseam of my jeans shorts was all I had for any crotch-grabbing, because he was scared to do it. All he could do was bite down on his bottom lip.

I grinded slowly and forward as if I was moving closer to him. He continued the fire. I looked up and down the street-still no one around. He never turned away or looked around, up or down the street. I went for it: "Touch it. Touch me," I whispered to him.

He was stunned and frozen, but didn't know what to do.

In my mind, I was kicking and screaming: "I *like* youuuuu! No-I *love* youuuuu-always have!"

But instead, I invited:

"Just grab it-one good hard time, please," I begged-innocently, while admiring how unbelievably good-looking he was: gorgeous and older-just like I liked 'em.

There he was, standing right there in front of me, having no idea that I ever looked at him in such a way-sure that I never even entertained the thought of him in such a way-because of the way I always ignored him so. As he continued to stand there, my mind envisioned him grabbing my crotch. I got more excited because he was sweating bullets fighting hard not to-paying attention to my body and forgetting to care about my age.

In a matter of seconds right then and there, he had slid my shorts over to the side, and manipulated my clit with his thumb until it got tired. He buried his face in it while I begged for mercy as he threw my legs back and shoved himself inside of me and pounded me mercilessly.

Thank goodness my jean shorts were too tight, because instead of that thought being in my head, I probably *would* have pulled my shorts over or put his hand up in them while sitting there in front of him to see what, if anything, he would do about it. I could feel his desire-it was burning about as hot as the cigarette lighter he kept flickering. I could tell that as long as he could not see (or touch) anything, he had the lockdown on making sure he was going to control himself. All else was fair-game.

He turned me on so badly standing there.

He grabbed hold of himself as best as he could:

"No. No. Stop girl. We have to stop. No. Stop it. Stop thisssss," he grunted; bunching his lips together angrily-in agony and with a frown of frustration on his face as if he was forced to withdraw out of the best pussy he never had. I wanted his dick so badly. I had been *dying* to hold one in my hand, my mouth and inside of me-his (to be exact). And here it is staring at me-inches from my face-erect and bulging through his pants and turning me on. He stood there clutching his fists tightly, doing his best not to touch me with his hands or touch himself.

His forehead was shining like glass. He was lit like the fire in his Bic. I needed to feel some part of him, so I slid my right foot from out of my flip-flop and with the back of my foot; I began digging into his leg-trying to pull him closer up on me to make him fall on top of me. I wanted him as close to my pussy as possible. His body was so strong.

I was trying my best not to lean forward, and come off my (now) sore palms that I had been leaning back on, to support me the entire time. He fought like hell standing there holding his fit body stiff as a super-hero, while gritting his teeth and biting down on his jowls. His head was still hanging down with his chin close to his chest as he kept staring smack dead at my crotch as if he had x-ray vision and could see my pussy from behind my jean shorts. It was driving me mad-so mad that I could almost feel rays of heat from his eyes-beaming at my pussy. Thank goodness for the thick inseam of my jean shorts pressing right on my clit while I thrust slowly into it for pressure and pleasure, because he was fighting too hard not to touch me, and was winning his own battle. He just kept staring into my crotch while I kept grinding slowly; gasping and moaning desperately. I could feel him, feeling himself inside of me.

I was fighting just as hard not to grab my own pussy or his dick, as he tried hard not to grab my pussy or touch his own dick. This was about as painful as it was pleasurable for him and for me. I was about to explode-hard. My pussy was pulsating vibrations that could bust an eardrum. The back of my foot was digging into the back of his muscular thigh-hard enough to dig a hole in it. I threw my head, back then clenched my teeth together to keep from screaming out loud while I came.

I collected myself, unwrapped my leg from around his, then sat up from leaning back on my sore palms. I looked at him with my watery eyes trying to focus. I closed my legs. My heart traveled from my pussy, back up to its rightful place: in my chest. He collected himself and finally took a seat in front of me-placing his head in his hands, wiping his face and grunting aloud. He then turned around, looked up at me and bit his lip: "Ooh ANGIE, I wish you were older! Just a little older!," he challenged, as if he would have definitely won this game.

"What are you-like, sixteen?" he threw in my face.

"You kill me. You're not even twenty-one yet. You're not so grown yourself!" I snapped back.

"And you're not quite eighteen yet-*that* I *do* know-despite…" he lowered his voice and stopped himself from finishing his own sentence, but tried looking in between my virgin and tightly closed legs.

I folded myself back up by wrapping my arms around my legs and sat my chin in my lap. He stood up and folded his fingers to give me a little affectionate thump on my forehead: "What's up big head girl? Get your chin out of your knees and that hump out of your back before you end up with bad posture-you don't want a hump in your back do you?" he said to me-turning his head to the side-being playful.

"Trying to act as if you like me now. You never even speak to me!" he complained and remembered-all too well.

"I *do* like you," I replied and stuck my tongue out at him playfully like a girl my age would-whom I snapped right back into being.

I stood up and yawned, stretched and pulled my shorts from being bunched at my crotch. I then began to slowly step down off the porch:

"I'm kind of tired. I'd better be going home now," I said.

"You and me both," he replied.

He then yawned and stretched like I just did.

I didn't say anything else. I just squeezed past him, turned left and began to head home without turning to look back at him.

I could feel him staring at me walk away.

Old Man Leroy's was good and closed.

There were no people standing around or sitting outside from the left, going down the hill-the direction I was heading to go home.

The only direction for him to head towards his home was to the right and up towards the top of that hill, only to disappear into oblivion as far as I or the situation was concerned.

This night with him was a one-night-chance and I couldn't *wait* to get home to write all about it into lines of my little red diary:

"Dear Diary: Progress."

7
TGGF & ME

Sun up, mom gone to work, brothers still asleep and me: lying there having barely opened my eyes-the doorbell rang. On the other side of it stood my TGGF, dressed, hair combed and a slight frown in her brow, looking as if we had made plans for the morning and inconsiderate-me, rudely overslept.

"Uh hey, what's up?" I asked, while cleaning out eye-boogers, lips swollen and face with that morning shine on it.

"Nothing, what are you doing?" she asked, sounding as if it was a "kinda" emergency, but feeling awkward for showing up at my door before 9am-fully dressed and with a disposition as if she had tossed and turned with me on her mind all night.

"Well, I *was* still asleep and my brothers are still asleep upstairs and all," I offered.

"Well, I was just making sure you weren't doing anything for the day so we could hang out all day and whatnot. School is starting back up in a couple days and all…" she said-not completing her sentence.

"Oh. Okay, that's cool. My lil' summer is over with. I don't have *any*thing to do today. When I get dressed, I'll be out-probably… around 12p okay?" I told her.

"Okay, that's cool. So I'll see you around 12p alright?" she verified.

"Sure, I'll see you around 12p," I confirmed.

I went back up the stairs and back into my bedroom to try and get a little shut eye at least for the next couple of hours. Later into the morning when I got dressed, I walked over to Leroy's to grab for my TGGF; all her favorite goodies and a juice drink before reporting over to her house at 12p.

No one was sitting on any porches around the basement apartment where she lived, so since it was wide-open, day-light and person-free; I could clearly observe the black railing over top my TGGF's basement apartment. For some odd reason, after all these years since Twin had Cable Boy wrapped around the railing; I stopped and took a moment to observe the deadly distance from that railing-down to the large rock-tiled bottom walkway that led to my TGGF's father's front door. The protruding cemented walls resembled a dungeon, ironically. I don't think my brother noticed the deadly distance either-he was just a madman that day. Anyone who would fall from that distance most probably would not live.

"Wow, scary thought. That could have been the scene of a crime had my TGGF's dad not come to the top of the stairs to save [Cable Boy] from Twin's angry stranglehold," I said to myself.

When I walked through the dungeon and approached the door with my hands behind my back, clinching the brown paper bag, before I could even knock; the door squeaked and swung right open like a scene of a horror movie. TGGF took a seat right back down at the dinner table and gave me a "somewhat" kind of

smile-not wanting to give up too much of a smile at all. She was still feeling about one month's mad at me I guessed, but she changed her mind when I took my hands from behind my back and showed her the brown bag that I was hiding behind it.

She grabbed it out of my hands and started giggling-sitting there with a blushing and embarrassed smile, nose squinted like Ms. Celie sitting on the bed after Shug Avery gave her a kiss.

The moment she put one of the Jungle Jollies in her mouth and after savoring the flavor, she removed her smiled. She still wanted to withhold it from me. Standing right over me and looking down at me with her two fingers pointed toward my face, she asked:

"What was up with last night? Why didn't you just pack yourself up and prepare to leave and go home when you saw that I had to go in the house?"

"I didn't stay long, not real long," I replied.

"Mmm Hmm," she said, looking as if she saw the whole thing that went down.

She paused and put her thinking cap on, looking like she was planning something.

"Who's at your house?" she asked.

"My two older brothers are gone to work and Twin is gone out in the wind some doggone where," I replied.

"Well, Twin pretty much stays gone until he retires for the night doesn't he?" she asked.

"Yeah, he does. Once he leaves the house, he's gone like he works two or three jobs!" I laughed.

She somewhat smiled at me and kept staring at me for an awkwardly long time:

"Let's go to your house for a second," she said, looking like she had something up her sleeve.

"Well...Okay," I replied-having just left from home a little less than an hour ago.

Still standing there, her awkward stare was replaced by a devious look on her face as she opened the bag of Jungle Jollies without looking down at it-still looking around my face and cooking up something in that awkward mind of hers. She placed a Jungle Jolly in her mouth. We then we began to walk out of her house, through the dungeon, turned left, then down the hill toward my house.

When we arrived at my house, I was walking up the steps in front of her. She made her way up the steps by stepping both her feet onto each step-slowly, still looking like she was up to something. She was almost playful.

When we got inside the house, she sat on the couch, crossed one leg on top of her knee and sat back as if she was about to start a serious conversation. I sat down, then stood up to go over and turn on the television. She grabbed my hand with one of her hands and with the other; frowned and shook finger then said: "Noooo."

"Why not?" I asked.

"Because, I just want to sit here for a second-what's wrong, you scared of silence!?" she sarcastically asserted and hit me in my forehead-affectionately.

She kept staring at me and while doing so; reached over and grabbed my hand. She then lay the back of her head on the couch and smiled at me-softly.

"Are you still mad at me?" I asked.

"I'm going to always be mad at you. I stay mad at you-that's just how it is," she replied.

"What! How is that? Why is that?" I asked.

"Because, as long as I stay mad at you, then next time I see you-you'll know how to act because you'll already know that I'm already mad at you-keep you in check!" she laughed-putting those same two fingers in my face.

I rolled my eyes and lay my head back on the couch next to hers.

She moved closer to me as if she was stealing a moment, and then got up on me and kissed me.

She then started giving me gentle kisses all around my face while I lay my head on the back of the couch; exposing my neck and shoulders. She began to move her soft full lips down to my neck and sinking her teeth in to both my shoulders and neck-passionately.

As she got more comfortable, she climbed on top of me and stretched my arms out.

With my head and neck still resting on the back of the couch, she began to kiss all over my face and sink her teeth into my neck, shoulders and arms-wildly this time; breathing hard, biting her lips-aroused and frowning. I was shaking so badly. It was feeling so good.

We're teens now-still loving all on one another since third-grade. She and I had been so used to hiding from the world and being balled up in a closet, or behind a couch kissing and grinding one another until we were drenched in sweat with sore pubes. We never got a chance to be in a wide open space in this way. This was new to us. It was amazing. I was so aroused and hot. I loved it. She loved it. She began purring like she wanted to cry and I was shaking from limb to limb. The feeling was incredible. I had been longing to be felt up like that for a while. I wanted to just piss my pants.

She then lifted my shirt, unsnapped my bra, grabbed my breasts and moaned out into the air like she was howling as she caressed them. My feet were curling and my hands were balling up. My heart had fallen down to my pussy and I let out a loud: "hellllpppp meee ahh!" She was going crazy all over me. Nobody was there to help me-but the one who was making me feel so good.

Every part of my body was jumping, and I could feel every part of hers jumping onto mine.

She then grabbed both of my breasts and held them together-trying hard to suck both of my nipples at the same time. The more my nipples grew longer and more erect, the more she kept yelling out as if her own heart fell to her pussy too. She was so aroused that she would occasionally arch her back and bend her body back as if she was being struck in the back while she was yelling out. She was *animalistically* aroused. I understood. I knew all too well how it was to play out a mission in your head then execute it, or have it right in your presence-accessible for you to complete it.

She was taking this moment all in-savoring it. She paused, and close her eyes-tightly-then folded her lips and bit into them. I could tell that her pussy was thumping. I wanted to grab it so badly and go crazy with her lips and clit, but she never liked for me to touch her like that, caress her like how she would caress me, or kiss her breasts like she would do mine-ever.

"Oh Angie, Oh Angie, Oh Angie, let me stretch you out on the bed so I can get you! Come on-please-come on, right now!" she asked-desperately.

We had never been unfolded and able to be passionate with one another out in such a wide-open space, so the atmosphere added to the excitement that we both were feeling. I was ready to just let her have her complete way with me.

Protectively, I stood up and grabbed her hand as if she was somehow going to get lost into the thin air on route to my bedroom. She sat me on the bed, kneeled beneath me and grabbed at the sides of my shorts while biting the top of my thighs like she was hungry for me. It was turning me on so badly. She then pushed me up on the bed to undress me while she undressed herself as I helped her. We were everywhere all over one another.

Ever since third-grade and up to this very day, our usual routine was to: kiss, allow her to caress my breasts and grind-for hours.

This time, her touch felt different. She had a lot of tension in her mind and body. She let herself go. It was wonderful, I loved her this way.

With my heart beating madly inside of my pussy, I practically growled at her-begging her to grab it: "Grab it! Grab it with both hands and shake it hardddd please! uhhhhhh!" I yelled out.

Even despite our private moments and unbeknownst to her-I had a thing for having my legs wide-open and having my pussy grabbed, shaken and handled aggressively, and I knew that if anyone would do it for me, it would be her.

A thousand times in my mind while masturbating, and on my "to do" list (as written in my little red diary); I had sucked the life out of her pussy and she sucked mine twice as senseless. With the way we were at this moment, I was hoping that all this would finally happen between us. I needed to get this off and out of me so badly. It was so agonizing to me because I knew that if she would never let me touch her with my hands-sucking her pussy would probably be out of the question. Quite frankly, I never knew if she knew anything *about* sucking pussy, because we never talked about those things, we would just get together and do what we routinely did-all above the waist.

She had been straddled over me-laying there going crazy from my neck, shoulders, breasts and stomach. I wanted her down on my pussy soooooooo bad. All I could imagine was her dropping down on me, aggressively chewing, gnawing, sucking and pulling; trying to put my entire pussy and clit in her mouth while I'd scream bloody murder. Instead, she gently crawled down slowly-as her tongue traced my stomach. Then by surprise and on her own time-she grabbed my entire pussy in both her hands and began grabbing and shaking it like I asked her. "Ahhhhhhhhh!" I yelled out. This time my back was arched and enjoying that shit. The pleasure drove me wild.

She then took those two fingers that she had been pointing in my face today and began playing with my swollen clit with them. I was crazy-shaking wildly. Then all of a sudden, she yelled as if she was about to ask me a question: "Angie-let meeeee!" …and started inserting one of those two fingers inside of me.

I jumped. She snatched back and yelled out in surprise as if she had been busted from trying to do something that she had no business doing:

"Oh my goodness!" she gasped.

"What?" I asked.

She then crawled up to me with those long legs of hers and put her face in my neck-whispering stuff that I could barely understand-like she was speaking a different language. She was so excited.

"What?" I whispered back.

"Shhh" she pressed her body into mine to gesture-as if I was breaking her concentration.

She kept her hands in my crotch while grabbing and shaking my pussy, aroused and gurgling into my neck while I opened my legs wider. I started thrusting my pussy upwards to give her full access to it without having to reach down uncomfortably. She began to manipulate my clit with those two fingers again. This time, it was so wild and non-stop that I was sure her hands had to have been tired-my clit was loving it. She would not stop. The pleasure was unbelievable to a point where at times, I would lay there with my mouth wide-open; in complete shock at how good it felt to me. She was making me moan and sing out in a gyrating and riffing manner that matched the motion of what she was doing to my pussy. She was biting down on her teeth; grunting some language in my ear as if while she was driving my pussy wild, she was driving hers wild as well. She was aroused to the point that, whatever she was doing to me-that made me feel good-she could feel it too. That made me crazier.

I then opened my left and right legs; making them both hang off the twin size bed. I then reached down with her to push and knead the top of my pussy and screaming out. Everything was driving me crazy.

"Damnnnnnn" she said.

"What?" I asked gently.

"You-you got your pussy open for me. Oh so beautiful. Angie-ooh. Oh. Ooh. Mine," she kept saying over and over.

She then grabbed my swollen clit and pulled it; shaking it while I yelled out-about to burst.

She knew my body was telling her that I wanted something different. She nervously moaned out and went for it. She quickly slid both of those fingers deep inside of me and let out a quick yell-as if it frightened her. She started to thrust her body into her hand with her fingers inside of me; moaning out my name as if it was me who was breaking her in. She was aroused, excited and nervous-all at the same time. I was cumming so hard in her hands while her thumb was manipulating my slippery clit.

Tears were rolling down my face, which to her, probably looked as if I was in pain because I was panting out loudly and cumming decibels-until the sound of my voice completely disappeared. I must have sounded like Prince at the end of "Darling Nikki," I didn't care. I was with someone who knew and loved me.

She was watching me while I was trying to regain my focus-fully.

As if she was sneaking, she kept looking at my pussy and my face back and forth; trying to figure out what was going on with it and me, while at the same time; those two fingers were still inside of me. She held them there as if she was supposed to hold them there until I told her to pull them out of me. I lay there and slowly relaxed my legs, closing them some-trying to give her a cue that it was okay to pull out.

She was busy staring at my pussy-admiring my swollen and exposed clit with those two fingers still down there. She slowly pulled them out of me and laid her body on top of my body-wrapping one hand around my neck.

She brought her two fingers toward me so that together, we could both look at them. I focused in:

"What?" I giggled.

"My fingers are wrinkled. Why was it wet like that?" she asked, with her nose squinted.

"Well, I mean you where down there for a while-I don't know," I replied.

"Oh. Boo…" she placed gentle kisses all over my face and neck-feeling happy about what just happened.

"That was wonderful, so, so wonderful," she whispered.

I paused for a second then asked her: "Soooo are you still mad at me?" I giggled.

She lifted her face from out of my neck and looked me in the face. She dug her knees into my bed, took both of her hands and grabbed my pussy as if she was snatching me up by the collar. She then said to me: "I **told** you that I'm **always** going to be mad at you girl!"

"Owwww," I yelled out loud as if she was hurting me.

She rolled onto the side of me and sat up on her side, supporting her head with her right hand as she traced my body and face with her fingers.

"So. That dude that everybody's crushing on-*including you,*" she emphasized.

"What was up with that last night?" she asked.

"I don't know why you keep playing. You like him too!" I accused her-laughing.

"You were pissed *off* that you had to go in the house!" I laughed out loud.

She then pointed those two fingers in my face like Celie pointed in Misters face and said: *"everything you done- done, done already been done to you.."*

The laughter subsided.

"What do you like about him?" she asked.

"I mean. I think he's cute. You know, sometimes I feel like I want a guy to have sex with me…stick it in…kiss it and stuff. I think about that sometimes." I said, immaturely.

She paused with a look on her face as if she was trying to picture what I had just said.

"I know, but, I stuck it in-my fingers," she offered.

"I know. It felt funny too!" I laughed and said with my nose squinted.

"Has anybody else ever stuck it in? Be honest." she asked.

"Never," I replied.

"If a guy does it (sticks it in) he can get you pregnant," she said-immaturely.

Long pause.

Crickets.

"Angie. I saw what happened last night. I watched it through the crack of the curtain in the window…" she admitted.

I didn't respond-I didn't know what to say.

She then asserted: "I think you *think* you like men, but you like women. I think your place is with a woman. You like it too much."

"Yeah? You think? I haven't been with any guys yet, so, how can you say that?" I replied.

"Well you almost did last night. But you didn't like it as much as you liked what just happened," she challenged.

Crickets.

Long awkward silence in the room.

We then got up, washed up, got dressed and hung out for the day as if we were just two cool friends-and we were-but just a little more than that.

8

DIVORCING DAD

I'm back in high-school now, feeling a little more mature, ready and focused.

I enjoyed my summer, because along with all the fun and experiences that came with it-it was the summer that I seemed to have grown up overnight.

Life was great and everything seemed right, in line, and as planned and mapped out.

The only eye sore, well, no…more like a heart scar, was the Saturday afternoon big blow up that my dad and I had shortly before school started back up.

Kenya and I had been playing around on her mom's vanity and makeup case while Kenya sat there imitating each and every move I made. I was looking all too experienced in how to apply the makeup and she loved it; having no idea about how sometimes at school during the day, my friends and I would be in the restroom applying makeup only to be worn around school because we had to wash it off before we got home.

Everything that I had learned in art class about the color wheel, primary, secondary, tertiary colors and how to blend from dark to light; I wanted to try on mine and Kenya's face.

I was so happy with my finished product on Kenya's and my own face that I couldn't wait to go home and show my mom, despite the fact that she insisted I not wear makeup.

As far as her eye-lined eyes and mascara lashes could see, I wasn't high-school enough to wear makeup just yet, but I just wanted her to see it (and in the back of my mind) hoped that she would like it enough to allow me to wear it this upcoming school year (so that I wouldn't have to sneak and apply it during school and have the daunting task of washing it off before I got home).

I knew that she would not have been angry at me when I walked in with it on, but whether she liked it or not (most probably by way of some idiom of hers) she would sarcastically ask me to wash it off.

Before I could even make it down to my house from Kenya's, my dad beat her to it-no, he beat me *for* it. He completely blew his lid in an instant. He practically chased me like a crazy man back up that hill. When he caught me, he tossed me around like a ragdoll so badly, that all I knew was that when I opened my eyes, I ended up against the banister at the same exact spot where my twin brother had Cable Boy wrapped around the rail across-right above where my TGGF's dad's dungeon of a basement apartment was.

Remembering the distance I had observed that day, I panicked.

Like déjà vu and I guess from hearing me scream like a banshee; my TGGF's father swung his door open-preparing to talk someone *else* into unwrapping another human being from over the top of his humble abode (that was starting to look more like a coincidental attraction for the scene of the next homicide).

Only this time, my TGGF's dad was met by an extremely good-looking, long-legged, talk, slim, grown man; man-handling his tiny, baby-faced daughter-whose face was painted with electric blue mascara, dark blue eyeliner and bright red lipstick-looking as if she had been playing in her mommy's makeup case.

With a John Witherspoon-like demeanor mixed with a George Jefferson walk, after my TGGF's dad took one look at my colorful face and obviously put himself in my daddy's place [and obviously] understood-unlike the way he saved Cable-Boy's life (the day that

Twin had him wrapped around that *same* railing that I was now being bent backwards on with his hands mashed into my tiny face); John-George walked right back down the steps to his basement apartment's cement floor and stood under the railing and watched my dad hover over my badly shaken and near lifeless body while I cried out like a stray cat.

My daddy may as well had killed me right then and there, because as far as I was concerned, from the moment he would remove his hands from me; I was officially dead to him as he was to me the moment he began chasing me up the street like some crazy man-in front of all of my peers. He could never imagine how much he blew it with me after that performance. It was a bright sunny Saturday and a sad surprise right in front of everyone's watchful eyes-they all witnessed it: My TGGF, Big Jasmine, T-Rubble and Collar Girl, Big Basketball Lena, Nina and all my umbrella friends, Rita and Charlene, the boy from swimming who had a crush on me, the older teenage girls who I would sing for, my friend's parents-even Leroy stepped out of the store and stood at the bottom of the hill to see what was going on. They were all there-startled; probably wondering what happened that caused my mature persona to be handled like some bitch in the street, slash, abused child. Confusion was on *every*body's face.

If Male Model was near, I did not see him. Oh-wait a minute…

I was hearing birds chirp and seeing stars. I believe his mirage was twirling in the circles of the vertigo I was experiencing at that moment, for he *had* to have been there. *No one* missed this sideshow because it went on for a long while.

I was worn out and all too confused.

In all my life, I had never seen him like that-ever. It was almost like some stranger had run up on me-not my dad. He had never even raised his voice at me yet, yet he went from 0 to 60. No, not 0 to 60; 0 to 120 in a matter of some long unforgivable minutes that day.

Regardless how close we had always been all my life, and no matter the: Star Wars, Battlestar Galactica's, Superman sequels, Ringling Brothers and Barnum and Bailey Circus,' shopping together, long drives and conversation, short rides on the back of his motorcycle, dinners, movies, and surprise bags of clothes from him being my personal shopper that he gave to me-*none* of that mattered anymore to me. That Super Saturday that he embarrassed me in front of my entire street of friends was the day that he exchanged everything we ever had. We no longer fit.

Because of that *one* Super Saturday, any closeness that we ever shared (as far as I could register) had now been exchanged for a permanent marquee emanating from my throbbing head that read:

"ALL SALES FINAL. SORRY, NO RETURNS…"

I made my way down the hill-tired and winded-with red lipstick, electric blue mascara and dark blue eyeliner outlining my tears. Standing on the top step, I pointed to my mother sitting there looking startled at the sight of my face. She didn't pay any attention to the makeup on it, but rather, the look on it. She had the same look on her face the day that Cable Boy, Tom-Tom, Bay-Bay, Day-Day, Ray-Ray and Kay-Kay attacked me. And just like that day, I placed both my hands to my knees as if I was in the middle of playing a rough game of football. I was wheezing, huffing and puffing like a toddler while trying to catch my breath. I was feeling a type of frustration that I had never felt, mixed with a sudden onset of an asthma attack and some conditions that I never even had. That was the feeling.

I closed my eyes tightly and clutched my rapidly pounding broken heart; fighting to assist my lungs in pulling any amount of air through that it could. While wheezing, some air came through and I said to my mother: "Daddy. Do not open that door for him if he rings the bell and from this day forward-I never want to see him in life again-*ever*…"

In that instant, I could see her face turn from empathy and concern for me, to some longing damsel in distress: sitting there waiting on that prince charming (who was once hers) to bring her some fucking glass slippers so that she could stand on her two feet to walk *and* breathe again-herself. Well after her heart was shattered like glass after him leaving her and given someone else a ring that once upon a time was hers, as well. I was livid from watching the expression on her face:

"Bull *crap*! Don't look at me like that. I never want to see him again and he'd better not *ever* come near me again-for **nothing**. And it's *your* duty to make sure of it!" I yelled at her as if she was the child.

"He doesn't have any *babies* in this house! I've got two brothers almost twenty-one and Twin is my age! So there are no babies here! What do we need him for anyway? We are all almost grown! You don't need him! How much longer is this fantasy going to keep going on in your head? The "babies" y'all had together are *grown*! The only reason he comes around you is because of me-and I don't ever want to see him again! Can't you see that he's moved on and started his life *and* started a business with somebody else *any*way. You're sitting over here crossing your fingers and toes, waiting for the day that he comes back to you! He's coming over here dangling you like a puppet on a string-*just* in case…and you've got the **nerve** to be looking at me like you are caught between a rock and a hard place!" I asserted-sounding like I got my mouth from her.

She paused and folded her lips-wanting to curse me out and spew a bad mamma jamma of an idiom from that mouth of hers to put me in my place. But she knew I was hurting, while at the same time-everything I said to her made the kind of sense that she needed to hear-a long time ago.

It was perfect timing because we were already about to start packing to move to a new apartment.

I made my mother promise me that she would not let my dad know where we were living-until I felt ready; when or if ever that day would ever come back around. I saw that happening next to never.

She digressed and agreed, but that mouth of hers was filling up with the kind sputum to moisten her lips that resembled mine-in preparation for forming an idiom to smack me with for talking to her sideways in my moment of my temporary insanity.

The expression on my face was like that of Larry Fishburne-frowning up at Ms. Sophia and begging her not to, before punching the mayor: ("Ah no, Ms. Sophia, Ms. Sophia No!"). My mother just couldn't hold it back: "You let me tell you something LITTLE GIRL! You are *not* grown! And if you ever talk to me like that in *your* life-**again**, I will turn your grown ass upside down and spit in your butt!"

9

YOU-KNOW-WHO

"Ms. You Know Who." You know what? You can't even imagine...

A tall, long auburn-haired, racially ambiguous, sassy, well-dressed, slightly bowlegged woman with an almost arrogant but self-assured walk. Everything about her seemed like the world did everything her way-at all times.

My friendship with Ms. You Know Who escalated to a whole new level a couple school years before this one in particular. One of my major courses of study ensured that I would see her for the duration of my years there at the artsy-school I had been attending.

We first met some years back when I was in fifth grade. She was always very "big-sisterly," slash, borderline "motherly" to me; a mentor-a "momtor" of such. She wanted all the best of everything for me and went out of her way to give to me, push me, as well as show me.

No matter what, she always felt like she knew what was best-not only in her area of expertise,' but she felt like she knew what was best for me (studying under her) as well: artistically and personally.

I admired her so much because she was like magic. My area of study was one in which, if you took the time to care, you could see that I had major potential, but it didn't come natural for me like other things did. She took that little bit, and like a magic ball; wove together: my potential + her expertise and made me an artistic force to be reckoned with. Step by step, she taught me "how" to do it from the ground-up. It was as if she knew how to take her mind and place inside of my mind-to help me see things from her a perspective that the average untrained mind and eye could not see.

The subject she taught went so much deeper than the surface (and as expected in the outline of the curriculum). She would interject the science or psychology behind what we were learning, so that we would know the science or psychology behind the art-itself. She interjected the study of hemispheres of the brain and how they worked for us in relation to how we could make it work for what were studying, all the way down to how the trained versus the untrained eye looks at lines, shapes, (primary, secondary and tertiary) colors-the whole sha-bang. She was full-on.

I trusted her and everything she taught.

I valued her and held onto everything she said-like I could take it to the bank.

For two hours a day, five days per week, nine months out of twelve, school year after school year; she watched me like a hawk. Come to find out, she had actually studied me school years prior, and now was the time she felt the need to intervene: intervene in my school life, my personal life and any other life that I had that could fit into my busy lil' teen schedule. My summer before this particular school-year was pretty full with a lot of goings on. My body, my emotions and my mind had seemed to change overnight. She too, could tell that I had a full growth spurt overnight rather than gradual-and she just *had* to know why.

As my momtor, something about me was just was not sitting right with her. And by the time I sashayed back and forth in her classroom *this* year; she was ready for me. Reminiscing on all those previous school years that she would start her classroom demonstrations by break us up into one big circle to surround her-then send us back to our seats; she would lean back in her chair as if to say: "my work here is done."

After which, she would sit back and scan the classroom, her eyes: observing. Everyone would be working diligently on their projects, and sometimes I would look over at her. She wouldn't quite crack a smile at me, but rather, a squint-as if to say: "I'm on to you/I got my eye on you..."

Her interest in intervening was almost like she had been a fly on the walls of my life up to this point and she could no longer act like she didn't know.

It worked out perfectly this school-year, because my schedule was more flexible-which allowed me to have her class for two hours. And since my study hall followed it, and my lunch bell followed my study hall; my busy little schedule eventually opened itself up to many a conversations with Ms. You Know Who. So when that bell rang for class to end, from the first moment she asked me to stay after, I stayed after every day.

While in class, she was warm-but detached and serious about her job. When classroom was over and everyone was gone, she would start her conversation as if she was taking her lab coat off and it was now time to break everything down to a science.

"Playtime is over bitch," was what she may as well had said to me, because when class was over and that door shut, with the entire class gone and on the other side of it, it was curtains: "show time." She wanted to know everything that was going on with me: my life, what I wanted to do with it, where I wanted to go, things I wanted to see, people I wanted to meet, what inspired me, what made me happy, what made me sad, my favorite color, favorite food, favorite movie-you name it, she was on it. I was comfortable talking to her because not only did I trust her, she did not smother and scold me like a mother would-but more like how an older sister would.

Our personal time started off as small talk to eventually: a tough love, slash, mini boot camp, slash, touch of etiquette class, and a dash of image consulting, slash, a crash course of: "Angie Baby Your Life is Calling What Are You Going To Do About It?"

Within a couple of months into that school year, she was on first name basis with my mother.

Before too long, one Saturday or Sunday a month, she would come by the house and chat with my mom for a minute and off we would go out on our girlie dates to talk about life, my life and her trying to keep me focused on it. Our monthly weekend excursions included everything from going to the movies and out to eat-where she'd sit across from me-teaching me dining etiquette. We would also go make-up shopping (for her) where at the counter, she mentioned how she had seen me a couple times trying to sneak into her classroom with goo-gobs of mascara and eyeliner thinking I was cute.

"Death by eyeliner!" she joked-holding her hands up as if she was describing a headline or marquee of some kind. We laughed so hard standing at the counter like two teenagers insulting one another without a care in the world about who was listening to us being downright unruly.

"Girl, that foundation was ten-twelve shades off from your complexion some days. I would look at you and say to myself: "What in the?!" we laughed. It was a fun day-bursting into loud inappropriate laughs mid-store, as if we were both thirteen.

"Angie, sweetie your mom said she didn't want you wearing makeup right now but just for the record, this is where I buy my makeup and when you do start, this is where you will get yours. I *insist*!" she emphasized and laughed again.

When the clerk to come back, Ms. You Know Who bought me some pink lip gloss and purse spray, telling me that woman's purse should always smell good as well. I felt like a princess that day, it happened to be one of our best weekends out

We had one of our weekend excursions over to her house. I was astonished when I walked in.

She lived richly. More richly than I already thought she did. I wondered how she could be a mere teacher but live in what looked like a mansion with all the trimmings.

When we first walked into the foyer of her home, there were two sides of spiral stairs that met a giant life-sized oil painting-a portrait-of her beautiful self, posing in such a way that her legs painted in the picture gave off the same mental picture as the long stairwell. It just worked. The stairs looked like they were built for the painting. "How vain," I thought to myself, but she was sassy anyways, so nothing less could be expected-coming from her.

She had a husband who was the Dean of College, a daughter away in her first year at Harvard and she loved to brag that her son was on his way to Yale or Harvard behind his sister.

Outside of class, more and more, she let her hair down.

She was so child-like and immature with me. We'd love to insult one another non-stop and if it was something that went wrong during a class demonstration or any imperfection or mishap; that would be my insult for her for the day. We were so fun together, but when she would get serious, she'd look me in the eyes and tap my nose:

"Angie I feel like it's something special about you and I wouldn't want it to go to waste. You're "different." Stick with me and if you want to dance-I'll make you dance. If you want to sing-I'll make you sing. If you want to act-I'll make you act. If you want to go to the best school to do whatever it is you want to do, I will see you there. I have two kids who are doing well. They followed my rules, they're well-adjusted, and success is a guarantee for them, as long as they have me for mother," she bragged.

"Success is guaranteed for you, too-as long as you have me as a friend…Oh!… Provided that you don't get fat!" we busted out laughing, again.

"No, but I do want to tell you a thing or two Ms. Angie. You stay dancing-but you also should stay watching your diet and even when you get older. And most of the girls who dance with you and walk the halls are still built like little twelve year-old boys. You have bells and whistles," she laughed.

She then got serious:

"You're different than them. Though you're slim and fit, your body is still more developed than your peers, so, there are things they do-that you cannot do, anymore," she explained.

I listened on.

"Let me ask you a question, Angie. Couple days ago, I gave you some interoffice mail to take to Mr. Richards, remember?" she asked.

"Yeah, I remember," I replied.

"Did he say anything to you-at all, like anything inappropriate or out of the way?" she inquired.

Long pause.

"Oh. I know-I remember. He was just joking," I replied.

"What was he joking about? What did he say?" she asked.

"Well when he took the envelope from me and then when I was leaving, he called out my name. I walked back in and he whispered to me: 'Angie, you'd better not come back in here in that leotard again because if you do-I'm going to start thinking different about you.' "

"And you didn't think anything was wrong with that man saying that to you?" she asked-looking me in the eyes as if she knew that I knew better than that-as if she knew that I was smarter than that, and if not, all this time, she had been giving me credit for being smarter than what I really was.

She had no idea the life I lived, so that comment had gone through one ear and out of the other-to a girl like me.

I didn't respond.

She was thrown, she scolded me:

"Angie, I know you didn't think that was appropriate did you? That was inappropriate!" she yelled.

"If it didn't register with you as being inappropriate-then hell yeah, you got bigger problems coming your way than I thought-where men and boys are concerned…"

I defended:

"No, let me explain. When you gave me the envelope to take to him, I thought it was some kind of note or something personal for him. And when he said that, I did frown up somewhat, but I didn't reply back to him. To be honest, I didn't say anything to you about it because I didn't know what was going on between you two…the mail and all…I…thought it was a personal letter or note inside."

"What!?" she replied, in shock.

"I mean-he *is* fine. And you are really pretty too. Soooo…I…thought that you too were passing notes or something-flirting," I explained.

"Girl, I don't even *know* that fool down there! That envelope was going around to all the staff and his name was next on the list to sign! I only gave it to you to take to him because you were headed that way when you left here. It didn't dawn on me, until you were good and gone, that you (with all your bells and whistles I might add) were in a leotard, going down to some man's office. I was hoping that the fool could contain himself and not say anything to you. I just know how some men can be. I merely took my chances and asked you what, if anything, he said to you and you just proved my same exact point that I am making to you!" she defended.

"Oh. Okay," I replied.

"I want you to quit walking the halls with that leotard on. Those other girls your age, walking around in their leotards after dance, have under developed bodies-they can do that. You: Angie-cannot. Do you hear me? You are getting to an age and stage of development right now where little boys are getting curious and excited about girls like you, and dirty old men are taking notice," she said.

I stood there and listened-taking it all in.

She continued making quote and unquote symbols with her fingers:

"And Angie, just because a man and a woman are both "fine" doesn't mean they have to be messing around either. Besides, did you forget that I was happily married?" she laughed.

She rolled her eyes in her head, rolled some assignment papers up in her hand, and smacked me on my forehead. She then gave me a hug and kiss on that same spot on my forehead before she interjected her bottom line: "You are my special girl. Stick with me-do what I say-and you'll go far," something she would always say: many variations-many ways.

After a few moments of silence, she placed her hands on her hips:

"Wait a minute. So let me get this straight. So…if Mr. Richards *was* my lil' man on the side, you mean to tell me you would not have told me what he said to you girl?" she said-sounding like some sassy peer of mine.

I began to shake my head "no"-repeatedly, then let out a loud and obnoxious laugh.

"You sneaky lil' strumpet!" she laughed out loud in unison with me.

With the rolled up assignment papers in her hand, she then ran up on me and started smacking me anywhere there was an open spot I couldn't defend and cover myself. I was laughing and giggling like a munchkin-trying to guard myself from her playful blows.

She then interjected:

"I can see right now that I have a lot more to teach you than I originally thought I did."

I kept giggling, not knowing what was brewing in the lessons forthcoming I still had yet to learn that were in the making-changes between us and my situation altogether; many variations-many ways...

10

FIRST FLINGS FIRST

Our pairing was odd. No one understood why or how I had his nose so far open. It took a lot of people at our school a while to adjust to our being together because he was cute and: popular. I was cute but: "weird" and "different." But let him tell it, that was why he liked me so much.

Some days I would wear normal clothes like skirts, slacks and such, but other times, I wore my pink Chuck Taylors with most of my jeans or shirts that I would splatter acrylic paint all over. I attended a creative arts school, so it was not out of the ordinary to dress like that. Some of us were into tightening our jeans with a gazillion (visible) safety pins on the outside of the left and right legs of our jeans-for style. It was nothing for me to wear a select number of jeans [that I had personally designed] by tying knots in them, then bleaching them so they would look airbrushed. I would then wash and wear them-leaving some pairs like that-but others; I would dip into a tub of clothing dye and let them hang dry for a couple days. After the bleaching process, if I applied yellow clothing dye-the jeans would look lime green, yellow and dark green. If I applied red dye after the bleaching process, they'd look pink and purple. After the dye job, I would wash them, then put them in the dryer. I would have myself an awesome looking pair of jeans that looked couture and to die for. They looked stylish, hot and store-bought, but you couldn't get jeans that looked like this from any the mall. Oh no. I never told my secret about how to do my jeans like that and I held on to my secret like the Colonel holds on to his secret recipe for the Kentucky Fried Chicken.

The other half of the school kids stayed on top of the latest designer fashions from head to toe. Santana was one of them. He *hated* the way I dressed. And what he could not buy me with his little work checks, he would steal for me: all those latest fashions (shoes included).

Santana wrote letters to me every day and would glow at the sight of me. He had to wait a while to officially court me by permission though, because my mother had a rule: no makeup and no boys until I was sixteen. But a year earlier, I broke both of her rules and eventually lost my virginity to Santana. I felt that my heart was safe with him and he would stay for the long haul, especially since he too, was a virgin. He was not quite a bad-boy but he wasn't lame either.

We met in the school library. I was standing high on a ladder-trying to locate a book that I wanted to read. He walked into the door looking from left to right, as if he was looking for someone. When our eyes met, I turned away really fast. He walked over to me and sat the table beneath the ladder I was standing on. I looked down at him and asked:

"Why are you standing down there under me like that, and why are you looking up at me?"

"It's a free country I can look at what I want to look at. I'm looking at you-I always like to look at you," he said.

I was confused because I never thought of him that way, and for that minute, my brain tried hard to scan any recollection where he looked at me for any length of time. I was so scared and didn't understand how to handle this because it was so storybook-like and boy-meets-girl-normal. Nothing in my life that I had experienced thus far was of this kind normal. I was so nervous standing there. I felt like about as awkward and out of place as Sissy Spacek in "Carrie."

Ms. You Know Who branded him the nickname: "light-bulb head boy." She knew him because he took her class at the last part of the day for five days per week. She refused to call him by his real name when discussing him with me.

He was charming, with a gorgeous smile, perfect teeth, carved, chiseled lips and cheek-bones, and what we would call "girl eyes"-because he had long eyelashes. He was a dead ringer for Phillip Michael Thomas in "Sparkle." He had deep-wavy and curly hair, his pretty grey-green eyes drooped in the far corners. His eyelashes made it look like he wore eyeliner. When he would smile, his right eye was lazy and his small dimples looked like little muscles in his face. To top it all off, he had a hairy chest (that was a rare find in a boy his age). His having chest hair was always the whispers and talk of the school. He dressed impeccably, with the latest clothes and always carried his backpack neatly across his back with both straps on. Everyone else wore theirs with one strap hanging but he didn't.

"Come down off that ladder so that I can talk to you-please! Please!" he pleaded.

Feeling shy and embarrassed-shaking and ready to fall off the ladder, I ignored him.

"Please talk to me-please!" he begged-this time with his hands folded; making me blush as I peeked down at him from behind a book in my hand.

Very slowly, I stepped down to him. Each step of the way that I was closer to him, my heart raced with the speed of a thousand Derby racehorses. He was tall, and when I got down to his level, he was looking down at me. Through my bangs, I looked up at him and he bluntly asked, in a tone that was too loud for the library atmosphere:

"WHYYYYYY are you so weird, man?"

"What do you mean: *weird*?" I asked, sarcastically.

"You dress weird. You act weird. What are you scared of?" he asked.

I was so embarrassed but I couldn't let him get away with talking to me this way, so I responded:

"I'm not scared of *nothing*. I beg your pardon," I said-trying to sound firm and menacing.

He had no idea this was my first normal, real-life, age-appropriate: "boy-meets girl" experience, and it was all so foreign to me.

"You dress kind of like-not goth-but like a rockstar or something, sometimes," he said-seriously.

I was standing there in a pair of regular designer jeans (about the only clothing item of I had on that I was sure he could understand and agree with) a wrist filled with black plastic and silver bangles, and one of my acrylic-paint sprinkled specialties for a shirt, (further proving his point). I really didn't know how to take what he said without feeling insulted. I felt called to the carpet with the evidence on, from head down to my pink Converse and light-blue shoe-stringed toe. I scolded him with my eyes. He smiled and interrupted me before I could speak:

"You do! But I like it. I especially like your pink high top Converse Chuck Taylors-your light-blue shoestrings and all. That's pretty fresh," he said, looking down at my feet and shaking his head up and down with approval.

He then looked down into my face and removed my bangs from my eyes and spoke softly: "I like your red hair and skin," he said.

I smiled, scared to say anything back-not even: "Thank you."

He laughed and said:

"You are soooo pretty but you *are* soooo weird, man. Something about you…is different. I aint gon' lie."

I frowned while biting my bottom lip-not knowing how to respond to that, so I defended:

"If I'm so weird then why are you here?"

"I watch you and I…I…always wanted to say something to you, but you're always with your friends. So, I watched come in here, alone and I…waited a few minutes then followed you here," he explained.

"That's weird," I jabbed. He laughed.

"May I have your phone number Angie?" he asked-seriously.

I stood there-feeling shy already-like Sissy Spacek in the movie classic: "Carrie." Having just been branded a firm "weird" by this cute boy and now having this same cute boy stand in front of me asking for my number was too much to bear. Like in "Carrie," I constantly looked up above me-waiting on the pail of pig's blood to fall on my head. The thoughts of Carrie's crazy mother were replaced by *my* mother going crazy and having a fit at the sound of a boy on the other end of my phone-calling my house before age sixteen. "Age sixteen" was the next level of freedom and access to accessories threshold that my mother [and dead father] always reiterated. It annoyed me since I could remember.

I couldn't say no to Santana. I was too embarrassed to say no. So instead, I took a deep breath and gave him the phone number with complete confidence, and in hopes that when he calls, my mom would be able to see him through the phone then decide that he was as charming and cute to her as he was to me-standing right there in front of my face.

Later that night and going forward; day by day, we got a chance to talk on the phone for a while without interruption or incident. I would be guarding the phone during the evening hours so that I would be the only one answering it, because he refused to sneak around with me. He had already warned me in many-a-jokes:

"If your mother ever answers the phone, I am going to be a gentleman and introduce myself. Then I'm going to tell her that I like her daughter a lot and she's being selfish!" Though he would joke about it, I could never argue with him about it-it wasn't even up or discussion. He was heaven-bent on making sure nothing was going to come between this chance we had. He liked me as much as I liked [and never entertained the thought of dating] him. Alone and to myself (and later into the courtship) sometimes in his arms; I would cry at the fact that I was finally in a normal situation with a normal, age-appropriate boy whom I liked too. The fact that I thought he never even looked at me, because he was popular and all the girls liked him so much, was nothing less than storybook special to me. And as it turned out-I had been a twinkle in his eye for a long time, without him being so much as a passing thought in my mind.

Santana made me feel "special" and "different" in the right way-opposite how I was so used to hearing that I was special and different: separate and unlike my average peer. But his kind of "special" and "different," made me feel included and accepted *because* I was "special" and "different" as I was.

We decided that we liked each other too much, to not go steady. I was still trying to figure out why he wanted to go steady with me, rather than all of the other girls who liked him who were cute and popular not "weird" "different." He would insist that he liked my being "different" and "weird," because he also thought I was so pretty but "pure" without even learning that I was still a virgin. After a while, the fact that he called me weird didn't bother me anymore because he would stare at me and hold me like he absolutely adored me. When he would remove my bangs to look into my eyes, I would see stars in *his* eyes. Before he would kiss me, he would bite his bottom lip and hold my cheeks like he was afraid I would leave and never come back.

I was so happy. I knew that this boy really liked me. For the first time in my life with another person; I felt normal and free of the covert and secret.

We made a pact that every school day, we would write a letter, a note or on a card of some kind, for one another-so that we would stay close. We both liked that. I did not tell any of my friends that he liked me because a tiny part of me was still not trusting of all this undivided attention that he was paying to me. He either kissed or flirted with all the girls, and all the girls flirted with and liked him-entire cliques of girls did. I wondered "why stop here?" [with me]. Because the fact still remained, I did not fit into his world.

My drug of choice was: r&b, pop, lite-rock, proper English, and creativity.

His drug of choice was: rap, broken English and slang, and conformity.

I was also afraid to reveal our liking for each other to my own friends and peers because each and every one of them either: liked him too, talked to him on the phone, or kissed him before. Actually, pretty much all of the girls in the school fit into one of the three categories.

Fortunately, for me-he stopped-here: (with me).

He was eager to prove himself different than my perception of him and to show me how different I was *to* him-than anybody ever was.

Finally it happened. He was not in the spot where we would normally meet. Instead, he came in front of my homeroom, then kissed and hugged me while everybody was around: my friends (who now, were all officially old news to him-mere girls in passing) and his friends (who would tease him about being two years older than me. They would call him "Chester child molester").

I got my letter, my kiss, my security, my confirmation that we were official and that no one else mattered but me. Weeks into this, he quickly learned my "way." He was so familiar with my uncanny ability to function covertly, that he could not take it anymore. All my life-that was what I was used to (as being a "normal" thing), so he couldn't understand it anymore than I had the ability to communicate and explain it to him. It was just a part of who I was.

He didn't care *who* knew. If anyone wanted a birds-eye view into our relationship and the goings on in it (the good, the bad, the ups, the downs, the virginity, the loss of it, the ins, the outs and the over's); all they would have had to do was read his letters written to me-word for word. If someone would have gotten a hold of all his letters that he wrote to me-they would have been singing our life from his words. Because each and every letter told everything about me, about him, and about us-apart, or together:

"To Angie, My Big Baby.

What's up? Nothing much here. Just got my math test back, another F. But anyway, I found your letter thought provoking and somewhat funny. But did you have to use such big words? (smile) Alright, so I get a little upset when I can't come over. I can't get in touch with you over the phone. It's just that I want to spend as much time as possible with you because I feel rather empty or lonely. (yes! Gigolos get lonely too) smile. (sike) but I think you understand.

Being called a Chester doesn't bother me at all just as long as I have some very special, sweet, lovable person whom I love and they love me back. When we first started talking (or whatever) I knew I would be pressured for being involved with a younger girl, but don't worry, no phase on my part. To be honest, I know I really love you but for some reason, when around your friends I sometimes feel scared to even come over to you to say hi. But when we are alone I feel just fine. About the making love business. I would never tell anyone about me and your sexual encounters (if any) because I put myself in your shoes I wouldn't feel good if my business was told to everyone. I would never do anything to hurt you or our relationship in any way.

Open up a little more? Who me? I have no idea what you are talking about. I don't know how to open up. Really I do, but I would rather not until I know for this (me and you) is what I really want. I mean I know for sure I want you but as you know, times change and people change and I would hate to be caught up in the middle one of those changes.

But that's what love is all about, so I promise you that I will work on it. (Dam! I can't write, but I'm trying just for you) two more minutes until the bell rings I'm 'bout to go. I'll get back and I LOVE YOU."

Still looking up for the pig's blood, I lowered my head quickly and frowned with an embarrassing smile on my face, so I covered it. This was too much like a popular: "Boy-meets-Girl. Boy-falls-in-love-with-Girl. Boy-tells-the-world. Shows-the-world" fantasy. This kind of wish or hope never even made it in the lines of my red diary. So it took me by surprise about as much as it swept me off my feet, because outside of my mom not knowing just yet; everything was at a normal pace with normal happenings: no rushing, no reasons to hide. This was all much too normal for me.

He kissed, held, grabbed me and pulled me away from the jealous onlookers and green eyed-monsters. It was then that I began to trust him and all the affection and love that he claimed to have for me. His letters matched his fears, his touch, his kiss, and the way he would look at me:
"The Stormy Nights
The stormy nights
The winter breeze
Holding you in my arms, relaxed and at ease
It seems so simple, no problems occur
But our love will endure
I want so much to see you smile
And take away that inner turmoil
You make me so happy unlike any other girl
You are my heart, my soul, my world
The stormy nights
The winter breeze
You touch my mind with loving ecstasy"

"Santana & Angie
What's up! I can't think of nothin' to write. I loved your letter. The only thing I don't follow is I thought you had already fallen in love with moi! Or do you mean falling deeper. But anyway, I love you so much also. What do you mean my fault! That we don't spend much time together you're crazy! I'll accept 50 but not 100% of the blame. I'm really sorry I played you about the telephone deal. My phone wasn't even plugged up and it won't be for a while. Cause I'm on the big two week P from Friday, my mother found out. So if you want to write me a weekend worth of letters, even if you don't have much to say just so that I have a feeling of being with you. It won't be the same but it will get me over the weekend. WHERE IS MY FUCKING WALKMAN. Sorry did I scare you. I'm just acting blowed. But I'll get back. Love, Santana."

"My Dear Angie
I take the pleasure of writing these few lines. I hope you love me now just as much as you did when I was there with you of Friday because my mind is with you day & night. The love that I have for you in my heart is greater than I thought it was. If I had thought I had so much love for you, I don't think I would have ever let the chance of making passionate love to you slip out of my grasp. All I can do is stop & look back and say what a fool I was for letting it happen. Sex...it's perfectly proper that when you and I make love, your own pleasure should be out of the utmost importance to you. Any sexual practices we engage in should be for your enjoyment, not just mine. When I whisper: "do you like this, whisper back the truth especially if the answer is no. Listen, I know this letter is just about contradicting at least one out of the three I have previously written but it's just a subject that won't let my mind at ease. Fuck all that deep stuff (for now) what's up! I love you. You love me too? That's nice to know. But um. What do I do that's so childish or stupid. When you say that, for some reason I feel as if I'm losing you. I know I'm not but it just seemed that way ya know."

"Angie
What's up! Me?! I thought you would say that. Well. I'm sitting here in
American History bored half to death and you just happened to pop
into my mind.
Nice letter I loved it. I read it six times already, (no lie) I really don't
*have too much to say but **I love you**! And from me you know that's a*
mouth full.
I understand about mom being over protective because you are her
only baby girl, I would be too but you are also my only baby girl and
mom's being selfish. I mean, just tell her how you feel about me and if
necessary I will tell her how I feel about you and we'll take it from
there.
But if you feel it is a rush then we won't push it ok!) Is that halfway
enough? I love you! (I said dick, not penis so stop trying to make
everything sound so less embarrassing)."

"Hi Angie how are you doing? Fine! I knew that. I missed you. Your
kiss. Your embrace. Your sexy smirk, your voice. And most important of
all, your love. Baby please don't be upset with me I'm begging you.
(Something I hardly ever do) Whatever I did I'm really sorry I am.

When I called you to say bye! (twice) you just looked as if to say fuck
you forever. That really hurt me and you just don't know how much. I
know I play too much sometimes but you know I never mean any harm.
Especially not to you, so I'll apologize once more. And again and
again and again if I have to accept this is it without the deepest depths
of my heart.

I know I'm sometimes abstruse (but lovable) I know I'm sometimes the
reason for you having a bad day but I'm sorry really I am. Ok! Let's
make a deal! Let's stop bullshitting each other and leaving each other
with a doubt in mind that we'll lose each other.

Let's talk everything out even in the most silliest things and laugh at the same mistakes later. I must admit through this whole relationship there has been little rain. Let's keep it that way. Let's start over. All grudges (if any) aside ok? Ok! I love you look up and say what you think! And then give me a hug and a kiss! Just don't smack me! Please.

PS I'm off my P so start calling! I love you! I'll get back Montgomery Moose! WRITE BACK PLEASE The letters here at the pad are getting old."

"Hello! I'm back, how are you doing? Fine! I know I'm alright. If you are wondering how I'm doing. I don't have anything on my mind right now accept you of course. Just putting pen to paper hoping something will come to mind. I LOVE YOU. Just can't live without you and all my dreams and thoughts are about you. Let's spend more time together in school. I just love being as you say "in the presence of your company."

It makes me feel even more like a man. In other words, my nature comes out even more when I am exposed to the female scent that you carry. Dam!

I'm sleepy but I want to complete this letter. I love you! (yawn)

Love is a passion you just can't hide (or don't want to) And I just want to express our feelings with kisses, caresses, hugs, eye contact, words and any way possible as long as I know how you feel about me I'm cool ya know! That's about it cause I'm dead sleepy it's 3:30 now but it was about 2:58 when I started. I just woke up thinking ANGIE, ANGIE. ANGIE something I've never (yawn) done before. I love you.

P.S Hope when I close my eyes I continue to dream about you.

Love,
SLEEPY SANTANA"

"Angie
Hi what's up? I read your letter. It was alright, nothing to get my
beaters up about. It was quite interesting. Your perspective on how you
plan on going about doing this was too crazy. It had me tripping hard.
But anyway, it did start my imagination to run, that I must admit.

My house? Why my house. I mean I don't mind but ya know, my bed is
dead broke. (Don't laugh) but other than that my room is in perfect
shape. So let me bust that ass over your house.

Naw! I don't care where, just as long as I bust that ass.

Boy! Do you have a mind for sexual fantasies. You would have thought
you have been through all this before (in real life) Hmm. Makes me
wonder...

But anyway! Hours of pleasure? I wish I could fuck you for an hour.
(Excuse me, I meant to say make love to you for an hour). But maybe
it's possible I wasn't in a daze or sleep. So there was no need for you to
write "wake up its only a fantasy!" But anyway, maybe your dream
about being pregnant means something but as strange as it may sound,
I would love for you to have my little girl. Really.
But you know! That's all I can think of, so I'll get back at lunch!
Love Santana
I love you!
PS- you're nasty!"

"Hi! This is Santana (Sap of the Year)
I'm sitting in the tub thinking about you and me (our future together).
It seems as though we will be together for a while or longer. Are you
positive that you want to spend your life with me. I'm sure. But are
you? Yea! I know you told me that you are but I would hate to keep you
from doing a lot of things girls your age do and that's meeting different
kind of guys. But don't get me wrong. I'm not saying I don't want to no

longer be with you it's just that I feel as if I'm depriving you of something special. I don't know what, but something.

As much as I've gotten around I deserve to settle down don't you think. But you can't say the same.

Sometimes Angie (please don't get mad) Never mind oops! You hate that don't you? LOVE YA!

But anyway. I need it bad. Every day I look at your ass looks bigger. Your tits look softer and much bigger also. This is torture. My dick gets hard when the wind blows, (don't laugh). Maybe there is an advantage to all this torture I am going through. I mean you know the greater the anticipation, the greater the satisfaction.

If I touch you, beaters up, when I kiss you, beaters up, thinking about you, beaters up and you think that shit is funny. Sometimes I think you be teasing me on purpose sometimes. Either that or this horniness is affecting my mind. But anyway I LOVE YOU!

P.S- next time you ask what's up you should already know before you ask right?
Love, Santana"

He started getting creative:

"EIGNA
Angie
STAHW PU? GNIHTON! I WENK TAHA ESUAC ER'UOY A PAS.
What's up? Nothing! I knew that cause you're a sap.
TUB YAWYNA I EVOL UOY. I LEEF HCUMRETTEB. WOHEMOS
But anyway I love you. I feel much better somehow.
I LEEF RO MI NWARD RESOLC OT UOY ESUACEB FO
YADRETSEY
I feel or I'm drawn closer to you because of yesterday

I WONK UOY TNOD NEVE TNAW OT REAH TI TUB STAHT EHT
YAW
I know you don't even want to hear it but that's the way

I LEEF. I DEZILAER WOH ESOLC I EMAC OT GNISOL UOY
DNA TI
I feel. I realized how close I came to losing you and it

DEPPIRT ME TOU. OS WON MI ANNOG TSUJ LLIHC TUO DNA
EB
Tripped me out. So now I'm gonna just chill out and be

YREV YREV ECIN OT UOY UNTIL I NAC TEG UOY KCAB
REDNU
Very very nice to you until I can get you back under

ETELPMOC LORTNOC. I EVOL UOY OS HCUM. DID TI KOOL
SA FI
Complete control. I love you so much. Did it look as if

I SAW GNIOG OT YRC. FI SEY I TNSAW STAHT TAHW I
DLUOW LLAC
I was going to cry. If yes I wasn't that's what I would call

RETTUB. UOY TSUM EB ENO LLEH FO A LRIG ESUAC ER UOY
EHT
Butter. You must be one hell of a girl cause you re the

YLNO ENO THAT SAH REVE TOG EM NWOD. OT LLET EHT
THURT
Only one that has ever got me down. To tell the truth

I DEKIL TAHT TUB REVE UOY OD TNOD TEG EVARB NO EM
I liked that but ever you do don't get brave on me

KO? I LLIW TIMDA I SAW A PAS TUB UOY TNOD EVAH
LORTNOC
Ok? *I will admit I was a sap but you don't have control*

TA TSAEL TON YLLATOT. MI 9.99 TNECREP DNA MI EHT TSEB
REVEN

At least not totally. I'm 99.9 percent and I'm the best, never

SSEL. KCUF ADNAY EHS TNIA TIHS OT EM EHS SAW BMUD
YAWYNA

Less. Fuck Yanda she aint shit to me she was dumb anyway

EM DNA IBEL KOOT SNRUT HTIW REH OS WOH SEOD EHS
WONK TAHW

Me and Levi took turns with her so how does she know what

SEHS NEEB URHT. UOY TNDID NEVE TNAW OT RAEH TAHT I
WONK UOY

She's been thru. You didn't even want to hear that I know you

TNDID IM YRROS

Didn't I'm sorry Love, Santana"

"Alright Angie
I liked your letter. It was alright. This is the last time our future as far
as relationship is concerned will be discussed. Let's face it, I'm stuck
with you and you're stuck with moi! That's hell aint it! Naw I'm just
acting blowed. But I'm absolutely, positively sure that you are what I
need and want. And that's final ok? Ok! But I love you.

Oh by the way. I'm never wrong. And I wasn't saying I wanted you to
get involved with boys. I know I'm a sap but not that much of a sap. I'd
be crazy to make a decision like that. I can't think of anything else to
say but I love you don't ask me to write no more, you can write and I
can read on, bet?
Love,
Santana"

"How are you doing today baby?
I'm thinking about you right this minute and just can't stop. Angie I
really love you and want us to live together, raise a family and be
happy. Cause I really feel as though it's gonna work really. Dam! I love
you so much. But um! We'll get back to dat! I can't: I LOVE YOU!
(smile).

I loved what you did to me yesterday. It felt so good. But I wanted
to...But it felt good. Real good. Very good. I feel that experience
brought us a little closer and deepened my love for you. But I want to
get to know your body like the back of my hand and you to know mine.
To know what each other likes and what we don't like. So in other
words, experiment with each other. Remember, you said that you were
creative.

Let's see how creative you really are. I know we will be in school and
that will probably limit your creativity. But don't give a fuck, and don't
worry about embarrassing moi. Because we're not supposed to be
embarrassed for no reason when we are alone about anything. Nothing
we say to each other, nothing we do to each other should be
embarrassing right? Right.

But when you did what you did to me, you knew what to do. But...I
wish we could have made love after that because I bet it would have
been so dam fulfilling and pleasurable.
Love,
Santana"

"Dear Angie
Fuck it! I'll be a client once more (and how many other times) I really
shouldn't say shit to yo ass, ya know. But that's no way to treat a girl
who will someday be your wife and the mother of your kids. So fuck it.
I aint gone say shit. Why did you play me like Jeff Leff? I know you

didn't take that shit serious you know? When I said I didn't like you anymore. If you did (which I know you couldn't have) that's a sap for ya! yea! Boy Angelo was down all night wonderin' what was up with the bitch that got up and walked away, and then you called...

I wish I would have answered the phone I would have fucked (and I mean fucked) you up! But maybe a couple of zzz's will mend me and Angelo's very hurt feelings. I don't know. Maybe shit like this is supposed to fuckin' happen but don't let it fuckin happen again ok??? Ok!!!! I'm 'bout to move out cause the more I think about what you did the more I... fuck it never mind and I did that especially cause you hate it.

Nyaa! But I fuckin' love you tho' (remember that)

P.S maybe it's silly for me to be mad but I am mad and I don't give a fuck if you think it is or is not you. Just don't fuckin' do shit like that to me anyway, ya know!
Good fuckin bye.
Love,
Santana"

"Happy Valentine's Day Baby!
I hope you loved the card and the earrings. I love you. Really I do. I've been thinking about today. I'm nervous but willing and ready. I'm sure you are too. You want it more than me am I right or wrong. (Answer out loud) That's what I thought. GOD! I can't wait to fill you with my hot and ever erect rod, I can't wait to show you how much I really love you. I'm scared but not as much now because I know you'll be there helping. But anyway, I hope I make you feel very good, inside and out.

Happy Valentine's Day
Love Santana
P.S -I would really love to pour my love inside you really."

He was getting even more creative. By this time, he had given our physical parts a name, parts to play and a relationship all their own:

"Dear Nikki This is Angelo.
I'm up because I'm lying here thinking about the time we got together and tried to boldly go where no penis has ever gone before. (I think) Psyche! But anyway. You know what? It didn't even work. Just before I was supposed to enter, I don't know what it was, maybe it was the very arousing sensual female scent that you carried or I was just too excited that I became weak and was not fully erect and I just could not penetrate. Don't laugh Nikki cause you didn't help much either. You were so tight that you caused Angelo to be scared causing Angie tighten up even more, which made it even more impossible.

NYAAAA! So it wasn't all my fault. But anyway. I love ya! Tight little cunt. But um. I'm 'bout to move out because Santana would like to talk to Angie. I hope we encounter again what we tried and so successfully failed at. Bye Bye!!
PS I'm not too big, you're just too small, too tight and too nervous etc. etc."

"Hi!
Angie I couldn't even tell you what Angelo was tripping off of but that's between him and Nikki, so let's not worry about it.

I love you and I've missed you so much that's the real reason why I was so sappish or giggly today cause I was happy to see you.

I really was. I love to talk about Thursday or should I say think about cause that's all I do cause that's really the first time I've ever been that and sexually (not all the way) involved with a girl cause I loved her and not cause I wanted my dick hard for a so called cheap thrill.

I mean when my dick gets hard (cause you caused it to be that way) I fall deeper in love cause I know you love me and you're not just there to satisfy your needs but ours, like when you performed on me I don't think any less of you cause I know you did it to express how much you loved me and not cause I said here's my dick now suck it!

When I sucked your tits I felt as if we were one, satisfying both me and you. Those sacrifices felt so good that I could have came right then and there.... ...."

"Hi Nikki it's me again, I'm not up but I'm thinking about you.

Did you see Santana's sweat suit? it's funky but a little sappish (that's what he thinks) Do you like it? It's alright if you ask me. But fuck all that lets talk about me and you before Santana wants to talk to Angie. But um! Are you still tight? I've gotten braver and stronger. Can't wait to take the plunge. I know you can't either. Your love juices smell so sweet (grape) and I'm sure it would make my penis feel good in return I'll give you a cunt full of hot thick semen. I'm rising just thinking about it. And when that's done and weak maybe a light but wet kiss would revive me then your soft smooth hands could jack me dry while you're doing his.........."

"Okay Angelo I'll take over now!!! Nikki, Santana has interrupted me cause he wants to talk to Angie. But I'll get back.......Hi Angie this is Santana, I'll just finish where Angelo left off. okay while you're doing this I would gently take a large but soft tit in my hand and gently suck it, playing with the nipple with my tongue, causing it to rise and causing you to whine out my name which would turn me on highly (which did turn me on highly Valentine's Day Thursday) after we would passionately osculate, fall asleep, wake up and start all over again, but this time more erotic than before. Bye!
Love,
Santana
Bye!"

"Angie & Angelo to Nikki:
I love when you jack me off. It feels so good. And I know you love the
control you have over my every action. I'm pretty sure you know what I
like and I have no dislikes about anything sexually you do to me. And
I'm sure I don't know all of your likes. I wish you would tell me your
likes or would you rather me find out when we're in a position for me
to experiment. But I love it when you talk nasty to me. It turns me on.
So just tell me cool?

Cool. I liked when you played with Angelo with your (stinkin' ass) feet.
Psyche! But it felt good, you liked it didn't you. The freak didn't come
out of you, not quite. There's something else you're hiding but when I
find out, I'll push the button. I love you so much. You're the only girl
who has ever seen me fully unclothed. And I wasn't embarrassed. I felt
as if being naked was the only way to be whenever me and you are
together.

Your pussy smells so sweet it drove me crazy. Turned me on. Now about
this pill business. After hearing about it, I don't even want to deal with
it. I know you love me, but shit like that you don't have to deal with I
mean if I don't want to use protection I get no injection. Zat's simple.
So stop catering to me and think about you sometimes baby! Girl I love
you so much and I want what you want for yourself.

Angie. It hurts me to see you making sacrifices that can't be avoided. I
mean fuck me. You won't be able to please me all of the time, just
because you don't please me doesn't mean that I'll stop loving you.

Tell me, the only reason why you do for me is because you're afraid I'll
say fuck it then, were threw. Baby, I'm not. I never will. You're mine
and I'll never let you go. I love the hell out of you. And nothings gonna
change that. I'm sorry if I got a little out of hand. Smack me if you
wish. I probably deserve it. But I love you baby. We'll talk more, and
out loud, if you want.
Love,
Santana"

"Angie. It's me, Santana.
I'll go first today and then Angelo will do whatever at the end. First of all, how are you doing. You look like you're doing fine. You look so good today. I'm dead up. you look...dam I can't even describe. There's no word worthy of how my P.Y.T looks. But enough riding (it's really butter so I can bust that ass) But anyway...I can't think of shit to say. But I do love you so damned much! Why did you leave me yesterday? I wanted to and would've made tongue love all day. Of course, a little grind here and there. I really hate to be away from you because like I said, whenever we're alone it seems as though we are in our own lustful world.

_____

Ok sap! That's enough of the butter, I want to talk to Nikki if you don't mind.

_____

Angie, I love you and will get back.

_____

What's up Nikki you know who this is. I just wanted to tell you how lucky you are to have a playmate like me because my love is long and Santana's back is strong and all that adds up to fun for you. Santana said you were a pretty pussy. Me, I say also but that scent I can't get over it. Anyway I love surprises and I'm sure Santana does too. Whatever it is I hope it's something that has almost never crossed my mind about being done to me and it sure better satisfy me. I wish there was more than one way for you and me to express our love for each other. I mean I know burying myself deep inside your sexy lips and doing all sorts of things to your clit with the tip of my head expresses a lot but I want something more. I don't know what, but with your creativity, it'll be easy. I'm about to move out and I love you.
Love,
Angelo."

"Angie,

Santana doesn't even want to talk to you so don't expect him to interrupt me while I'm talking to you Nikki. Nyaaa!!!!!!What's up Nikki, I guess you expect me to make up erotic fantasies or bring up old encounters but not this time. You fucking make me sick this is the second time not the first but second time You and Whatchamacallher stood me and Santana up. Make it so bad, you promised me.

I expected to be with you, make your love juices flow, you make my love liquid flow but as usual you disappointed me. Santana was really tore up. If he would have saw Angie, talk to Angie, the day after it would have been dick for her. but knowing Santana, he would have hugged and kissed her and told her how much he loved her, knowing his clienting ass, but if not, she would have been up a fucking creek. As for you, I don't know what to say. I really did miss you.

I mean we couldn't have done much but at least I would have felt good with the thought that you were just outside the zipper of my pants. But fuck it, everyone should have made up by tomorrow.

Kissing, hugging & feeling each other's heads with sweet thoughts (that is Angie & Santana) while I (Angelo) see if I can make you (Nikki) More wet than you can make me hard. But you know we (Santana & Angelo) still loves yall! Nikki (& Whatchamacallher)
Love,
Angelo."

"Hi boo!
How are you doing baby? Fine I know. I love you. It's been a while since I've put pen to paper to converse. But anyway, this morning I saw you from down the hall. Angelo started getting warm and restless, (cause you had on them tight jeans). But nonetheless, everything was cool. Hold on...ok now I'm in math class, I'll act like I haven't read your letter.

We'll talk about that face to face (Angelo and Nikki).

But anyway I feel like…(not a client) we are going to get together real soon. I mean I'm ready to try again. I need it bad. My house or yours. Most likely mine. Either will do. Cause I need it.I love you. I feel lousy in a fuck, don't ask why I feel like staying home with you and experiment. I don't know what for you mean whatever you want. I don't feel like fucking writing but I'll finish….

…I'm finished.

I love you, Santana
and Hi Nikki from Angelo."

Our failed attempt at trying to make our "special day" be Valentine's Day: February 14, ended up happening on March 14th instead.

Santana and me were close, but he had no idea the agony my body had been going through-probably more than what his words and hormones-combined. For many months and Sundays, we shared everything. He knew of my other lil' boyfriends that I had (that were peers). He knew about the kisses I had shared with them and talks of losing my virginity to them. But they were fast boys, and I couldn't see myself sharing myself with them. They weren't "designed" for me like Santana ended up being.

In my mind already, I had my type of guy and my type of night pre-planned, and they just weren't good fits.

I did get a chance to reveal to Santana, my lust for Male Model and how I wanted my first time to be with him, but that was the extent that Santana knew about the secrets in my past and my desires from the red diary.

I anticipated this March 14th day for more reasons than Santana could ever imagine. He was in receipt of residual frustration from all that happened and all that did not happen with everybody from Ms. Beautiful to Male Model to my TGGF. He was all that I needed to cure the tingles in my body brought on by my past that he knew nothing about-and that (at this time in my life) I didn't fully understand as being reasons.

That March 14th night, I handled Santana like some sexual instruction manual that I had studied very well. The only thing we had in the form of music and candlelight was the sound and light from the television in the next room while Dr. Huxtable was giving Rudy and her buddy's pony rides on his leg as fat boy Peter hung on for dear life. With my mom gone out for the next four hours, I had all the time I needed with Santana to experiment with and on him; all that I had been fantasizing about doing, but merely writing in the crevices of my mind and lines of the red diary.

After our experience, we both thought we were everything short of being married and having walked down the aisle:

"Dear Angie
Today I enjoyed and appreciated your company very much. I love you so much...God! I just can't explain it. I don't want to say good because it was more than that. The things we spoke of made me feel even closer to you. I'm glad you saved yourself for someone special (and who can be more special than me)? Of course that's what I myself was doing.

(And who could be more special than my baby!) No one ever! I got a little mad about the times you almost gave yourself up! But I thought to myself Santana? This young lady (Angie) after so many close calls still managed to save her virginity for someone who would care, love and respect her afterwards and whom she would love dearly afterwards, just be grateful she's here now, pure and innocent and smart instead of used and naive. Every time I think of your plump pretty cheeks adorable eyes and the sexy way you look at me through your bangs just

make me want to make love to you, not make love but make love to you. Angie I love you so much baby I love you so much. I wish you were there in my bed in my arms and we could just sleep in each other's arms knowing that when we awake, we would be in a safe, warm loving and caring place in each other's arms.

Baby I don't get tired of you. I regret being used to a very bad habit that you will break me of. Just looking at you while you were in commercial art class drawing my picture for me, your body looked so wholesome and it just made me shake, quiver and everything else just knowing it's mine (your wholesome fulfilling body) I also love you more than anything else in the whole wide world. I wouldn't give you up for a fucking thing. You're all I need, and of course a couple of brats to make me happy in life. I love you baby! From now on, we are going to speak our most deepest feelings out loud to each other. I mean letters are cool but voice to voice face to face are so much more exciting and much warmer. I promise to love you babe, so much.
Love,
Santana (Bucky)"

"Changing
Hey, here's looking at you and what you want to be
And what you want to do but I need some time to grow
And live and give you all I want to give
If you don't see things my way that's alright
I understand but please don't turn away
When I hold out my hand because you're my baby
I have nothing to hide
If you want, I'll be standing there when you're hurting inside
So baby remember changing isn't a crime
It's a wonderful experience that happens with time
Santana
(Bucky)"

For a long time, I had gotten away with sneaking around with Santana: talking to him on the phone at night without my mom ever knowing, being at his house, him being at my house, us-staying afterschool together. You name it, we did it. We had literally been there-done that; everywhere. I always knew how to do that covert thing right under my mother's nose since ages seven to thirteen. So now, she was certainly no match for me. I was past covert, I was "pro-vert."

But sneaking around to be with Santana was beginning to be a bit too tough, we had so many close calls. It seemed like the only pressure and stress in our relationship was getting around it all.

I had to break it to my mother gently, and as soon as possible. Because between school, friends, and sneaking to be with him; my schedule was way too full and poor Ms You Know Who was barely getting any girl-time with me anymore. But if I were able to see him freely, time spent orchestrating the covert could have been spent with-if not her-on something else; even if it was time alone, or some extra rest.

By this time, we were full-on-seven days per week: taking pictures of each other every moment of the day, going to the movies, out to eat and visiting his relatives-that was pretty much our routine.

His bedroom was a little cul de sac garage-like extension at the back end of his mom's home.

We'd be huddled up in there taking pictures, eating, and taking naps in each other's arms. Other times, he would be sitting on top of his giant speakers from behind all his DJ equipment, rapping, beat-boxing and playing air-drums while I would be dancing about for him. He would put on his classic Beastie Boys, LL Cool J and Run DMC records, then I would put on his b-boy hat and vintage Adidas Run DMC running suit; standing there looking like "Cousin-It" the way it would be draping over and drowning my body like curtains. I would break into this lil' borderline corny but sexy b-girl dance that I made up; trying to impress him and fit in to his b-boy world-he l.o.v.e.d it. Santana was my love and one man show: cheerleading for me, smiling, laughing, and making bullhorns with his hands to shout through and cheer me on for when I would break into a break dance stance; folding my arms and tooting my lips while nodding my head. He'd bouncing up and down cheering me on and screaming: *"GO BA-BY! GO BA-BY! GO! LOOK AT MY BABY! LOOK AT MY BABY! Aw man you are the SHIT! I love you girl!"*

He would grab me tightly and hold me in his arms as if I was trying to run from him: "Don't ever leave me, don't ever leave me, don't ever leave baby-never leave me," he'd would hold me and say-all the time.

We were like two peas in a pod nearly seven days a week, so I had to let my mother in on it. I had to tell her that I had a boyfriend that loved me-madly.

It was getting kind of hectic and cutting it way too close; those days of us leaving school, coming over to my house, making love, and laying in each other's arms until the alarm clock rang to wake us up so that he could get dressed and head out the back door in time before my mom would enter the front door.

My two oldest brothers had gotten their own apartment together. Once Twin finished up his mini lock-up bid at the school for disorderly boys; he was due to move in with the wifey and Mr. Super Saturday: that 0 to 120 blast from my past. After roughing up one too many guys for stepping to him-trying to test him, my mother did what she knew to do best: save *her*self the trouble; send it or ignore it away. That left breaking in the new apartment for just my mom and me. We had been there for quite a few months-since around the time I had first met Santana. The way the apartment was situated, it was perfect for me and Santana: the back door was at the back end of the small kitchenette we had-which was right by my bedroom. My mother would say that it wasn't big enough to cuss a cat in, so she'd cook and take her plate into her bedroom or the living room. The living room, my mom's bedroom and the bathroom were all in the front: perfect and convenient for her. Outside of the fact that in order to get to the kitchen, my mom had to come through my room; all else was perfect. Once she was done cooking or preparing a meal-I didn't have to see her anymore.

So when Santana would come over afterschool, he could easily slip out the back door once we heard my mom come through the front door. The only downside to having Santana do that though, was Mrs. Cochran: the little old lady across the hall from us. Her back door was opposite and faced our back door and she didn't missed anything or anybody coming in or out of it.

It was obvious that our back door was freshly broken in from being painted shut. That joker was hard to open. It was so tight around the hinges-built for looks and a mere apartment amenity listing rather than for opening and closing. Sometimes when Ms. Cochran would be in her kitchen, she would peek out her back door whenever she would hear me tugging at it-each and every time-as though it was her first time hearing it and she was alarmed.

Santana and me would twist our lips and roll our eyes in our heads while trying to balance out his back door getaway and my mother's front door entrance with Mrs. Cochran's watchful eyes. We got crafty in those few minutes of time; tugging at the door to let her see me sit the trash out, then wait a few minutes to let Santana squeeze out of it. Our alarm would wake us up at 5:45pm and by 5:55pm Santana would be dressed and gone out the backdoor. My mom would be walking in the front door at 6:05pm. By that time, Santana was always good and around the corner and on his way home-never having to run into her.

It worked like magic for months, until that day my mom got in the house a little sooner than that 6:05pm time. There we were, cuddled up and napping. Me: "Goldilocks." Him: my "Papi Love Bear. The sound of someone tugging keys and juggling bags-startled me. My bedroom door was cracked open a little bit, so I got up and peeked through.

I could see my mom's lunch bag in clear view.

"Santana, get dressed! It's my mother! She's coming inside the door!" I screamed.

In an instant, I grabbed my sweats and t-shirt that I would normally slip into afterschool.

He was busy turning in circles trying to find every article of clothing that I was tossing to him-one by one-while I was forcing him into the kitchenette and trying to get him out of that dreaded back door without Mrs. Cochran hearing and peeking out. We had zero stall time-this time.

In a matter of seconds, I had Santana standing on the back porch with his underwear and socks on, catching cotton, while Mrs. Cochran opened her lace curtains and looked out-but not to her surprise as wasn't mine. I expected her, and from my peripheral vision, it looked like she expected us too because she merely looked and walked away. I always avoided looking right at her because I knew that the moment our eyes met (in this daily thing that had gone on most of the five days a week for months now) she would have used that as leverage and permission to reprimand me about it or feel obligated to tell my mom. I wanted to be the one to deliver this situation to her-first.

So I kept right on tending to Santana, not wanting him to know that Mrs. Cochran had seen his naked ass-that would have only slowed him down.

I could hear my mom yelling my name-she was right there in the bathroom. The small, clear, stained-glass bathroom window was, too, *right* there on the back porch-right *next* to Mrs. Cochran's-both facing Santana out on that back porch, and at anytime, if either one of them wanted to raise their window up, look out on that back porch and simply say: "boo!;" "Boo" would have simply been busted. "Ssshhh," I placed my finger over my mouth, looking at Santana with my lips folded tightly.

By this time, he was completely dressed but demanded a kiss goodbye while I was trying to step into the house and shut that back door enough so the hinges would meet, but not all the way. I needed him off that porch:

"Leave!" I whisper-laughed; pointing out into the air, needing him to follow the direction of it.

He kept making silly faces and making me laugh because he could see my mom's silhouette in the little bathroom window-but she couldn't see him.

"I love your daughter!" he pointed at me while whispering and giggling; then pointed over at the little bathroom window with my mom on the other side of it.

I raised my hand as if to strike him. He reached to kiss me again, treaded lightly down the steps, and around to the front of the building.

When he left, I pushed the door up on the hinges and yelled out to finally answer my mom. The alarm clock was sounding off and served as my theme music for this hell of an impromptu performance that we managed to pull off. I yelled out to my mom: "I'm taking the trash out Ma-I'm coming!"

Sigh.

I was sweating bullets-happy that this scene was over.

Cut.

11

IN THE LION'S DEN

I decided that it was time to get that last part of our perfect little wide open relationship [that everyone knew about-including Mrs. Cochran] out in the open. My peers at school, his family and friends, and my friends already knew that Santana and I was a serious item.

I was becoming self-conscious.

I had always prided myself on being mature and brave. Where my mother was concerned, part of me felt enslaved to all the freedoms and responsibilities I had been entrusted with for so long. I was the little lady of the house since I can remember. She secretly had me keeping an eye on the pastures: babysitting Twin and my older brothers over the years-despite the fact that I was the baby. I would hate for her to find out from someone else's mouth, that for almost a year now-I've had a serious boyfriend that I've been going steady with. I sure as hell didn't want her to find out from my belly steadily growing. Despite the fact that Santana and I were using condoms, we would occasionally get careless and resort to the rhythm method too. So with that, I was eager to throw it all in the bag: tell her that I was going steady, tell her how long it had been going on, tell her I lost my virginity, tell her how long I had been sexually active, and then tell her to march me up to the clinic to get some birth control pills before something happened that would change my life altogether.

I was becoming self conscious.

As I was thinking, I began to wonder if Ms. Ananda (who lived beneath Mrs. Cochran) knew too.

I wondered because she had two middle school-aged kids. I began to wonder if either one of them had ever run into Santana in the back of the building, or see him leave down the front steps any time at all-all these months.

Ms. Ananda and me were pretty close (instantly) from the moment we moved in. She was a few years younger than my mom, but was youthful and fun. We talked about everything. I just never told her about me having a steady boyfriend. As I thought deeper, I knew that if she knew I was sneaking around, she would have laughed and told me that her kids told her. I was over thinking and getting carried away with my being subconscious.

When we would talk about it, Santana's would say he thought it was pretty "gangster" that although Mrs. Cochran knew about us for a while, she never said anything to me about it, nor did she snitch on me. She very well could have, many-a-days, because she and my mom would talk in the small hallway area at the front door in between both of our front doors-sometimes for hours. That old lady kept her mouth shut for many months and seasons! I think I was growing all too comfortable with it after some time, yet, I didn't want Mrs. Cochran to have a slip of the tongue one day. Every now and again in the evening hours, she would occasionally pour herself a lil' something to drink. She could talk you to sleep then awake all over again. I didn't want that to happen on some random evening, after all this time, and have my mom find out that she was the last to know. And to add insult to injury, find out by anyone else but me.

I was becoming self-conscious.

Santana and my relationship and ability to date openly was too easy and smooth-sailing for too long for my mother not to know.

But not know-no more.

Without any hesitation or fear, before my mom could get comfortable and undressed, I cut to the chase.

I walked to the bathroom door, knocked on it with the back of my knuckles and simply said to her from the other side of it: "Ma, I think I'm ready to go steady."

There was a long awkward moment of silence. My mother had way too much mouth to sit quiet for too long. I knew something was going to echo from behind that door in due time. I could feel her wanting to say: "You must be out there on the other side of that door with a pork-chop suit on!" but instead, with bass and a grunt in her voice, she roared like a lion from a den:

"Angie. Wait until I get the hell out the bathroom before throwing some shit like that at me!"

I didn't reply. I honored the moment of silence by standing there with my hands folded behind my back. My lips were folded tight; ready for this battle that was about to occur when she came from behind that door. Outside of what I had just dumped in her lap, she had no idea what my mind had been going through. I fancied myself as being so mature, that it was beginning to annoy me that I was sneaking around like some thimble-toed kid. I was getting so annoyed with the fact that although I wasn't sixteen, I was "age-sixteen" threshold-worthy (in spite of all the "age-sixteen" threshold types of things I had been doing).

"Make it snappy now, I haven't got all evening," I may as well had said to her-but instead, I broke the moment of silence by replying: "Alright then. I'll be in my room."

I went into my room and pulled the door just wide enough for her to peep her head in to call me when she was ready. It must've taken her a long time to peep in, because I had fallen asleep and woke up a couple hours later to find her nowhere to be found. Looking at how I had my door cracked-it looked as though she never even came into my room, or stuck her head in the door-which means she didn't even go to the kitchen either. "Where could she be?" I wondered.

A short while later, while I was in the kitchen, I heard a peck at the back door. I pulled the curtain back, it was Ms. Ananda standing there with a very nosey look on her face-looking as if she was about to laugh. I wrestled the heavily painted amenity open: "What? What's so funny?" I asked-even before she could get anything out of her mouth.

"Girllllll, what are you up here doing. You know what's going on don't you?" she said, sounding like she was one of my nosey peers-fresh from a huddle of gossip.

"No. What?" I probed. I wasn't offering any information. I always had a "won't ask/don't tell" policy.

Ms. Ananda asked: "Girl, you got yourself a little boyfriend and didn't even *tell* me! Why not?" she finished-gasping and sounding concerned at that point.

I laughed: "No, I was going to tell you, I've just been so busy!"

She replied: "But Angie, you've been down to the house and you never said a thing!"

I laughed and coyly replied: "I'm sorry, don't kill me Ms. Ananda."

She smacked me on the side of my head.

"But girl, your mother is over there talking to Mrs. Cochran, right now," spilled Ms. Ananda.

She stretched her eyes open wide as mine.

"At first she was down at my house-telling me that you asked her if you could go steady with some lil' BOY! I think she wanted to know if you had ever said anything to me about it-but you didn't even tell me!" she laughed, then turned her voice down an octave:

"After that, she went upstairs here to Mrs. Cochran's house and called me from over there. Turns out, Mrs. Cochran told her that she had seen this lil' rock head boyfriend of yours already! A *long* time ago! Oooh Angie! You sneaky lil' hussy you!" said Ms. Ananda.

I covered my mouth and laughed out loud then asked:

"What! She told her…like that?"

Ms. Ananda continued: "Girl please! Mrs. Cochran told your mama like: '*You need to go' on and let that gal' see that boy because if you don't and you force her to sneak around and see him, you are asking for bigger problems that you will NOT be able to handle!*' She is over there up *in* your mother's shit!"

She then asked quietly:

"I don't want to be evasive and all-you know-since you kept everything from me. But I thought I was your girl," said Ms. Ananda, sounding sarcastic and slighted.

She continued:

"Angie, I'm right downstairs if you need to talk. Don't ever keep stuff like that away from me, as much stuff that you share with me. That kinda hurt me that I didn't even *know*," confessed Ms. Ananda.

I stood there in awe about all of this; pissed at my mother for her cowardice after all this time that I was letting my conscious get the best of me-fighting hard to be the first to talk to, and tell her. I took the initiate to open up dialogue about it and just like her: she ran. And she ran off and got the news from somebody else-anyway. She loved to ignore away important situations. As much mouth as my mom had, it baffled me how she went about (not) handling this like an adult, but instead, handled it as if she was some silly little girl with a gossiping mouth, taking hay to everyone else but the horse.

It had been quite some time since I had seen her-no, as a matter of fact, I hadn't seen her face since the day before, because we spoke from on the opposite sides of the door, when she came home from work.

Just to know that she wouldn't even face me, over my merely asking her for permission [to do something that I had already been doing for some time already-anyways] annoyed me even more.

At this point, I was merely being courteous to her by inviting her in on a secret that everyone else [in school, his world, my world and in the very building she lived and paid rent in] knew.

Into the night, Ms. Ananda, Mrs. Cochran and my mom met over Mrs. Cochran's house. My mother simply refused to come back inside the house to even fix herself something to eat-because my bedroom was right by the kitchen.

I lay in bed preparing to turn it in for the night, with the bedroom door still cracked open enough for my mom to peek her head through it. Instead of her, Ms. Ananda appeared, peeking through it. She pecked on the door: "Angie, may I come in for a second. I have something I want to tell you," she whispered in to me. "Sure Ms. Ananda, what's up?" I replied.

She pushed the door open, closed it tightly behind her and sat at the end of my bed:

"Angie your mom wants to meet your new boyfriend tomorrow," she said.

"I will talk to him about it at school tomorrow. It shouldn't be a problem getting him over here within the next two days or so," I replied.

"Where is she right now, still next door?" I asked.

"Oh, she's up front in the living room. She said she was about to go to bed in a minute," Ms. Ananda responded, relaying for my mother and trying to cover up for her inability to look me in the face as yet.

I lay there on my pillow, squinting my eyes and shaking my head back and forth about how shameful this thing had gotten. I mean, she never even came to the kitchen to eat or drink anything since she had arrived home at 5:45pm that evening. The house was set up such that if she didn't want to eat or drink anything, she didn't have to see me at all. I didn't have to see her unless I got up to use the bathroom, and that would only be if she were in her bedroom, rather than up front in the living room.

Our usual routine-anyways-during the morning, would be for my mom to have her bath then breakfast. That is the time she would be waking me up with the aroma of breakfast food cooking and the sounds of pots, pans, silverware and water running in the kitchen sink.

On days she didn't eat breakfast, the norm would be for her to bathe, get dressed and before leaving out the door for work; bang on my bedroom door to make sure I was awake to get ready to do the same.

Well, she didn't eat breakfast the next morning either, and I did not get that bang on my bedroom door to wake me up (either). I guess she felt like I would inhale the morning aroma of the fumes she was still exhaling as breakfast. The way she slammed the front door as hard as she could, I guess she figured it would be all the alarm that I needed (to wake up).

In school that day, when Santana and I met in our usual spot before classes started, I gave him the good news: I told him that my mom agreed to meet him. I purposely neglected to tell him that she was so upset, and that I hadn't even seen her face in the almost 24-hours since, and as a result of her finding out about the two of us. I just wanted to pass on the "good news" and let Santana feel good about the two of us being able to see each other freely without sneaking around, when everywhere else in both of our worlds; we were openly a couple and as far as we were concerned: "grown."

So, his meeting her was indeed going to be like him walking into a lion's den, especially without him knowing that her finding out about us didn't go over to well. As far as how she would act when she met him-I wasn't sure. I just hoped that his pretty face and eyes and charming smile would warm her up. Bless his heart, he was so excited:
"Dear Boo.
About me coming over (if I can) I'm not scared just a little nervous. I hope she does. Tell her that I'm shy and don't laugh me. Am I to tell her that I'm in love with her (my) Baby Boo! That would be hard for fear she would ask what made you fall in love how do I know its love and what does love mean? Not that I couldn't answer her. I'd be…uncomfortable. I hope she likes me. Maybe I'll ask her if the garbage needs taking out you know, the usual "butter." Should I say yes ma'am! Or does she prefer yes and no! I would prefer yes ma'am! No ma'am! Should I call her by her last name? Should I shake her hand or just say "hi how are you doing?" I've been through this many times but this seems like the first. Maybe cause I'm wondering if she'll disapprove of me and ask you to stop seeing me. That would hurt (I'm paranoid)

Is this the right time or should we wait… I Love You.
I hope mom likes me.
Love, Bucky"

After school let out, we behaved like the "grown" responsible "adults" we thought we were. And instead of us running home acting like jack rabbits, he went home to get prepared to come over to my house, and to pretend that it was his first time ever there. Unbeknownst to him, from the outside of the lion's den looking in; he was going to be walking in [most probably with an Adidas] pork-chop suit on. He had no idea that Mrs. Cochran kinda-sorta snitched and charged her gangster to the game last night. If he knew, he would still probably give her some "cool points," because it was still be*cause* of Mrs. Cochran that my mother was forced to change her mind to allow this meeting to happen.

I just wanted it all to unfold naturally.

I cleaned up the house in preparation for "company" and eagerly anticipated my mom's 6:05pm (or early-5:45pm) arrival time home.

Santana was due to arrive at 7:30pm.

When mom arrived home, I was back in my room with the door opened about halfway; because it would usually be cracked just enough for me to peek into the living room while Santana would (usually) be preparing to leave out the back door. I knew she had already found out that he had been coming over afterschool, so closing my bedroom door (completely) would have rubbed her the wrong way, or sent her the same message that she sent me yesterday when she shut me out: "I do not feel like dealing you or this situation."

So yeah, leaving it open about halfway was perfect, because when she would come home from work, my door was never left wide open-she would have definitely noticed that. It would have screamed her name right out, leaving it wide open for her to say: "Oh, you got your bedroom door wide open now that your lil' boyfriend's not sneaking out the back door today huh?" I knew her moves-I'm her child.

I was anticipating a good night and wanted it to go smooth, so I made sure that with every detail, everything was everything.

6:05pm is when she began fidgeting at the door-doing her usual: dropping her lunch bag and whatever else she had in her hand onto the living room floor until she would get done fidgeting at the door from trying to get the tough key out of the keyhole. Her bad key bought us a *lot* of stall time many-a-day.

I let her get all the way into the house and into the bathroom while

I went back to the kitchen to wash dishes and give her some space. I could imagine all too well the horror and flashbacks that would have gone through her mind had I started another conversation on the opposite side of that bathroom door. She would probably hear "Psycho," horror-movie music, in her head.

When I got done washing the dishes, I knew she would be good and out of the bathroom, so I walked right through my bedroom and opened the door (wide), walked through her bedroom and then into the living room. She was sitting there watching television while going through her bag.

"Hey Ma," I said, while I kissed her on the cheek and balled my fist up and gave her a little nuggie against her forehead.

"Don't be kissing me!" she yelled, playfully.

"You still love me baby?" I asked her.

"What time is this lil' boy coming over here tonight?" she demanded to know.

"He'll be over about 7:30, Ma." I replied.

"Mmm." She mumbled and rolled her eyes, tightly.

"Lighten up-acting like an old battle axe!" I laughed. She laughed out loud. That cut the tension in the air that she got right up and walked through. She then walked through her bedroom, through the (wide-open) door of my bedroom then straight to the kitchen (that she hadn't seen-going on thirty-six hours by this time).

7:25pm came.

Santana knocked at the door like a gentleman. By this time, my mom had been resting in her bedroom.

I was in the living room watching television. I sat there and made him knock once more-having purposely ignored the first knock.

"Oh don't try to act like you don't hear that knock at the door-whore! Get up and answer it!" she said, halfway serious and halfway jokingly.

I laughed loudly and opened the door to Santana standing there looking like the fourth member of Run DMC with that Adidas pork chop suit on.

"Hey Red," he smiled, with his eyes sparkling like diamonds.

"Hey Santana," I replied, with a smile.

"Ma, Santana's here…"

I looked into the slightly opened double-doors that separated the living room from her bedroom where she lay.

"I love your daughter and she belongs to me!" whispered Santana, playing around.

"Down boy!" I laughed and pointed.

The two of us sat on the couch at a distance between us like we were two virgins who were still corny and nervous around one another.

The lioness slowly opened her bedroom doors just wide enough for her to walk through it:

"Hi. Hello," she purred, while walking towards Santana.

He stood up nervously and began walking towards her-so as to shorten her distance to him, as a courtesy.

"Hello, Mrs. Angie's mom," he said.

"I asked Angie what I should call you and she never wrote me back to tell me-and I wanted to make sure I addressed you the way you wanted to be addressed!" sounding like the juvenile he was.

I shook my head back and forth as it rested in my hand with my elbow on the arm of the couch-chuckling to myself at Santana; standing there with that pork chop Adidas suit on like a dunce cap, still knowing nothing about the storm that had blown through this very same house over the past forty-eight hours was the same one that just blew him through the door and into the wild.

I eagerly awaited to hear what my mom was going to say to Santana, as he stood there looking like fresh meat. The awkward long pause and stare ended:

"Yeah you lil' fart! The next time you bring your tail to *this* house, you make sure you leave out the same way you came in! You hear me?"

Santana turned to me-startled. Just about as startled as I was when I looked up at him-having no idea that she would spew that out of that mouth of hers. He had no choice but to think that I told her, so he merely replied: "Yes ma'am." I lifted my hand from my head and shrugged my shoulders as if to say: "Well, the cat's out the bag now." I played along with it.

Mom continued:

"That's not gonna fly in here! You farts aren't making any feet for socks up over in *this* establishment where *she* does not pay any rent!" she pointed over at me-making it seem to Santana that I just told her *everything*-every detail.

She wouldn't let up:

"I'm the only grown-up in here that's got permission to be laying up-because I'm the only one in here who's paying up!" she said firmly, but in a way so as to not scare him off too bad.

"Yes, ma'am," Santana replied, having no idea what the hell any of that meant. My mom spoke a language all her own sometimes.

Something only my brothers and I could translate its meaning.

After she fired, she retired to her bedroom and grabbed the double-doors; hesitantly at first. By the middle of closing them-she looked in at us. And though not with her full blessing, pleasantly nonetheless. She backed off-leaving us alone for the evening, even without giving me instructions on what time he should leave or how close not to sit.

Though my mom was upset about what she found out, she always knew I was mature and could handle many things on my own without probe or prompt.

She remembered.

As a kid-unusually responsible; I was always busy, had a full schedule and trusted-why stop now?

She remembered.

She knew that come morning, I would begin the same responsible routine as every morning, five days a week: using her movement through the house, in the kitchen or the bang of her knuckles to my bedroom door to wake me up right before she left out to go to work-all with the surety that I was responsible enough not to lay back down the moment she closed the door to go on about her day.

She knew she trusted me.

She knew she could trust that from behind those double-doors, no feet for socks were going to be made opposite where she lay.

She trusted me, despite her angry feelings about it all. I never knew them all-we still never talked about it-remember? I could only assume and speculate.

The fact that she was the last one to know probably pissed her off more than anything.

Who knows, it could have been the fact that I gave her, what I felt, was a reasonable exit away from her love: my [dead] dad. Yet, there I was, all booed with up my love: Santana-sitting there smiling and looking all scrumptious-moving closer to me and acting silly.

The television watched us while the radio played one of our favorite classic love songs: "Crazy for You" by Madonna. All the while, my lonely mom lay beyond doors opposite us, probably listening in on us until she fell asleep.

Still, without us ever having a conversation about Santana and me, I could tell she was never going to be more comfortable with it at sixteen than she was at fourteen and fifteen. Because from this day going forward, she showed me better that she could tell me that she never did and never will forgive me for it…

Meanwhile, in other safe pastures, what a sigh of relief this was for the both of us.

School the next day felt different for us. We met up at our usual spot. When he first saw me, his whole face smiled. He hugged and kissed me and twisted me all around; lifting me off my feet-happy-like Richard Gere and Debra Winger in the "Officer and a Gentleman." It felt like our relationship had started all over again. I was very happy too. I felt so normal, so loved and so adored.

He reached in his pocket to give me my letter:

"What's up Boo!
Man you ate my KitKat and Doublemint. I was looking forward to that.
You should have made the Kool-Aid to wash down the KitKat. But I
love you. I like your mother, she's real nice. I enjoyed being there with
you. I felt so good. Let's go outside at lunch somewhere to be alone if
you want to, but you probably want to be with your friends and I
understand but it was worth a true try.
…Hold on man. I sound like a sap talking like that, fuck it, it's gone

work because I'll make it bye!
I'm 'bout to move out.
I Love you
-Santana"

...and into the days following:

"Hi Boo!
How ya doing baby. You look good today (everyday) just some days
you look extra special.

I'm sorry if I hurt you yesterday. I mean, you said bye first so I took it
as if you didn't want to be with me so I said ok. And when you took
your picture...man! That hurt, I felt bad. I felt like acting like a bitch
(crying) but I didn't so I guess the tears caught up to me in my dream
last night. Dam! I woke up crying and that tripped me out and I looked
in the mirror and said you sap! You got it badder than I thought, (the
love bug) I love you so much. I just got through taking this history and
map test and I iced it. It was dead easy. Man, that kind of shit that
happened yesterday we shouldn't allow to happen because that's how
ice melts. I mean if shit like that keeps going on one of us (I know
you're goin' to say me) will get a attitude like I don't need this no more
and just walk away out of a very warm and loving relationship.

Man! Angie I'm getting bored, maybe I'm just talking to be talking but
it seems to me as though were going through a routine, what do you
think. But anyway, I love you! Oh! I hope you've been telling your
mom hi! Even though I haven't but if you haven't, tell her I said hi! And
not to forget to feed the fish! But Boo. You're my every...um let me
see...you are my everything. I had to think about that Psyche! You're
my everything and I love you.
Love,
Santana

(Nikki this is Santana, Angelo is on a punishment until he learns how
to control himself. But I told him about yesterday and he said)...

Love,
Santana."

"Hi Boo!
What's up? How are you doing? You looked good this morning. Real
good. I love you.

I really don't have much to write about, but I'll come up with
something...OK. When I come over today and if your mothers not
home I would like to try to make love to you again without protection
and I hope that I don't pre-mature nut. I think I can control myself. And
if I can't then,?!!?!?

I don't know but I know that I love you and will stand by your side if
you become pregnant, it would bring me close as close can get. Man!
You can kiss. You have improved since the first time. But even then,
your kiss was alright but now when you kiss me, a funny feeling goes
through my whole body. I love that. I love you.
Love,
Santana
PS-I'm not sorry this is so short, I had nothing to write.
PS-I love you
PSS-I love you
PSSS-I love you
PSSSS-I love you
PSSSSS Don't worry I'm just a little toasted.
Love Santana."

"Dear Angie
Hi baby how are you doing? I've missed you greatly and I love you oh
so much these two days seem to me as though they were weeks. I was
so alone, unhappy, and felt very empty. God! I love you so much. And I
hope your absence from me will no more be withheld so long. Baby!
I've missed your warm slobbery lips and large beautiful eyes and the

softness and warmth of your body. And most of all, I missed that I love you! Which seems like only you have the power to make those three words (special) work for me.Angie from day one, my love for you has grown not all at once but gradually.

The things that we speak about lets me know that you trust me enough to tell me about very personal matters. That makes me feel so dam good! I've finally found a lady who will actually treat me with the utmost respect and love me dearly. One who is in my life for a purpose. Not to burden me, but to help lighten my burdens. I've found a lady whom I wish to spend my entire life with, a lady whom I want to mother our beautiful children (2) and I thank God for allowing you to walk my way. Angie you are a very special and lovely young lady to me. I am building my whole world around you and without you here, it would crumble into nothingness. But I'm not worried because I know you would do nothing to hurt or jeopardize my (our) future HOLD ON...

Ok I just got out of hot shower and speaking of showers, would you take one with me some time soon. It's something I've never done, something I've always wanted to do. And I want to share my first experience with the lady I love: YOU! Well get back to that but anyway, I just got out of the shower, it feels good (my whole body does) I laid in my bed with no clothes on thinking of your warm wet love juices running down my erect shaft. I laid face up eyes closed. When I opened them, I expected you there to touch and violently caress my very warm and hard dick (If that word is too harsh) Angelo But you weren't this thought caused Angelo to dwindle down to its once placid state. I need you and your erotic tongue love. I love you baby! I love you! And I miss the hell out of you! I'm sorry I stood you up today. But I'll make it up to you as I already promised...Can I stop and fantasize for a few seconds? Ok! Hold on...I'm back to tell the truth, I went to sleep and woke up...But anyway. I love you.

Love Santana"

"To Angie

How are you doing? I know fine cause you good as ever. Baby your kiss feels more provoking than ever. I mean, the way your tongue touches mine chills go up my back and my dick gets harder than a sack of quarters and your body feels different to the touch.

It seems as though I have been overlooking something or just been so wrapped up in sex that I have not took the time out to really notice things like your kiss or your sensual supple body. When I say sex that really what I mean because when you said I could be a little more romantic, I thought to myself as I do now I was fulfilling sexually (at least not completely) and that's going to have to stop. I mean anytime my lady tells me that I'm not romantic enough; after making love many times, there is a gap in communication (your fault for not telling me and my fault for not asking). To tell the truth, there is no romance in you taking your own clothes off and me mine.

I don't even attempt to put you in the mood. I don't tease. It's just a routine we go through and if I really love you, Ill change my unsexy ways, which you better believe I will, because I love you. I promise to stop being selfish as far as sexually satisfaction is concerned.

W/B Quickly
Love, Little Bee..."

"Dear Angie.
How's my angel? (you little devil) Fine I hope. Provided you forget about yesterday at least for a while.

Baby I was just violently upset yesterday. I was totally confused and didn't know what to think. I mean when you (and them) was in the bathroom asking if he looked good (I think it was you) then you told Chara that if I ask again who was she gone say and she said I'll just say it's one of my friends.

It sounded like y'all were making up a lie. I tried my best to just say she knows nothing (which you didn't) God! I was so scared. I thought to myself that finally I found the right girl and she turned out to be

the wrong girl. God I needed you with me to ease the pain, to ease the fear. Why me! I never took nothing of nobody's. I mean life is not fair! You find someone that is your world and someone else tries to make there's. I asked you before we got started was there anybody else and you said no.

The reason why I chose you to be wife and the mother of my children is because you're special and different. Our relationship was to be unique and far more superior than anyone else's. I mean shit like this aint supposed to happen.
I love you dearly.
W/B Whenever you have time
PS I'll get myself together, I promise
PSS Sorry if I'm acting stupid."

"Dear Mami
What's up? Damn you look smashing and that's no lie. I couldn't believe you were mine. It seemed as though you were too good for me. I was in a daze. But I love your sexy ass. Sunday was fun. And so was yesterday. You know what, I'll be dead happy when we live together because now I don't care if I spend an entire day with you it doesn't seem like enough and I'm sure you feel the same. Ha! People don't feel we'll last and that's a laugh. Some of the best couples do eventually break up, but us? Shit they must be crazy. I aint giving you up for the world, you are the right young lady for me. I guess commitments must be lame this generation but I'd rather be lost in love than lame. This morning I wanted to hold you tight in my arms and just say 1,000 times I love you (which is not enough for me) I want the best out of this relationship material and (uh! What's the word) "personal."

Our babies, money, a nice home, cars, family fun and family love. And a promise I have made since I was little I'll never leave my family no matter how bad things get, and they won't get bad.

My father left us I didn't know the difference then, but now I resent him for that he was supposed to be my example as a man. I won't let you down never.
Love Papi
PS-A Daddy is a man who brags about his wife and kids.
A father is a man who supports and gives."

"Hi Angie.
Your letter was alright, but I expected more. When I said I "hope" about us getting together in the summer I meant if I'm not working half of everyday, but I'd love to spend my whole summer wit choo.

But anyway, I'm also pressured when it comes to promiscuous behavior, but I just swallow kinda hard and the temptation is no longer there cause I know even though you aint there with me, messing around sure won't fill the emptiness. Cause it wouldn't be the same. Don't worry about those poems, they will never cause I wuv u and I always will I'm 'bout to move out cause the bell is 'bout ta ring ring Bye Bye I wuv u.

PS. No mistakes
PSS. I was so happy to be with you this morning and the stuff you did to me felt so good.
PSSS I wuv you
PSSSS I wuv you
PSSSSS I wuv u.
...alright I'm back. Can you promise me that...
I've been thinking about this every since my father talked to me about the air force. We could get married before I went away or would that be rushing things.

Getting married would probably only be done cause we would be scared to lose each other. I want to be married freely, not scared into it. Now that we know we won't lose each other. Tell me what you think about getting married before I go (or if I go) or when I come back. I love you so much baby you're my everything and I love you. Man did you hear that punk ass cryin' last night I was laughing at him.

But Angie, be strong for me ok. Baby I'll be even stronger for you.
I wuv you,
Wuv,
Santana
PS-Promise (remember) no more tears."

Although my mother allowed me to go steady with Santana, she was always straddled with giving me the full "okay." It was agonizing sometimes, but weird for the two of us because we were already a happening lil' couple by this time-even before she was let in on our big lil' secret.

The only things about us that really changed was that I had retired my pink Chuck's with the light blue shoe strings for every color Reebok high-tops that he could afford to buy me. The only thing that changed was that I substituted my bleached and dyed, and acrylic paint-splattered jeans and shirts for the designer digs that complimented his style-courtesy of him. The only thing that changed was that I traded in my black rubber and silver bracelets in, for countless cool designer watches of his-that he would let me wear. He had them in all prints and colors and insisted that I wear every color of his to match whatever I was wearing, until the day could afford to buy me the one pretty yellow one that I wanted.

That day came.

That day came just as sure as the day came when I wanted to be the first to tell my mother about the sunny yellow relationship with the boy who loved me-so that I could avoid just what she was putting us through.

Not only was she the last to know, but she was caught by surprise and coerced [all thanks due to Mrs. Cochran] who by way of connecting dots and reason; made my mother approve of something that had it been asked by me, she would have simply said "no, not until you are sixteen."

Off and on, she would make it her business to say or do something to rattle my comfort where Santana was concerned, when he would be over some evenings.

7:30p-nothing different.
The usual: retiring to her bedroom, pulling the double doors closed.
Me and my Boo all booed up-sitting close enough on the couch so as to not cuddle up.
Madonna on deck.
Television.
Us.
Out of the blue, the double-doors opened and the lioness began to roar:

"Nah, this can't happen. It's just too much. Much too much-I cannot approve of this. You two are entirely too young to be this serious. You can't see each other no more. You see each other in school already, and I don't like that, so that there is more than enough," she said, uncaringly.

She continued:
"Come on here, let's go. Santana, you have to go. None of this here, no phone, no courting, no coming over here after school and sneaking out my damn back door. Seeing each other in school-in passing-is enough! Come on, let's make it!" she asserted.

Like a deer in headlights, we were both startled and looking at one another as if at any moment, camera men were going to come running in with key grip and microphones pointing in our faces to tell us that we had been punked.

That never happened.

So we sat there looking at her, waiting for the punch-line, thinking she was going to burst into a loud laughter and tell us that she merely wanted to see how we would react.

That never happened.

After coming to terms with the fact that she meant business-serious fucking business, like Nettie and Celie in the "Color Purple-" wrapped around one another while Mister tried to peeled them apart; Santana and me practically re-enacted that entire scene. We stood there in the middle of the living room, crying and mumbling words to each other with tears racing down our face and our smiles turned all the way upside down. We held on to one another tightly, and as if she was standing between us with a crowbar trying to pry us apart. But instead, she just stood there with her arms folded tightly, while Santana held me to his chest and pulling my hair like he was guarding a baby while running through a lion's den.

"Oh cut this dramatic bullshit out already!" she growled.
She bit harder: "Come on, right now, let's make it!"

The sound of her apathetic and uncaring voice hurt both of us even more. We weren't used to being treated that way-anywhere. In his family and amongst our peers at school, our relationship had always been about as respected as the love that everyone knew we had for each other. She had no idea that by this time we nearly relied on one another for the air we breathed, so this was a complete culture shock. We stood there and cried out louder this time-still holding each other as if we were going to become one.

I nearly wanted fight her. That scene was much too abrupt and uncalled for. I was so angry with my mother because this was all so God-awful cruel in my eyes and I hated her for this one.

It was a sad sight to see Santana slowly packing up his snacks and goodies to put in his Jansport backpack. As he approached the door, he put his baseball cap on, and grabbed my face. He then kissed me with a combination of rebelliously striking at my mean mother and like he was on his way to leave and serve his country-helicopter on the helipad: spinning loudly.

When he closed the front door, I immediately walked back to my bedroom and closed the door (tightly) while my mom was on the other side of it, yelling as if she had just got done passing out two ass-whippings. I could swear her shoulders were most probably hunched with her fists balled, while on the other side of my door she was talking-talking *just* like she should have from the other side of the door when I first knocked and asked her if I could go steady. She always knew how to get worked up and talk shit at all the wrong times. But the things that required diplomacy, parental advisory or conversation; she had no ability to handle. I was already (secretly) developing a special kind of disrespect for her inability to assert herself over situations where, when her authority was needed; she would run away, ignore it away or send it away for someone else to deal with it-for her.

Where Santana was concerned, she never wanted things between us to seem like everything was everything-like everything was merely back to the drawing board of life as we'd known it before she found out that I was no longer a virgin, and had sex in her house, who now had a cute boyfriend that went to the same school that I did, and therefore, had access to me over eight hours a day (evenings and weekends included provided that he didn't have to go to work).

From night 'til morning, a lot of things change. We repair, prepare and renew, despite our ages or situations.

Santana and me probably *were* a little dramatic the night before. But everything really *was* everything the very next day-we got over it. Because we knew we would still be seeing one another soon. As long as I was "pro-vert" and he was in love with me, nothing could come between us:

"Dear Mami Love Bear
This is non-other than your main lover: Papi.
Mrs. Harrell gave me a whole bell to write you a letter (laugh).
I'm sitting here crushing monster chews, slobbering all over the place
but they're good. Last night must have been truly rough. I felt for you
after I left. I felt so helpless. I wanted to take you from all this. I know
just run away but where are we gonna live? $50 a week aint gon' get
us nowhere but when I graduate I promise I'll take you away, 'cause
you have two or more years in that house. If things get worse, I'll
provide for you. I'd love to tell your mother a thing or two but who am
I, I'm not grown. She gives you no encouragement. She's not proud of
anything you do. That's what I'm here for, to give you all the
encouragement, love that you need. Fuck your mother, my mother,
everybody.
Love,
Papi."

12

COLD SHOULDERS and FROZEN DANCING FEET

"Hey! Angie

Remember me? Santana? About 5.9 wavy/curly hair, cute face, grey eyes? Yea! That's the one. Hi ya doin! I feel lousy in hell. Baby I'm hurting real bad. Hurtin' real bad. Something's wrong and you're not telling me, and that makes me feel as if you can no longer confide in the man you love (or do you?)

I feel as if I'm no longer any help to you. I'm supposed to be right? It's either that or you're trying to change your image or something.

All the times today I've tried to speak to you and you say nothing and the look on your face is saying get the hell out of my face and this morning when you resisted when I tried to bring your lips to mine that fucked my insides up. But I said what the hell. I should start getting used to stuff like that 'cause you are the lady who my entire life will be about. Wont you?

I've thought about giving up but I can't Angie, I love you so damn much and you're hurting me with whatever you're hiding, could you please stop. If it's something I done, can it not be undone, can I not be forgiven. Please. I'll do anything to bring our relationship back to higher grounds. Ok?

Fuck the Air Force. I won't go. Fuck everything. I've got all kinds of shit (emotions) building up inside me, confused, angry and sad. All that mixed is pain that I'm bearing. Help me baby please. I love you and I'll never let you go, not even if you wanted to because you are my wife, me your husband and together we are our child's parents. Please Angie, don't fuck my life around. Please stay with me. Am I losing you. Huh? I know I'm not but…to tell the truth I don't know I just can't get through to you and its hurting!

PS If I'm blowing everything out proportion I'm sorry.
I'm sorry for false assumptions and everything right now I'm just confused
PSS I love you
PSSS You're not my same Angie, today.
PSSSS I'll stay away for the rest of the day if you want me to!
Love Santana"

…as long as I was "pro-vert" and he was in love with me, nothing could come between us except for the silent treating that I was giving him and the thinking that I was doing-brought on by Ms. You Know Who in one ear and my mother in the other.

Santana was feeling the remnants of that rollercoaster ride. Things were getting very stressful for me with Ms. You Know Who because just like at home with my mom-we began to fight about any and everything.

She was so upset with me and knew that this Santana thing was bigger than she could have ever imagined-just like my mom couldn't. Just like my mom, she was straddled with her role as my teacher versus her slowly diminishing role as my momtor and bridge between the gap of me making and being [in love] versus me making something of myself [in life].

Having still never had a conversation with my mother about Santana, and nothing but two to three hours of Mrs. Cochran's liquor and low-down to play in her mind; I couldn't even imagine the version that Ms. You Know Who had gotten (from my mother). Regardless of whatever version she was in receipt of, my inaction and inattention was enough to prove what*ever* my mother said to her-right.

During my whirlwind with Santana, she continued to grade and critique me fairly, but I had pushed her so far away from me, that even if my mother never said one thing to her about it; she absolutely, positively refused to care anymore. She even refused to sit at her desk and stare anymore. It was strictly business of the "I can't wait until this is over," kind, with her.

With the huffs and puffs and the sighs in her voice plus her frowned brows; I could feel her thoughts.

If it wasn't for the fact that I was mere child and subordinate to her (that at one time-she really cared for); the sound of my voice would have sickened her. She did not want to see my face-she was hurt-very.

A momtor, she was no more. There were no more once a month weekends, movies, house visiting, beauty counters makeovers and long drives discussing my plans for my near future. The bridge between the gap of me being in love, and making something of myself in life-was broken. She meant business: instantaneously.

She treated me like everything we had was a fable. My being serious about Santana definitely was not a part of the design and she proved to me that where she was concerned; my life would definitely be lived by default-all by my choosing... I was still hopeful. Hopeful that there was still a little bit of a chance that she cared. I needed her attention-just one more time; something to pick her momtor-brain.

I wore a pair three-inch burgundy boots into her class. My [dead dad] had bought them for me some time ago. I refused to wear them ever. They remained in my closet, new and with a $200 price tag hanging from them. They sat there, annoying me-representative of the total oxy-moron he was; how he could kirk out at me from trying out a face full of makeup, yet buy me sexy swimsuits and boots with three-inch heels-despite the fact that the heel was chunky. He was now a moron who had been dead to me for quite some time now, but at least he was good for something that I didn't want to let go: Ms. You Know

Who. So I pulled the boots out of the closet.

I knew that she would have a problem with me wearing some boots like that to school or around her-period, but I was desperate. I was pulling out any stop I could-to try and get some attention and a rise out of her-in hopes that she would try us again.

When I walked into her classroom with my boots on, she frowned at me and began to scold me:

"Angie…what are you doing with those boots on?" she asked.

"Wearing them. You like?" I stuck my right foot out and looked down at them-so that we both could admired them.

"They're too grown for you-you look ridiculous," she insulted.

"I like 'em, my dad bought them for me a long while ago," I offered.

"Your mom know you walked out of the house like that today?" she asked.

"My mom leaves the house before me," I replied.

There was a long pause.

"Don't come in my classroom with those boots on-ever again," she warned me.

I didn't reply. I didn't care-that was the plan. I had that glimmer of hope that we were on our way to fighting like we used to and all would be well again. Instead, this fight was more of an annoyance to her. And those three-inch burgundy boots seemed to remind her that I was just trying to be grown. Whereas many months ago-before the light-bulb head boy; she would have merely saw it as me going through growing pangs and trying something out that was too much before my time. But the fact that I was now sexually active and with-boyfriend, in her eyes, it was no longer the innocence of a girl who had a lot to learn. It was merely me wearing a pair of boots that were too grown for me-trying to impress my light-bulb head boyfriend when I should have been focusing on keeping up with the formula of the dainty sweet little girl that she was grooming for success as a woman.

Considering the fact that Santana had her class the last part of the day, I could only imagine how she was treating him-but I never asked him. I figured if anything significant were to occur, he would tell me anyways. Although Santana was two years older than me, Ms. You Know Who felt that he was way too young and immature for me. She had no problem warning me that in time, I would see.

All she wanted for me was to graduate high school and concentrate my efforts on college and a career by my design and her direction. I wanted that too, but I guess I didn't want it bad enough to resist my chance with the light-bulb head boy who chose me to stay with, and be his official and steady girlfriend over all the other girls-many school years. I was just happy. I felt normal and what we had, felt "right." She didn't understand that, and Santana and me we were much too tight and serious at this time. It wasn't open for discussion as far as I was concerned any more than she cared about or understood it. I started to accept the fact that she absolutely positively refused to contend with or even work around it, with what she had in mind was best for me.

So eventually, my study halls would be substituted by my being hugged up in some corner kissing and making out with Santana. My lunches would be spent in its entirety; eating, walking, talking and or cuddled up in some corner with Santana. Every now and then, I would drop by to see if she would be in her classroom-sometimes she would, be most times she would not. The times she would be there, she would let me hear the radio playing from the other side of the door. I would knock a few times, then walking away feeling sad until I'd see Santana. The times when she would not be there, I would expect a note on the door explaining her departure and projected return times, but that never happened either.

She gave up on me so quick and swift that if I didn't know any better, I would have sworn ours was a mirage or dream of some sort. She closed down shop with me as if it never was open, so, I let go, too.

As my teacher (during class lesson demonstrations) she would practically set me up. She would purposely forget to bring an item to the demonstration circle so that I could volunteer mine-my desk was always closest to the circle. One day she needed scissors. I hurriedly reached over to get mine (trying to ingratiate myself to her). I handed the scissors over to her like an orphan begging for porridge and acceptance. She sucked her bottom lip and smirked at me as if to say: "Got'cha!" then underneath her breath (but loud enough so that the class could hear) she said to me: "these aren't the best scissors in the world." The class laughed. She then slid them back to me and went to her desk to get her own-as if my scissors were nowhere near worthy. I was so upset with her-she had her payback coming, I tell you. I was steaming mad.

My turn:

One morning, she was strutting up the steps on the way to her classroom when some wild boys had come running through the hall and bumped into her-causing her to drop her bag. An individually wrapped sanitary napkin came flying out, and everybody (including me) pointed and laughed. She looked around at the immature kids as she reached to pick it up. When she looked up, our eyes met. She gave me the look of death-squinting her eyes and turning her head in total disbelief that I would participate in such silliness. I froze like a popsicle and turned away from her gaze. I can't lie though, I did feel a little vindicated for her cutting mylifeline to her.

I wasn't done with her yet, vengeance was mine-I was still steaming mad inside. When the next opportunity arose, I was still going to be sure to take it. I needed some attention from her so badly-but she turned completely cold. I never felt so completely ignored in all my life. She kept my heart nervously beating.

It's still on though. My long-awaited opportunity of vengeance finally back came around.

My turn, again:

While in class, we found an acrylic nail that happened to have matched her nail polish that she was wearing. We knew it was hers. Everyone dared me to walk up and give it to her. Obviously I was glad to do the honors, seeing as though it was in front of these same people-that she embarrassed me, too.

So two minutes before the bell rang for class to let out, (when it got quiet), I walked to the front of the room, nail in hand, and handed it to her. Everybody laughed so loud. She just looked at me with no expression whatsoever. I knew she was shocked at my childish behavior-but I didn't care. I stared into her face and it didn't move and inch, as if all that I did-had no effect on her. I knew better though. I knew she was hurt, and that it took everything inside of her body to keep from snatching me up by the collar. She couldn't, however, because the entire immature class watched while I smiled at her as if to say: "Got'cha back, bitch!"

My timing was perfect after handing her that fingernail. When the two minutes hit, and the bell rang; I blended in with my fellow immature classmates-hoping that she would form a beak at the tip of her nose and lift me by the skin of my neck. That didn't happen. No white flags were rolled out, and no olive branches were extended. Instead, she let me out of her classroom door on a straight and narrow path and no resistance. And that was the last time we had anything personal, or anything resembling: care, concern, contempt or scorn, ever again. All was lost-any interest in or for me: gone-as if it were never.

I had to learn to accept that…

I loved her to life, but during this time-we had underlying issues far bigger than the heel of my boots. Only about five percent of our issues had to do with the sanitary napkin, the boots, the fingernail and my disrespect. Throughout those months of my dating Santana, we fought about boys and babies and how a situation as such would ruin my life-all my dreams would go down the drain. I didn't want to listen. Although I needed her, I wanted Santana, and I wanted her to accept Santana-but he wasn't a part of the plan.

I had to learn to accept the consequence of that. Santana was worth it to me...

With just a short time before the school year was coming to an end, for five days per week and two hours per day, she was merely my teacher-nothing else. Outside of that, pretty much the only thing we had in common at this point was the fact that my birthday was the same date as her wedding anniversary. If it was left up to her-I'm sure she would have probably thrown that away too, if she could.

I heard that after the school year-she would be moving on to another school to become principal there.

I do know for a fact that she never said goodbye to me and neither did I, her.

Sometime later however, I felt like all that time we had been momtor and mentee, she had either been playing a cruel joke, holding on to a big surprise or both. Because one day I sat in my living room flipping through the pages of a popular magazine and turned it to a picture of Ms. You Know Who with: you'll never guess who...

Turns out, Ms. You Know Who was a sorority sister of, and did business of some sort with my dancing idol who I loved to watch every Saturday. Tears filled my eyes as I focused in and brought the magazine closer to my face: "Got'cha back bitch!" I imagined Ms. You Know Who saying (back at me).

There, on the glossy picture was Dr. Huxtable's wife on the right, Ms. You Know Who in the middle and to the left-there she was: Dr. Huxtable's real-life sister who in my mind, at that very moment, pointed her stick [at me this time] like she'd do every Saturday from the television screen; screaming her notorious line: "YOU WANT FAME? WELL FAME COSTS AND RIGHT HERE IS WHERE YOU STARRRRRT PAYIN'IN SWEAT..."

13

PILLS & FRILLS

July 14

"What's up Chick? Nothing much over this a-way! I'm just kidding. But seriously, what's up? Are you and Santana still kicking it? How long has it been since yall started going together-gosh!

Me and Ken Grant still don't go together yet. But, we are talking and that's good enough for me you know Vern? It's just like we go together because I've been up here for three weeks and he hasn't messed with anybody.

Girl I couldn't believe it. He told me he loved me. I almost had a fit! Girl you're gonna have to come spend the night with me before the summer is over! I asked Ken who had he kissed and he said "my mother, everyday!" I said ha ha very funny. I'm serious who? And he said nobody, I haven't got my beaters down or kissed anybody since you left!

Girl do you know how glad that made me feel? Well go ahead and imagine had good that made me feel. (Stop laughing) I hope you haven't forgotten my phone number or have you? Well in any case, I forgot yours so you can write me back before July 25, (because that's when I leave to come back home anyway) and give me your phone number.

You know I'm gonna go fuck happy when I get home you know why? Cause I miss him, his dick and just making love itself. Angie stop laughing. Tell Santana I said chello! Oh! My brother saw your picture and said, "Damn that girl is bad, she got a boyfriend?" I said yeah she

does, he said, "Shit!" I said, "Too bad." Don't laugh. But girl you know what? After me and Ken had made love that Sunday, he made me have my period about 3 weeks earlier than I was supposed to. Do you know what? I got 3 weeks earlier than I was supposed to again. I don't know what's wrong with my cycles. But when I get home, I'm getting on the pill! Have you started yet? Do they make you fat? Do they also change your period cycles? Because I sure don't want to be fucking fat!!!!! I'm going to tell Ken and see what he thinks about it. What do you think, I should get his opinion? Or just go ahead and get on it? I don't know how to go about telling my mother without having to hear **why?** *That's a killer question...as you well know. But I have to go so be cool sweetie!*
Love Always Sis
Aya Nile (Grant)

Aya was a hot lil' number. Her mother *had* to keep her busy and preoccupied. For the summer, she had gone away to some creative arts camp to be a youth leader for part of the summer. She would write me to catch me up on how things were going with her, as well as following up on the subject we agonized over most: "The Pill."

I was very secretive about everything (and especially where Santana and I were concerned). Aya and I had been friends for many years-even before Santana started attending our school. We told each other (most) everything. Aya was good for always slipping in the invitation to meet or hookup with someone else if ever I wanted to. She, like a lot of girls and mutual friends of ours in school, had been in the league of girls who had kissed Santana before. And because he kissed so many girls, his kissing me, at first (to all of them) was nothing more than me being the next girl up to bat, while everyone waited hear about who he would be gone on to kissing next. The expectation was that I would be just another girl on his roster, but much to their surprise, I hit the home run: Santana did the running and everybody else had to return to the dugout-Aya included. Almost a couple years had gone by and we were still alive, in love, and kicking it. Because of the fact that we were steadily going steady; I could only foresee trouble ahead for Santana and me at the rate we were going. No babies for me. So without trepidation and despite knowing my mom would rather I not be with Santana; the fact (still) remained all which was sustained: our relationship-and we were still together in it. I had no time to worry about my mom's silliness about such a subject as the next one I was about to dump in her lap. I went to her to tell her that I needed to get on the pill. *This* time, I didn't ask her from the opposite side of the door. *This* time, I asked her face to face.

She practically pulled the classic soap opera stance where the two actors would be talking face to face about something emotional and one would turn his back to the other actor-his hand holding his own shoulder. She confused me so-all over again-the *same* way. Rather than answering me, she did what I figured she would do: she ignored me all day as if I never said anything to her about it. I was so annoyed.

Into the evening and night, she still ignored me. But when the sun came up, I raised up. Mom was gone off to work. The telephone rang with Ms. Ananda on the other end of it, asking me to come see her the moment I got up to get my day started.

Later into the morning, I reported downstairs to her apartment where she stood with that same deer in the headlights look on her face-feeling too embarrassed to laugh and joke with me about what she had to say to me this time. She broke it to me gently:

"Your mother told me that you wanted to get on the *pill*?..." she asked-emphasizing the word: "pill."

"Yes. I do." I confirmed, confidently and simply.

Getting straight to it-nervously-Ms. Ananda said my name in an almost whisper: "Angie... I'm going to make an appointment to take you because your mother just wasn't ready for that question okay?" she finished, with an almost identifiable motherly plight, as if she understood what that feeling would be like (for her) the day her own two daughters proposed that same question (to her).

I know Ms. Ananda-very well. The other half of her was more embarrassed to be forced into handling a situation that she knew should be handled by my mother. She just couldn't tell my mother that. My mother was so many ways out of line to have Ms. Ananda face a situation that she had yet, years, to have to contend with-with her own daughters. My knowing Ms. Ananda though, I was more than sure that the topic of gossip on the phone to her friends later that day would be what she was unable to defend and say-to my mother: "that's yours and Angie's situation, I can't step in on that."

Well (for now), she was in on it. And I know that to alleviate the pressure of this whole thing, she probably wished that by the time I made it down to her house, I changed my mind about wanting to get on the pill so this whole thing would be over, but that did not happen, I confirmed and I agreed:

"Okay then, Ms. Ananda, you can take me," I said to her, as if I was challenging her.

She told me that she would let me know the time and date she set up the appointment for shortly.

Santana and I had already gone over the birth control pill conversation several times throughout our relationship, but this time-this summer, we were serious. I talked to him about this situation that my mother elected to put Ms. Ananda in on, and how uncomfortable she really felt about it.

He got his youngest auntie, whom he was close to, in on it. She made the appointment for all three of us to go the clinic for the end of that same week. Later that day, I lifted that load and responsibility off Ms. Ananda-that my mom dropped in her lap, by telling her that I changed my mind about needing the pills after considering all the

the precautions and side-effects and that, condoms would better suit us "if or whenever again..."

At this point, I just didn't want my mom or anyone involved with my mom to know anything about me and the goings on in my relationship with Santana going forward. Everything was more messier and crazier than I ever could have imagined. I was ready to just shut my mother out of this completely, since it was obvious that she couldn't handle it-any of it.

My plan to weed out and hoodwink didn't go over well-for too long, after my mother found out that Santana's auntie took me to get the pills. I confessed it when she found them in my room on my nightstand-amongst some papers and such. I think I got too excited with the idea of the maturity and responsibility of taking the pill that I tried to match my situation with the picture on the brochure where the pill pack sat out in open view on a night-stand and under a night lamp, so as to remind the woman not to forget to take her pill before bed. My situation was a whole lot different than the fantasy of a picture on a brochure and I should have know better than to try something like that.

Although this thing with Santana and me obviously blind-sighted my mother, I too, was blind-sighted by the thoughts I entertained of that "mother-daughter bonding" and closeness that occurred at that time in life when the daughter began to like boys, and all "age-sixteen"-like things that came with it.

I guess I had watched one too many movies and soap operas that summer, because it was nothing like that for my mom and me.

14

YOU KNOW WHAT: I TOLD YOU SO

Santana's senior year had finally come. And just like Ms. You Know Who would constantly remind and promise me-he would soon be "smelling himself" and his immaturity would rear its light-bulb head. She was right-as usual.

From school years past, unlike the few alter-egos that he would spring on me in many-a-letter back then; when he became a senior, he seemed to have a new alter-ego every other day. I could barely keep up with who "he" was, who "he-he" was, or who Santana was, in conjunction with the constant bullshit that would find its way into our "love bubble," as he would call it (back then).

If I watched one-too-many movies and soap operas about how the mother-daughter bond occurs at certain stages in life, Santana must have watched one-too-many movies or read some book I hadn't heard about called: "The Boys' Guide to Senior Year High-School Life." This school year-his last one-our entire relationship was being tested-everything about it: everything about him, everything about us, and everything we had built thus far. Everybody (secretly) wanted to get their last chance with or back with him. He didn't know if he was coming or going with all the female attention [and inattention he was getting-used for bait] from girls who were pulling out all the stops-like landmines: doing any and everything (from being rude to inviting), just to get a rise or some attention out of him that, for nearly two school years now; he had been too steady with me, to slow down and give or see. Him being "off the market" in a way like he had never been, was apparent and real to them. But his last year at school, everybody damned near wanted to be the exception to the rule, and Santana was breaking some of our rules-exceptionally.

His senior year was the biggest and most unexpected roller coast of a ride of our entire relationship. Nothing about him was making sense to me: nothing he did, nothing he said, or nothing he wrote in his few letters to me during his senior year. But what did make sense to me was how he had become a walking open book. Although the reasons behind the personality changes and rollercoaster rides were never written all over his face, or in his actions toward me; like never before- still, it was written (all between the lines):

"I Love You. And you know it. First shit that doesn't even matter, that one bitch Lisha! Talkin' bout why did I tell you what she said. And I think she wants to fight cause she said to tell you what her homeroom was. But I told her that nobody was pressed for that shit! God I felt like socking her ass. Damn school just started back and people are already starting shit. Now down to business. Baby I'm sorry but I was just playing. It seems as tho' you're worried about me running off with her. I don't care if she has a little place somewhere. Nothing could turn me away. Nothing. God dam! Can't you see that? I love you and no one else. You know I felt like saying what the fuck do you think I'm gonna do run off with this chick and just forget about my true love. (I love you) sheeet you must be crazy. To tell you the truth, I was hurt (real) That's why I walked away cause I would have started to act like a bitch...Dead up. I'll try to call.

Love,
Santana
I Love You"

"Alright!
What's up? What choo thinkin' bout. I hope cause I'm thinkin' bout you here in math. I don't ever get no work done cause I'm always writing you, that shits gone have to stop. I left my bus card at the pezad. I'm gone bum some money. Yezes! Me The Rock gon' bum sum change.
I LOVE YOU SO MUCH."

"Hi!
How you feel? Me, I feel like fucking my baby! You looked so pretty
today, I wanted to take you to the pezad and just Do you all day! I'm
thinking about holding out...Ok my minds made up we're making love
today after school, but I didn't bring any protection.
I'll find some somewhere, don't worry. I'm 'bout to move out cause the
bell's about to ring.
But I'll write back.
Love,
Santana 10:22am"

"Dear Angie
What's up! Sorry for not writing for a while, but I just wasn't up to it. I
love you and you're my heart. No one will take you or keep me from
you. This marker is kinda sporty huh? Baby I Love You.

Yesterday, I was happy to see you. You looked so good. When I get
some protection I won't take Angelo out like I've been doing cause I
know that leaves you unsatisfied. And me too in a way but girl the way
you do what you do...

You know I'll do anything for you go anywhere and go against
anybody's word to get to you and make you happy. ***I'm getting kinda***
tired of this color I'm switchin' to a color I can relate to. I can't wait
till the break, I'm gone fuck you senseless. I know I'm 'gon bust. On
my bed there is nowhere to tie each other up too Angie. We'll
probably make due. I'm 'bout to move out.
Love, Santana
PS- Think we should hold out til Wed?"

"Hi Gopher.
What's Up! Baby I'm sorry for upsetting you with my so called "hard
rock roll" maybe I do that subconsciously. But I must I admit that it is

rather silly and sort of immature. I'll try to stop. Promise. Naw I'm sorry about you too I was only thinking of myself. That won't happen no more. I felt real bad about doing you like that but I promise this weekend we'll go.

I enjoyed being with you Sunday. My love for you overflowed deepened and everything else. And I wanted to fuck the hell out of you God! You looked so good and I just wanted you to feel how much I loved you. I LOVE U LOVE U LOVE LOVE U LOVE U LOVE U LOVE U SO MUCH. I felt so damn stupid for doing you so wrong Sunday. I'm sorry, yesterday was a trip. Do you think UUUHHH! You threw up on me. We'll have to do that more often caused it felt kinda good. Gross but good. I like fucking you like that, it feels good. I know you liked it so I was trying to do it harder to make you feel as good as possible.
Love,
Santana"

"Dear Red How do ya do!
I'm alright. But my thumb fuckin' hurts! That's why my writing is so sloppy. You do look fine today. Finest of the fine. I'm thinking about yesterday. That was one of the best experiences for us both.

It felt good to us both. Especially to me. I felt sort of dominant but not fully. I wanted to hurt you and make you cry. But then again, I didn't. But next time, I'll show no mercy..."

"Hi! How are you? Yo! You look high.
You really do. Your eyes trip me out.
I asked Rochelle for some paper and she said no so I'm writing on no line paper. Baby you looked like you felt down 2ⁿᵈ bell I was trying to figure out a way to cheer you up. And I came up with maybe a hug, a kiss, and I love you would work and sure enough, you smiled from ear to ear. I was so pleased that I had made you smile. I love you so much.

Maybe instead of making love we could just get fully unclothed and get into the bed under the covers and just talk about you're so much of a woman and you're so damn sexy.

I doubt that talking would get my feelings across. And I am so much of a man and so damn sexy I doubt if you could keep your legs closed (smiles) My nature rises just thinking about it. You got some money? I don't! You do?! Good give me some.
Love, Santana
B.K.A Dennis (your) Menace REEBOK NIKE LEGEND"

"Hi!
What's up Surprised you this morning Huh? Should I come get you every morning? I mean there's nothing at school and at home. I have a better attitude and it is sustained throughout the day. But if not, that's okay. It helps me feel closer to you knowing that we're leaving the same place at the same time to the same destination almost as if we live the real one, just us. But my imagination will just have to keep running till it happens.........Do you want it bad? Real Bad? Real Bad?. I do too. I love you so damn much! I can't wait to see and hold your naked warm body in my arms and smell that sweet aroma of sex and love juices. I fuck as hard and as long as you want provided that you climax!

If you do...if not, I won't. Deal? Deal. Move your hips to meet my every thrust and you'll get what you want. You'd like that huh I'm sure. It will feel like a hot spray of liquid being sprayed inside you both filling you and fulfilling you. You'll be on fire ready to fuck again even harder. You will start doing things that you have never done before. I know you want it but you'll have to cum get it (work for it). Maybe if you fuck me hard enough, I'll forget and climax right inside you but I doubt it!

Love, Dennis The Menace"

"Red!
Baby you look so damn good today. I love your hair and your bulging
cheeks and your big pretty sexy sensuous baby doll eyes! Just thinking
about it makes my love tool feel as though it would rip through the
skin. The way you lazily blink your eyes...Damn! I could probably full
ejaculate just by looking at you.

I can't wait to get between those thick soft supple thighs with my pelvis
violently smacking yours with every powerful thrust and your soft
round wide tight ass ripping you apart with just a powerful thrust to let
you know I might cuss you out just to add a little excitement and I
expect you to cuss back or do what you feel no matter what you wanna
do no matter how erotic I'll follow.
Love, Dennis Your Menace"

"I love you (a hell of lot) damn! It's been so long since I've held your
supple body in my strong and very secure grasp. I miss you! I miss
you! I miss you! Your kiss, your sexy eyes, your sweet way of speaking
or saying how much you love me. I sorely miss it all oh! This is not a
diamond ring, a car nor a cheeseburger (smile) but the way I feel now,
it's the next best thing or maybe better! I love you! I love you! I love
you! I'm gonna treat you like a queen even though you're just my
princess and me your king. I'll never leave you! Never cheat! Never
lie! Or anything to hurt my precious princess. You better had came
over cause my feelings for you are bubbling over and i need you to sit
back and open your sweet sexy legs and let it all pour in.
Love your man Santana

PS-what are you waitin for? Take your clothes off lay down and enjoy
the show.
PSS-the real surprise was a blue convertible sports Benz but you
wouldn't, someone stole it! (smile)
Love,
Santana Papi Love Bear"

"Dear Angie
How are you. You look fine. You feel fine, you taste fine so you must be
fine huh! I was just wondering what time you had?

I have the new watch's time. You know what. I read your little thank
you card you wrote me. I don't believe I've ever seen it before which
means I don't pay as much attention as I used to.

I really love you, it's just that there is so much going on in me. I don't
open up to you like I used to. Because you have your school life and
after school life and me mine. What I don't understand why we can't
attract more when we do find time together I read your more recent
letters and began to think to myself why? Why has our relationship
gone so much more downhill instead of up and over the hill.

Don't deny it hasn't gone down because that would just make it worse.
We pretend too much. For example: when your friends come around,
we act like so much in love but after they leave we fuck up again.
Sometimes it doesn't last we fuck up when they're still standing there
because you are so stuck on being the most loving couple.

Nothing is wrong with that but let's be true to ourselves first. Then
other people. My suggestion is for us to take our time and go slow and
build up the relationship up and beyond.

The love is there (strongly) but not the right attitude.

Baby I love you. Baby let's try harder, please cause I want to be yours
forever and vice versa.

Let's work real hard, talk openly. Express hates, loves, likes, dislikes,
whatever, let's do it.

Love,
B-Zerk
Senior 9:40 (my new watch's time) "

"My Darling Red

Hi baby, and how's my pretty young lady. I'm feeling better, really. And I'm sorry about my dumbass attitude. And yea! I respect myself to a certain extent. And I do care to a certain extent. And yes I respect the hell out of you, but I'm getting the feeling that I am not respecting you as my fiancé' am I right? I thought so. I just don't want to unload my problems on you and then we would both be under. I mean I know you love me but there are some things that I have to do for myself in order for me to become a man (your husband) and after I master that, your help would be much appreciated. Not that it's not appreciated now. Yea I remember the promise and I am keeping my end. I do my work. But anyway. This pertains to the above. All I need is you by my side 100% and I know you'll be there always and I will expect you to, just as would me. I LO———VE you to. No I take that back I LO————

————— ——————— ———————————VE

YOU. You haven't put me through nothing, you just want to be a part of the problems and it won't work. I promise to confide in you. And I put all my trust in you, but I just think there is no need for me to burden you too. Make it so bad my problems are sappish and if I can't handle them, I'll never be the best of anything to you. But I want to be the best to improve myself as a person as well as a friend, lover and fiancé.

Love,

Santana

PS It's easier said than done, but I'll do it.

I LOVE YOU RED"

"Dear Angie

I know times are not as good as they used to be, but just to assure you that I love you just as much, if not, more. I'm sorry. I'm not saying I'm sorry cause you won't believe me but I hope things get brighter.

Love,

Santana

B-zerk"

"Hi Angie.
It's me. B-Zerk again. I'm really happy to know that were gonna try to
work out a beautiful relationship. Yesterday I thought all was lost. But
there was a glimmer of hope. I really love you and that's true
(strongly). Today when we make love, I want it to last, to be the best as
if it were our first time. We really need to try to understand each other.
We seem to be strangers in love. And I hate that feeling. You are so
pretty. God! Are you pretty.
Only reason I don't write as often is because you don't respond quickly.
Well Bout to move out Mrs. B-Zerk
I'll get back B-Zerk B-Zerk B-Zerk
SENIOR CREW!"

"Come out here! Come out here!" demanded Aya-standing in the
doorway of my classroom and looking in at me with her eyes squinted-
wiggling her index finger. I had never seen her like that, so I knew it
must have been important. She interrupted my class session despite
knowing that lunch was in twenty minutes. Since it couldn't wait that
long, I rushed to the front of my classroom door, expecting her to
whisper something in my ear. Instead, she forcefully grabbed me by
the arms, and held my shoulders steady as she turned me around to
face her. She then rested and squeezed her hands on my shoulders;
positioning me as if she was about to tell me something that, like a
soap opera, was sure to force me to place my right hand upon my
forehead and pass out onto the floor. She went straight in for the kill:

"It's Santana girl. He cheated girl. Santana **cheated**!" she yelled
out angrily, anxiously.

My heart was beating faster than a mile a minute, my eyes
stretched really big.

"What! How? With who?" I asked her.

"Carmen! The girl named Carmen who still comes down here every day afterschool-the one that got kicked out last year!" yelled Aya-with the kind of intensity and anger as if it was she who he cheated on too...

"No. You are lying to me," I said to Aya.

"Yes, it's true. I overheard Carmen's friend telling someone else while we were in class! That bitch didn't know that I was right behind her! I was listening to her tell her home girl about Santana and Carmen fucking at *her* house last night. She and Santana's friend Tony were hooking up, and while there, it's a **fact** that Santana and Carmen fucked too!" reiterated Aya-whose heart was beating hard as mine and looking as if she, too, was about to place her hand upon her forehead and faint and fall to the floor. She nearly dared me to discount this could be true and I sure as hell wanted to. Because we were reporting to one another when we were apart and hogging up so much of each other's time, I couldn't figure out how and when he had enough time to do this. And to think that he did-he *had* to make room and a way for it. My mind was running a race with my heart.

Santana had never met the queen bee in me and he was sure as hell about to meet her.

I couldn't *believe* what I was hearing, because everything was so busy and so were we. We were busy and overwhelmed with preparing for his prom, other senior year extravaganzas and excursions, as well as his graduation. We were busy preparing phase I of our fairytale and on to the next level-getting married and moving in together. Where did all this fit into the equation?

My mind was winning the race right now. My heart had dropped and gone away.

Eagerly, I approached.

He sat by the doorway of the class he had before lunchtime.

I walked right to the doorway, reached in and grabbed him by the back of his shirt, catching him by surprise: "Come with me, right now, right now!" I whispered forcefully.

He took a deep breath and his face totally surrendered and dropped to the floor-almost like a kid that knew exactly what he was about to get an ass-whipping for. Aya was standing there with her arms folded and rocking back and forth; waiting on an answer from him that looked more like an apology she expected to be given to her...

I didn't shed one tear. I was angry-way too angry to cry.

"Why did you do it Santana?" I asked.

He wouldn't answer. He was standing there biting his lip-looking at me like he needed to hold me. I could feel the dramatics coming on-but I wasn't having it. I backed away from him some, so that if he reached for me-he would drop to the floor.

"Why'd you do it?" I repeated.

"I didn't, I didn't," he kept repeating, as if somehow, repeating it over and over would work for him like going home worked for Dorothy after repeating: "there's no place like home, there's no place like home." He sure as hell wished he could click his heels and do the same.

He couldn't even look me in the face. That's when I knew that he *did* do it.

I could feel Aya's energy-it was much too involved in [what was now] our busted "love bubble."

Santana looked so pitiful-like if he could snap his fingers and rewind this moment to make it all be a bad dream-he would. He was that ready to faint.

"Come with me," I said to him, nodding to Aya-so as to excuse, but thank her. I lead him into our school's darkest room where mime class and performances were held every other day. Santana was unlucky-this was that "every other day" and I was all up and in his face with *my* hands-while he was mute as a mime.

The dark room was all one color. The one and only window that the room had was painted to close out the light, as well. The only things with any color in that room was Santana, me and what we had on for clothes. We entered, I turned the lights on:

"I've got to have it, Santana. *What* the hell happened?" I said, standing over him as he sat on the wooden stoop. The darkness of the room was filling up my head and my body. I was fuming. My brows turned up like he'd never seen before. Finally, he began to speak-looking at the floor:

"Me and Tony went over to her friend's house because Tony had just started hanging out with her friend. She happened to be over there," he mumbled.

"Oh, so this wasn't planned? Is that what you're trying to say (in other words)?"

"No! No! It was *not* planned," he answered.

It got quiet.

"So what happened? You heard me. *What* happened?" I demanded to know.

He mumbled some more: "Tony was in the room with her friend and we were in the living room talking," his face was still looking to the floor. "We, who? You scared to say her name?" I jabbed.

He continued as if he didn't hear a word I had just said: "…Then all of a sudden we ended up being upstairs and that's where it happened," he finished.

"We-who? Santana" I yelled.

"Carmen," he answered.

"These girls have been at you even harder-by the *day* and you bit the bait! Santana *why* would you do this to me-to us? When you know that ever *since* the very day we've been together-*some*body up in this school was *itching* to get a hold of some news like this. And now-you scratched it for 'em! **Id**iot!" I yelled in a tone like he had never heard before and with a facial expression that he had never seen before.

Feeling the anger from the thought of all that could have happened I decided: to hell with probing him bit by bit; this bastard will sit here and recite every fucking nook and cranny and detail. The anger I felt at the thought of the mere summary he thought he was going to give me, sent me into an angry tailspin. To keep from crying, all I could do was yell. I refused to cry.

I began to yell in his face as if I was interrogating him:

"Okay, you said: 'where *it* happened...' *what* happened Santana. I didn't ask for a summary!

E-LAB-OR-ATE-DAMMIT! Every single detail! *Tell* me what happened!" I forced. I listed how I wanted the details:

"What did you say that lead to you both being upstairs."

"What did she say?"

"Who lead the way?"

"What room did you go to?"

"Who got who undressed?"

"What was said?"

"Where did you touch her?"

"Did you kiss her?"

"How long did you fuck her?"

"What positions did you fuck her in?"

"Did your hands touch her pussy?"

"Did you suck her titties?"

"Did you suck her pussy?"

"Did you moan at all?"

"Did she?"

"Did you enjoy it?"

"Did she enjoy it?"

"What were you saying to her-during?"

"After?"

"What did she say to you-during?"

"After?"

"So how was the pussy? Was it wet, dry? Loose? Tight?"

"Awkward?"

"Did you kiss the bitch before you left?"

"Did you make plans for another hookup?"

"Did you talk to her on the phone when you got home?"

"I know goddamn well you didn't tell her you were breaking up with me!"

"Nawww! No!" he interrupted me.

"Well, tell it! Tell it all! Tell it all! Tell it all! Tell it all!"

...I yelled, with a force so strong that I could damn near feel him levitating up off the stoop right where he sat. He began to grab his head and crying-telling me how sorry he was-over and over; looking as if he was about to have a nervous break-down, I did not care at this point.

I had every thought going through my mind about all the things I gave up for him, fought for-for him, and how much I loved him for all those years; only for it to end because he cheated. I would've accepted the downfall of our relationship being because he got tired of me or me-him. Our relationship had no signs of tiring even through the day before I found this out-no indication that there was (this kind of) trouble ahead for us. The only trouble ahead I foresaw was getting pregnant.

You don't fall out of love and do anything to cause a downfall in love-in the middle of being in love. I might be young, but I know that much about love-regardless the age (if it is real love). So, that confused me. I thought we had (real) love.

Because of that, I wanted to punish him. I wanted his head to bust open like my heart was. I wanted to rip him from the inside-out, and to make sure that before we left that dark room, the two of us would be walking into whatever light was left in this, and like this was all a bad dream. I wanted it to be.

With his head still covered and crying, broken-down and regretful, he threw it up and admitted:

"Nobody lead anybody upstairs, I had carried her up the stairs."

I interrupted: "You romantic fool! You carried her big tall ass?" I shook my head shamefully-at him.

He continued without pausing; listing all the details as he slammed his right index finger into the palm of his left hand:

"We were downstairs talking about it, and during the conversation, she told me she was still a virgin."

"That was the only reason I persisted because I wanted to see if I could get her upstairs."

"When I did get her upstairs-I did kiss her."

"I *didn't* eat her pussy."

"I *didn't* put my hands *on* her pussy."

"I kissed her-*only* for a minute."

"Then I kissed her neck."

"*Then* I kissed her breasts and *only* for a minute!"

"And I didn't even get to finish because she was uncomfortable. It was kind of greasy-not wet. I don't know what she put in it when she used the restroom or whatever-beforehand-but it was," he said.

I paused-not know what the hell to say to that. I went on to ask: "Did you make her think in any way that this could continue to go on?" I asked.

"No, I did not," he said, with his head still hanging down, exhausted and sitting there biting his bottom lip looking like a sad puppy. I replied: "She's a girl-I'm a girl, I know how girls are. So I know that she expects *something* from you. She may not go to this school anymore but she's down here afterschool as if she just walked out of the *same* doors that we do-so you are *going* to run into her. That being said Santana-you'd *better* handle that shit! Get her gone-or we're through! Make her wonder if that really ever happened-because I don't give a damn," I demanded.

"I will! I will!" he yelled eagerly.

I drilled in:

"She, like all of her other lil' goofy-ass friends liked you when *she* attended school here. Now, those silly rabbits are left with something to talk about. The *school* is left with something to talk about. You let them all in. We are nothing sacred anymore," I said, while he kept shaking his head-refuting what I said.

"Yes you did! You can't be in denial about it Santana. We kept everybody out and now they're all-in!" I said.

He still kept refuting-in total denial. "So do you want to be with her?" I asked.

He used that as his perfect opportunity to stand up and hold me in his arms, because for the entire time since I first started to grill him, the closer he moved in to hold me-the further I would back away.

He caught me this time. He hopped off the stoop to overpower me; crying and holding me, rocking me from side-to-side while repeating: "No, no, no, no-please, no…" squeezing me tight until I almost couldn't breathe.

My heart had returned and was winning the race now.

With my chest pressed up against his; tears shot to my eyes and rolled quickly down my face. My heartbeat must have played the sound of the saddest song of heartbreak ever made: "I'm Only Human" by Human League. Nothing fit the situation and danced with the beat of my heart and matched my tears-more, at that moment.

I was winded like the air let out of a balloon, and feeling just how one looks-as a result of.

I was crushed that day while crying in his arms-feeling like everything I had given *to* him, I wanted to take back: my heart-and everything up to and including my virginity. Everything I had given up *for* him, I certainly could not get back. I wanted *so* badly to reverse everything and place myself right back on top of that ladder in that library.

My life would have gone entirely different. But the reality was-I could not take anything back from him any more than I could reverse life and put myself back up on top of that ladder. So I held him back, with my world was crushed and crumbled. This was something I never entertained the thought of happening. He continued to cry and hold me tightly while grunting in my ear: "Don't leave me, don't leave me, don't leave me, please....."

He then grabbed my face and began kissing all around it, with my tears.

We left the dark room, cut the lights back out and walked into the light (somewhat).

The nightmare was over (somewhat).

Our fairytale-for me-was as well (somewhat).

In just that instant, it wasn't quite the same for me anymore.

My mind told me to walk away but my heart begged me to stay.

I was willing to try.

After school, we went home (he-to his home and me-to mine). I couldn't imagine him coming home with me just yet. He wrote:
"Dear Angie
Hi! I won't ask how you're doing cause I know. I know you love me and as far as my stupid ways, you will have to put up with it order for us to succeed (our marriage) but it's not fair for you. I really know how you feel. And you wonder why I feel like killing myself. Am I of no worth, but my love for you is priceless and I would die for you and when I die it will be for you.
You know life has been alright. I've had my share of fun and good times and bad times and it has really been nice knowing a lot of fun people and I thank God that I have met you baby.
I love you and today when you said you can't take it anymore, that's

when I decided that I am nothing but a burden, and burdens only make people miserable.

You know. I am really hurting. I just could not live with knowing that unhappiness is what I'm putting you through. Yes! We've had good times. It makes me cry knowing that we could come to this after all the "I love yous" and smiles and the feelings we've shared in bed where our true feelings just overflowed. I can't live knowing that the lady that I love does not trust me.

You say you do to convince yourself, but you really don't. I'm hurting. But you're tired of that line so I'll keep it to myself.

And I mean, I just don't have the heart to say to someone that I don't like you. I mean they have feelings too. But it no longer matters because I love you and I'll tell her flat out.

And if I never get to have wife and kids and necessities and luxuries in life, at least I know I had the chance with a very special and most attractive young lady. I'm not giving up, don't get me wrong and I don't want to die, I have so much to live for. You, our family, our kids, and our family life but I don't

want to ruin or mess you up! I love you, please believe me.

I won't say I'm sorry again (although I am) because that's something else you don't want to hear. And don't say that killing myself shows how much I don't love you 'cause you are wrong.

I love you and I love you so dam much (I'm crying) but I'm making you unhappy and I can't live with that.

Love,
Santana"

15

DICHOTOMIES & DAZES

We made it through his senior year and all the plans, and excitement that came with it. I didn't want to be a Debbie Downer at a time in his life that he would never be able to repeat, but would certainly be able to hold onto the memories of-even if we ended up being a memory to each other.

I continued to be the doting girlfriend; wearing his class ring around my neck while being in receipt of anything else he would give and do to solidify our relationship and rebuild our "love bubble." Santana was trying hard to prove to me that what we had was built to last. It was working for the most part. He was my man and I was his girl-"Angie and Santana" were household names in both of our households and throughout our extended families by this time. It just was what it was.

If I had any plans on leaving him, they were halted shortly after prom. All that sex we were having and my-on again-off-again relationship with the pill: straddled between gaining one pound and panicking or getting sick from taking them every morning, was proving to be a bit much for me. Over time, Santana and I would see-saw between either using condoms or resorting to the old-fashioned rhythm method until our beat went off the track. In between time, we would just take the plunge and cross our fingers since it had worked for so long.

Well after prom, when I didn't get my period-we already knew. Ooh if Ms. You Know Who could be a fly on the wall of my life right now.Part me was disappointed in myself because my life was headed in one direction but then Santana and all things that came with it-in the name of "love," took me in another direction and my heart followed it. I knew what I should have been doing and should not have been doing, but we were so tight and no matter what, I knew he would have my back. He loved me crazily, and he also fulfilled for me, that fairytale girl-meets-boy fantasy that every girl dreams about. Now, we were on to real-life and needing to make real-life decisions.

After he graduated, that summer, my mom found out that we had officially made feet for those socks that she would talk about. The decision had to be made as to whether or not I would abort, put it up for adoption or have it.

Our Madonna classic love song "Crazy for You," eventually turned Madonna-tragic, singing: "Papa Don't Preach." Down to the very last lyric, it was as if that woman's songs brooded over our relationship and every aspect of it from love and now life: the feet that were being made for socks. As irony would have it, Madonna rode with us from conception of our relationship and the theme song for it, all the way through to what was a kind of immaculate conception growing inside of me: the product of two virgins who made love and a baby from love-regardless our interruption and situations. I could not hear "Papa Don't Preach" without crying uncontrollably and clutching my stomach. Everything about it resonated with what I was feeling about, Santana, our relationship and me being estranged from my dad-who, if he found out I was pregnant; no question about it, would have forced me to stop the music for all dancing feet involved-immediately. Thanks to me being estranged from him, along with Madonna singing all up in my relationship, with abortion omitted from the list of options; the fact still remained that my belly was going to grow bigger. Her goal was to deal with first things first: pull me out of that school. The dream was officially over, as far as she was concerned.

As far as the school itself, the dream had been over long before I even *met* Santana, little did she *or* my dad know. That was a big secret

I kept from him over the years of my even attending the artsy-school. Because he had a different perception of my inclusion at that school than what actually was. Although I didn't abort, I still had a second chance at life and a career going forward-hence why I chose adoption as an option. My father however, though estranged and out of the know of it all; the dream would never be over in his eyes-oh hell no-over his dead body. He was far too obsessively ambitious and loved playing fantasies in his head; his idea of success in the making (being cultivated vicariously through me).

Reminiscing on the time from back in third grade when his insatiably ambitious self interrupted me from my language arts classroom with a bunch of papers in his hand. He had the kind of excitement on his face as if he had hit the lottery. I was his lottery ticket: his golden-child.

He grabbed me by my tiny hands and dragged ninety-five pounds of skin and bones down that hallway so fast that dust probably followed us. He sat me in that empty lunchroom with the packet of papers telling me about this new school that was exclusive to kids with talent of a wide variety.

All my dad knew was that I could sing, I could dance, I could act, I could spell, I'd won spelling bees, I was articulate, I was theatrical, I had a lot of personality, good penmanship, nice handwriting, I was loved by my teachers (parent-teacher open houses were big to-do's and major strokes to his paternal ego)-my hood loved me. So in my dad's eyes, that was all the ingredients it took to make "Star Pie." So he signed me on for the school, when little did he know, my: acting, the written test, my dancing, my creative writing, my music and my drama portion of the audition that opened the doors for me to step right in to the world of non-mediocrity (from the outside looking in) wasn't what it took to actually make it in that "exclusive" school that he felt was built just for me.

All of that was merely behind (the entry) to door number one. That door merely squealed open to let you in the school-to separate you from the "mediocrity" of the traditional neighborhood high-school.

Door number two slammed behind you: hard. It consisted of politics of the economic, political and social kind:

The: **"Nobody's":** usually quiet, exceptionally multitalented, kept to themselves. Fashion was *definitely* not a priority or forte'. Most of them wore tattered and recycled clothes. Some were groomed acceptably rather than exceptionally well, other's-not. For many of them, their circumstance was visible and on their sleeve. They were friendly, stayed out of the way, probably had one hell of an opinion about the remaining cliques:

The: **"Why-The-Hell-Are-They-Here-Don't-They- Belong-In-Some-Neighborhood-School-Rather-Than-This-Exclusive-Schoole**r(s)": This was Santana's group. Hardly anyone in the school knew what their special talents were. Amongst one another they knew (I think). But to all other groups, you kind of just wondered why in the hell were they even in school but more importantly: *our* school. This group consisted of those who were most probably poor to middle class but wore the latest fashions that seemed to camouflage what, if any, talent they really had. It was *such* a mystery. They were the typical/local/neighborhood high-school type of group that seemed like they floated into the artsy-school on some island and got stranded there. Some of them laughed at the "Nobodys" and other cliques for not having the latest clothes like them and thought people outside of their cliques were lames or just flat out weirdos. They speed dated amongst each other and would rather be caught dead than to date anyone in the "Nobodys," but would occasionally date or speed date some in this next group:

The: **"Artsy- Talented- Popular-Attractive-Part/Nerd-Part/Hood-Part/Normal**'s": This was my group. We cared nothing about the latest fashions, but rather, expressed our fashion sense through what we could do with our clothes to create our own style. Some of our friends were in the "Nobodys," outside of that, we were friends amongst each other-that was of the utmost importance to us. Our group dated amongst each other, some would date within the "Nobodys" and the "Why the Hell's" if they summoned (and only if *they* summoned).

The: **"Wanna-Be's"**: Sigh. Rhetorically, I would have to ask: where do I start…

For starters, if this group of people's fashion choice consisted of white top shirts, white bottoms, white tennis shoes and (whether guy and girl), if they wore pink sweaters tied across their shoulders and they walked around with tennis rackets; it wouldn't be too far off from all their personas in school.

This was a pretty cool group (a very small part of them). The large part of this group would literally sicken you to your stomach if you let them (or hadn't eaten yet). They weren't trouble makers by any stretch of the imagination, but the large part of them would rather fight Goliath or ban together to hold open the mouth of a whale and fight tooth and nail than to digress to the clique in which *many* of them *really* belonged: "Nobody's," "Why the Hell's" or the "Artsy's."

It was funny because in truth, this large part really *did* consist of a mixture of "Nobodys," "Artsy" and "Why the Hell's" but you better not tell nobody God, because if you brought that truth out, you probably would have been in for a knock-down, drag out whatever-you-wanna-do-about-it-off.

The "Wanna-Be's" had one goal and one goal only: to be friends with, known by, connected to or connected with and/or besties with the "Be's." They *lived* for that. The "Wanna-Be's" dated amongst each other-period. The black guys (and black girls) in this group would rather be caught dead than to be caught dating a "Nobody," but would [in secret and *only* in secret] let it be rumored that he or she dated or kissed a black girl, or black boy, or an "Artsy"-and only *if* that "Artsy" was an "Artsy" that wanted to *be* a "Wanna-Be" or a wanted to *be* a "Be."

Eventually, most "Wanna-Be's" would get their chance in being a "Be," but the *actual* "Be's" were set in stone. "Be's" had the social power to make a "Wanna-Be" feel like a "Be" and especially depending on that "Be's" popularity at the time.

The bottom line was-since the "Wanna-Be" wasn't a set in stone "Be"-they would still have to take their place back in their "Wanna-Be" spot and remain happy that they were friends with, known by, connected to, connected with and/or besties with the "Be's." And in order to maintain their "Wanna-Be" slash want to be a "Be" image; it was best that they: deny that a "Nobody" existed, ignore the "Why the Hells" and act like they didn't know any "Artsy's" unless it was one of the "Artsy-10."

The **"Artsy-10:"** They were like: "reverse-moles." Moles of about ten guys and girls in our "Artsy" clique who if given the chance, would do anything to be a "Wanna-Be," and would *kill* to be a part of the "Be's." You could always tell when one of the "Artsy-10" got a chance to step out and hang out with the "Wanna-Be's" or "Be's." Because (for a short while) they would talk different, walk different and carry on a whole persona befitting of a "Wanna-Be" or "Be." They would feel *so* accepted and grateful that they stood a chance (even if it was a mere conversation with a "Wanna-Be" or "Be"). That would be enough to send them on these highs that (like clockwork because it was all a matter of time) the "Wanna-Be" and/or "Be" would send them *right* back into the clique to which they belonged: "Artsy- Talented-Popular-Attractive-Part/Nerd-Part/Hood-Part/Normal." Their little fantasies and hopes of actually being a "Wanna-Be" or "Be" (for good) never-*ever* came to fruition and they would steadily try: year after year. It was crazy to observe. Aya and my other friend Carren were two-tenths of one such type. It would be a mixture of pathetic and painful to watch their ups and downs as a result of it all.

The **"Be's"**: They were a mixture of *three types of people* and it was just this simple:

1-Either their parent or relative worked at the school (and/or had some control over the school program or any particular performance art or academic).

2-They were the kids whose parents were on a committee of givers who donated significant monies to the school (on a continuous basis).

3-They were close friends/besties of both. I repeat: close friends/besties of both. Not: known by, connected to or connected with. Their real friends and besties *only*.

"Be's" had their way with about 65% of the teaching staff. The teaching staff was kind of like a teaching staff at a college. In college, you have some professors who may have athletes as students, who pretty much have a "pass" in their class no matter what. Athletes' schedules are methodically chosen by their coaches and the athletic staff on a "preferred professor" basis: the professors who would always cut the athlete some slack because they are in cahoots with the sports program (secretly).

It was like that here, at our artsy school.

Probably about 65% of the staff was in cahoots with parents or relatives who worked at the school and/or had some control over the school program or any particular performance art or academic and as well, parents who donated money to the school.

So having to take a class with a "Be" could be quite the experience. Not as a result of the "Be's" behavior or presumptuousness (because they indeed were). The "experience" would come from the "Be's" real friends and besties or the "Wanna-Be's" behavior-that was the irony of it all.

The "Be's" besties, real friends and "Wanna-Be's" *loved* for it to be known that they too, were exceptions to most rules. Most all "Be's" were very assuming and presumptuous (subtly so). But they weren't pathetic or painful to observe. The "Wanna Be's" and the "Be's" real friends and besties were-at all times. "Be's" never had to do anything but just: be. They knew their place and knew it was solidified, and knew they had the most social power in the *entire* school-effortlessly.

All of that was what my dad did *not* know about this artsy school that he was so eager for me to get in. The doors had shut behind me, and the politics of the economic, political and social kind was a well-known secret that none of us ever talked about (in *either* group). It just was what it was. I'm just breaking it down (to *how* it "was"). I never explained it or broke it down to my dad because he would have taken my inclusion into that school to a whole new level, and I wasn't interested in that kind of fighting to get in and fighting to stay in kind of illusion that I was watching. It was really a circus act that neither one of them even understood.

When my dad had come to grab me out of my third grade class to do that school's paperwork, got me auditioned and in; he thought he knew-but he had no idea...

He merely expected that because I was multi-talented, I would get early training at a school that would hone in on that in a big way and from there-the world would be my oyster.

Well, unbeknownst to him, getting trained for the world to be my oyster-did not happen outside of evening recitals from well-rehearsed dance performances, drama recitals or art-exhibits for required classes. I tricked him into thinking that these performances, demonstrations and exhibits were major.

The bigger training and experience took place on the stage. That gave you the feel for what it would be like gigging in New York. The closest I got to that experience and on that stage (outside of my evening dance recitals) was auditioning for the major/school box office plays.

A callback list would go up. It had gotten to the point where I never had to check the first or second callback list-I made all of them. But when that final list would be posted, it was always 77% populated with the: "Be's" and "Wanna Be's." 10% Artsy's, 10% Nobody's and 3% "Why the Hell's".

Unbeknownst to my dad, by eighth grade (many years before Santana was ever a twinkle in my eye and had even started the school), when I started to take notice of the social politics and began to pay attention to the list of student's parents who donated big monies to the school-I totally quit auditioning. I would be obsessed with strolling that first floor area near the administrative offices watching rich parents with full-length mink coats stroll in and out of the principal and artistic director's office; either cutting checks or finding out why their child was the understudy rather than the actual lead in a major. I would run to the front of the building just to take a peek at their big expensive Jaguars, Mercedes and BMW's parked sideways-presumptuously knowing that the meeting they came for wouldn't last-because they knew all too well how their money talked and bullshit runs the marathon.

By eighth grade, I refused to be the bullshit running the marathon through callback list number two and higher. I started turning a deaf ear and a blind eye to it all. If you understood the social, economic and political dynamics (that at the age, I didn't have name for); you would have understood-like I did-how that social politic game went. I had zero interest in being a "Wanna-Be." I found too much comedy watching, listening to and hearing about the pressure and rollercoaster ride that some of them would go through to be where they were socially. It was so pathetic to me.

In hindsight it was *all* so pitiful; watching the five cliques outside of the "Be's (including me). The pathetic way that those who were in control of the performance art program, would come to classrooms and stand there like big suits-folding their arms and looking down from their eye-glasses and placing their hands on their chins, looking around at everyone and squinting their eyes like they were about to pick their next superstar. We would sit up with our backs arched straight and one-hundred watt smiles (looking all stupid and shit) from being told in advance that they would be coming through scouting for local commercials. No words were ever spoken, it was a classic case of the psychological Pavlov Dog Experiment.

By eighth grade, I quit barking and jumping. It never phased me anymore. I started turning my head to the direction of the window when the suits would show up. To myself, I would crack up laughing when they would leave-from how stupid some people looked-having no idea how that social politic game went. It was sad-watching my peers do just what I would do my first five years there for those suits (that were merely looking for the kid whose parents just strolled through with the mink coat-double-checking to see if the kid had the look for the next commercial they had just promised rich mom, rich dad).

It was hard not to, but I never told my dad about the politics that existed there because secretly, he too, was classist, elitist and insatiably ambitious and so was I, to an extent. Though I hated that school because of it-I understood what was going on.

And my dad (secretly) never forgave himself for having kids by a less than ambitious mother, so he was going to make at least one of us pay for it. Between Twin and me and my other brothers; I was the best fit. So he executed his plan, set me on the mark, put me in position and threw me into doors-that once closed behind me-he knew nothing about. He just knew I belonged and would have paid top dollar to put me where he wanted to see me: on a main stage even if it was up on a harness flying across that auditorium with a diaper on and sprinkling glitter throughout-that would suit him just fine. My dad played the game-always had. He had a formula for success and life: no sleep. To be the boss, you have to pay the cost-and usually, by any and all means necessary...

The only thing that made me happy there, were my friends-I loved my friends and two other teachers [outside of Ms. You Know Who, who respected me, knew my worth and talents]. I had nothing to prove to her outside of following her rules.

When I got home to the where I lived, my experience was altogether different.

If I say to someone (who is not from my hood: "my hood held me down,") that person would probably think I meant that my hood stifled me. But no, that school stifled me, but my hood "held me down" (up-in the highest esteem). I was fortunate because of that. And I always knew and was grateful for that.

Without my hood, I would have had no self-esteem or confidence, because that school would have broken me. When I left that school at 3:40p (many years before meeting Santana) my show began there-that was my main stage and bright lights with people cheering me on and appreciating being entertained by me at whim and request. My hood was my main stage, but while in school from 8a-3:40p; I was amongst a game of social politics that I refused to be the butt and bullshit of. That balance kept me grounded. Everything I learned and any skill I honed was the result of the ones who truly loved me, respected me and knew me-not the school I attended. My hood was merely disillusioned, bedazzled, and dazed by it all, because I was the only one from it-able to make it through those doors, that they (like my dad) knew nothing about-once they closed behind me.

In secret, I continued to let my dad (and even the people from my neighborhood) think that it was the school that was grooming me to blossom. Even Ms. You Know Who (who taught there) thought the same thing. I was learning, dreaming and inspired by way of her and my hood-not the school.

I wasn't learning shit at the school. I wasn't inspired there. I didn't dream there. That school wasn't preparing me for a life of what she and my dad thought I was attending there for. The school only taught me one thing and one thing only: the game of social politics, where by age thirteen, I was a pro at it and recognizing it. I *knew* my worth to people, my talents and what I was capable of. I didn't need that school to validate that for me-all for a financial, social and emotional large fee.

As far as I was concerned with my [dead dad], my faith and disinterest in the school plus my estrangement from him all worked out. I was no longer under his pressure in more ways than he knew (and little did he ever know)...

As far as I was concerned [with my mom on pulling me out of the school], it was a favor to me. Because little did she know, after about my eighth-grade year there, it only became important for me to attend because of the school's reputation and big name-in the eyes of other people. The school was something I could most certainly live without.

But now, I was faced with a decision to make and to decide if I could live with or without: this growing child inside of me. My mother merely felt that it would be distasteful for me to be in that type of school with a growing belly. She not only did what was best (and a favor to me), she also did what was natural for her and what she did best whenever she was faced with an important issue: run away from it, or ignore it away or send it away. So plans were made for me to be sent away to a home for pregnant girls that had a school campus but to me-was more like a pregnant jail filled with other pregnant and mean big-nosed bitches who like me, had a decision to make as to whether or not we were coming home with our brat, or give them to some happy couple waiting in the wings (which is what most did-as was my prospective decision) because I still had plans for a real life, with or without "real" love.

Couldn't necessarily say that Santana had any serious and major plans for his life after he graduated, because although I personally knew his creative and artistic talents; they were about as obscure to other people as about as obscure as what he was going to do in life *with* his talents.

Although I played a part in creating the feet for socks, mending socks were not in my plans. All I could see was a hard life, and a hard-working man; working hard for a minimum-wage job, coming home stressed, over worked and pissed at and resenting me.

No thank you (to that "life")...

16

SITUATIONS, TRANSITIONS & DECISIONS.

In the meantime during preparation for my transition and decision making process; my mother was up to her same ole "let me fuck with Santana" Jedi Mind Tricks. He was hard-working his ass off-continuously trying to be for me: a good man and a good dad. He took a job in the vicinity where my mom and I had moved to-which was in a whole other community a ways away from all of my school friends, umbrella friends and my TGGF.

Santana had come over to my house one day while I was gone to the mall with one of my big brother's girlfriends. By the time I made it home, Santana looked like he had been held hostage. The look on his face when I walked into the door was the type of sigh of relief that you can imagine from being rescued after being tortured. I found out that my mom and her friend Ms. Andrea-Dana's mom-had told Santana that I was gone out on a date-trying to explore my options, since it wasn't set in stone that I was going to keep the baby.

He had no reason not to believe her, because my stomach wasn't showing at all. Immediately, he had flashbacks on his cheating on me, so, he didn't know what to think. When I walked in on it and found out about what they had done to him, I screamed at my mother and her friend. I then walked back to tend to Santana and his hurt feelings, and there he was: standing there in his funny-looking work uniform, with the funny-looking polyester pants and the funny-looking pancake cap; looking like he was about to have a not-so-funny looking panic attack. Since the beginning of my pregnancy, he was about as pregnant and emotional as I was-we were both pregnant. I felt so bad for Santana-he could hardly breathe, he was so hurt. He just looked up at the ceiling at the light and held his head back; trying his hardest to hold his tears back. I reached out to hold him and he broke down and cried in my arms. I cried so hard with him. It was a sad day for the both of us. We had already had a lot to think about and were going through so much already, and my mother couldn't have picked a worse time to fuck with his head like that.

~~~~~~~~

Twin had still been on his send-off and vacay spot for rambunctious boys that my mom sent him to, and once he returned home, plans were still set in stone for him to go live with my [dead] dad. Mom was still on my don't ask, don't tell policy that I had asked her to adhere to-and especially at this time. It had been a couple years that I had been knee-deep in with this boyfriend of mine and now pregnant since last my dad saw me, so now was just a good a time as any for my mom to keep her mouth shut. She knew that by the time I would be showing, I would be good and gone off to the pregnant jail anyways.

My send-off would be coming around the time the new school-year was beginning.

The pregnant jail was a campus located about a half-hour drive away, where on the weekends, Santana and his mom (or sometimes Santana alone) would come get me. I would sometimes go home to my mom's house, and other times I would stay over in Santana's private cul de sac, neglecting to talk about what I was deciding to do with this "thing" growing inside of me. My way of not attaching myself to it-was to refer to it as an "It" or a "thing" versus referring to it as a baby or a child, as yet. I replaced getting attached to "It" by keeping in mind, my plans for a life that had no room for new feet. Because the first order of business was to complete my senior year of high school. I was insistent on graduating on time and the same year-as if my life hadn't been put on pause with this thing growing inside of me. With all the schooling I had missed (because of my mom wasting no time pulling me out before my belly even got a chance to get a bump), I had a lot of work to do.

Although through the pregnant jail, I could earn school credits, but the credits would not be enough to graduate on time-night school was my only option in addition to day school (full-time) plus summer school. I had already been looking at colleges I wanted to attend out of state and a couple nearby and in-state just in case this trial time away in the pregnant jail became too much to bear for Santana and me. That would let me know if I could handle being without him, although I knew in my mind-chances were-that Santana and I would not be together. For me, for a while, though I loved him; I was getting to the point where I was just going with the motions and being lead by my heart. I knew these mixed emotions weren't because of my pregnancy, because I never felt that way until he cheated on me. The newness, specialness and sacredness wasn't there for me like before. And even through the day before I found out that he cheated, I used to see forever with him.

17

UP, OUT & AWAY

The campus was so private, dim, and quiet that you could hear a pin drop.

I was so lonely that pregnant jail-one of the loneliest times that I could never imagine-it was claustrophobically unbearable and depressing. It really *felt* like "jail."

I spent a lot of time crying and sitting in my room alone: just-thinking...

After some time, I dried my tears and tried to toughed it out.

Though phones were free, and the comfortable little phone area was always available, I never used it anymore, after the one day and one day only-I placed a phone call home; crying to my mother about how lonely I was. She spit new idioms that she had thought of since last I saw her-all of them created to remind me that my being in the predicament I was in was a consequence of mine and Santana's actions.

No results or comfort with my mom, so I called my friend Dana whose voice had an all-too familiar sound, sort of like mine once did: as if the sun was calling her name and together: she, the sun, life and our friends, were playing a game of tag and running with the wind blowing through her free fingers. I did not want to interrupt her joy by dampening her sunshine with my tears that were falling like rain. I still managed to get through the conversation with a smile in my voice, but the truth was-I was now in a different element and my mind was echoing my mother's reminder that I was in the middle of a consequence of mine and Santana's irresponsibility. Dana had nothing to do with that, so I let her go as if nothing was wrong with me on the other end of that phone, but the truth was; everything was wrong-everything.

In search of comfort rather than conversation-just someone to listen to me while I sat there shaking and crying uncontrollably from feeling like I was about to have a nervous breakdown, who better to call than my accomplice and partner in my crime: Santana. He wasn't home. He too, was out with the wind blowing through his free fingers-most probably feeling the newness of being unattached at the hip that we stayed at conjoined at for many years. He probably didn't know what to do with himself, with me gone and put away for five point five of his seven days of the week.

I had to tough it out. I never liked feeling sorry for myself. So, after that day, I vowed never to pick up that phone again. I never even looked at it anymore. I decided it would be best to deal with the predicament I was in as best as I could and on my own. I was beginning to feel far too emotional for still having not made my final decision about whether or not I would be giving this thing up for adoption. I didn't want my emotional state to force me to give it away any more than I wanted my emotional state force me to get attached to it and keep it; merely out of being temporarily emotional.

I tried mingling with the other girls. I made friendly with three of the girls. Nobody really wanted to be friends with anybody. The way the pregnant jail was structured-we all had the option of having so much privacy that you really did not have to make friends. Most everyone took the privacy option, and so did I after a while. There were two other girls in particular that refused to be nice to me. I think they knew each other outside of the pregnant jail. They were unbelievably rude and mean on purpose. I think it was because they got jealous when they'd see Santana come get me every Friday, and kiss me guiltily as he'd leave on Sunday afternoon's after dropping me off. It was obvious that we were in love, at least once upon a time. Those two mean bitches never got visitors. One of the girl's fathers would pick them both up for some weekends home, but they'd remain on campus on the weekends, most of the time-snapping at one another.

Every girl was so full-bellied, pregnant, tired and mad. I was still able to make my way around just fine because I was barely showing-you could only tell that I was pregnant if I undressed, and then you could see a tiny little circular protrusion in front of me-from side view, only.

It seemed like overnight however, that thing sprouted inside of my belly like the sun hitting a flower that blossomed in a day. It made its presence known one morning after I woke up and masturbated. I lay there on my back while my stomach began to flutter rumble. It turned around and poked its butt in the air-sort of like how babies do when they are taking a nap. I felt so embarrassed. I was wondering if it knew what I had just done. The moment was cute, a little bit scary and a little bit creepy at the same time because I was at my bottom and it was in my belly-resting…in a child's place.

Considering the way I had been feeling, I needed that little bit of attention that thing inside of me gave me for that moment. I hadn't smiled and laughed like that in a while.

I proceeded to bathe and get ready for my day, and it did not move about anymore throughout that day. I guess it decided to rest…and stay in a child's place.

When morning came, I wanted to see if it would show its butt again. So I did it again.

I then lay there and waited to see what would happen.

It began to rumble just like the day before.

All of a sudden, it turned around and poked its butt in the air again. I sat up some so that I could see it better. It had poked its butt out so far that I could see where its little butt cheeks separated.

I covered my mouth and giggled-not wanting it to hear my voice and laughter. I felt so happy that I had some company-*finally*.

It hid throughout the morning and then all of a sudden, while I was in history class, at exactly 11:10am; it began to move about as if it was waking up. It ran to the left side of my stomach and kicked its foot.

That startled me. It then ran to the right side and kicked its foot. I tried to grab it. It ran back over to the left: kick! To the right: kick! It was so funny. I covered my mouth and laughed over and over again.

Day 3 and 4: It slept. After I did it-it woke up with its butt in the air. I smiled and lightly spanked its little booty and then rubbed it. It could feel me nurture it through my skin as it lay there and it went back to sleep while I bathed and prepared for my day.

11:10am into the morning. History class. It began to move about-waking up. "Time to play!" this rambunctious little must've thing said. It ran to the left side of my stomach and kicked its foot again. I was a little startled, but somewhat expecting it. It felt so funny-this life inside of my belly-this "real" life and living thing growing and moving about inside of me.

It then ran to the right side and kicked its foot-I tried to grab it. It ran back over to the left: kick! To the right: kick! Still, I covered my mouth and laughed-again.

Day 5 and 6: It slept. After I did it-it poked its butt in the air and I rubbed it gently. It was like I calmed it down because it went right back to sleep. I bathed and prepared for my day.

11:10am. History class. It began to wake up and start moving about-again. It ran to the left side of my stomach and kicked its foot, then ran to the right side and kicked its foot. I never could catch it, but it was fun trying though.

Throughout these days and moments, my mind started to play out scenes in my head of holding this thing in my belly from behind my belly and into my arms. I started feeling emotional about all inside of me that was literally protecting it and giving it life, while knowing that soon after being born into this world and right after taking its first breath of life; it would be handed over to be held not by me-but to the arms of someone else who is somewhere in this world having no idea about these special morning moments that I was sharing with this child, and wouldn't bit more understand the experience if I explained it to them.

I was feeling myself getting attached to "it"…my baby...

But into the lonely night by day 6, my mind began to play out the realities according to how things were looking in my life at that *very* moment; my mother's voice ringing in my head-continuously referring to my predicament as a "consequence" as if it were a punishment rather than a human life. I couldn't *imagine* what life would be like-bringing a baby into that house with her-that was punishment enough. I could see so clearly-her trying and make me feel punished for it every single day. From behind a door, if she couldn't handle my asking her if I could to go steady, then telling her I needed to get on the pill; there was no way in heaven she could handle a real-live crying baby from behind another closed door.

There I was, sitting up in that pregnant jail while life was still going on at home. My friends were living life and enjoying theirs, just like Santana was living his. If ever I needed time and attention-this was that time and the cure for feeling claustrophobic and lonely was merely a half-hour away. I wasn't that far away in distance that Santana couldn't make it during the week (in the evenings) for a visit or two. But he never took the initiative to do that. He was out in the wind enjoying his five-day a week, born-again freedom. Although it hadn't been decided as to whether or not I would be keeping the child, he never put up a fight or stood his ground about me giving the baby up for adoption. Yet he stood on many-a-floors of my mom's apartments crying *ugly* cries; holding on to me like nothing but death could keep him from me. I had seen him fight before. I knew how he could do when he fought for love and something that he really wanted. He didn't fight for this baby at all-not like he fought for me. He wasn't fighting the wind to get up here and see me with this child in my belly-not like the way he would fight to see me when I wasn't with-child. He was nothing like he would write to me in many-a-letters-talking about how he would fight for our (future) kids. That future was growing right now-inside of me without a fight being had for this kid, me, and from what I could see: our future, either.

I began to think about love and the reality of it and how it is never "forever." I reminisced about how when we first lost our virginity, his light-bulb head use to be sitting in that chair in my bedroom beaming just like one. I couldn't peel that fool off of me. We spent so much time honeymooning, letter-writing and all things unimaginable in our fairytale; yet he found it easy to lift a six-foot tall bitch off her feet and carry her upstairs as if she were a bride simply because she told him she was a virgin (too). So he stuck his dick in her-in the midst of us still honeymooning and me having lost my virginity with him (too), as if it didn't matter anymore and he was on to something new. My lonely lil' vacay at the pregnant jail plus what I learned from his cheating episode was slowing teaching me that whether it be love or sex; it's all good and right as long as it is in front of you-in the moment. Love seems to be only as good and true as it is in your face. Because the moment that the moment is over-it roams free. The biggest reward you get out of love is if somebody loved you back. But in the bigger scheme of things, you didn't do anything but teach them how to love and make love to another person. Virginity and the newness of things are physical trial basis' with expiration dates of the heart. People are here to learn love-lessons from each other until they end up with the one person [later on who at that time] will be in receipt of that person having finally gotten right: all that *you* taught *them* about love and making love. Santana and were merely were one another's first stop. I began to understand that no matter your age, "love" must really be this way.

I wanted and searched for a bright-side in this. But outside of a pretty baby in my arms-conceived by two people who once upon a time in this fairytale-loved one another, and were inseparable; I saw none. Except for the fact that the baby got a chance at *life*, so here we are, as we lay:

I'm back on "it," again…my tears and feeling sorry for myself is over. "It" lived, and I have to make it and take it from here…

Day 7: It slept through the morning because I didn't do it. I didn't do it because I did not want it to wake.

I did not want to see its butt. I did not want to smile. I did not want to touch or nurture it. I did not want it to expect me to nurture and touch it going forward. As if we had already bonded; it still raised while I lay there-as if my masturbating had nothing to do with waking it up anyways. This time, it raised as if it could read my mind and feel my resistance. This child insisted on waking with its butt in the air-regardless. I sat my head up some to look at it but I still refused to touch it. Instead, I gripped the sheets with my fingers and just stared at it like I was peeking; wanting it to put its butt back down. But this time, that baby wiggled its butt slowly and stretched it out farther than I had ever seen it do as if it wanted me to touch and smack its tiny little cute booty. I still refused to.

It lay there in its place…and went back to sleep. And I did the same.

Still, at 11:10am like literal clockwork, and while in my room watching television; it began to wake up and start moving about: "Time to play!" the rambunctious little thing must've said. It ran to the left side of my stomach and kicked its foot-ready to play.

I was stiff and stoic.

I didn't expect that…

My laugh from the 11:10am days previous turned into a frown.

It ran to the right side and kicked its foot.

I didn't reach for it.

It ran back over to the left: kick!

To the right: kick!

I still frowned and remained stiff.

This time, I tightened my mouth with resistance rather than covering it with my hand (with surprise, joy and laughter).

While I resisted, it insisted. Like never before, it was kicking and playing games in my belly as if was kicking conversation to my mind:

"You mean to tell me that you don't want me?" (kick!)

"I won't be a problem-I promise I won't get in your way!" (kick!)

"These pretty eyes-these little fat thighs?" (kick!)

"You mean to tell me you don't want me?" (kick!)

"Look ma! No hands!" (kick!)

"How come you don't want me?" (kick!)

"Wait'll you see these chubby cheeks!" (kick!)

"My skin is as smooth as my butt!" (kick!)

"When I'm out of your belly and you hold me underneath my arms, you can look me in my face while I yawn and stick my butt out in person!" (kick!)

I remained stiff.

This time, it tried something different. Instead of it lying on its stomach and sticking its butt out the front of my belly; it turned sideways and stuck its butt out on the side of my belly-as if was showing off for me.

Still, I did not reach to rub it or spank its little booty, although I thought about it.

But then, I gathered my thoughts, emotions and attachments to it-and in my mind, I said (back) to it:

"Nah, I've got living to do. After I hand you over, I get a second chance to do it right this time. Can't mess it up. I love you and I gave you a life to live."

"Look ma! No hands!" (kick!)

I kept my hands in my lap...

"Look ma! No hands!" (kick!)

I continued to keep my hands in my lap-balling my fists tightly.

"Look ma!"

I kept my fists balled up-no hands.

It rested in its place…

Day 8: Morning came.

It slept.

I did not do it, even though I knew It did not need me to-to remind me that it was there.

I did not want it to wake.

I did not want to see its butt.

I did not want to smile.

I did not want to touch or nurture it.

I simply did not want it to expect this of me going forward.

Unlike yesterday and previous mornings when I'd wake and lay there, shortly thereafter-it would wake and raise. But this time-it did not.

I got scared.

I gave in, and did it-just to see if it would wake and raise.

It still did not wake or raise.

I sat my head up some to see if it would, but it did not.

I lay there and went back to sleep, right along with it.

11:10am.

It's history...

Into the morning it did not move about or begin to kick and play-at all.

I lay there waiting to see if it would, but it still did not move.

"Ma...no hands?" (no kick...)

I lay back down with my fists balled up. Tears rolled down my face but I held on to the sheets between each finger tightly...tight like the rest of my life depended on it..."

1) How did you come up with the idea for this book? The original 'idea' (which began in 1997) was this same story and pretty much the same concept. However, as a novice-then; my writing style was indicative of what was "popular" at that time: the self-help/spiritual guru craze. And even though my story *was* what it *is* (then and now), I had the book broken down as such that I was kind of "evaluating" each chapter and speaking to my readers as if I was identifying a problem & providing a lesson by finding a solution for it. There were three big chapters: "Innocence," "Naivete,'" and "Sophistication." But the "lessons" were listed in categories of how we evolve. First by: learning ourselves, then earning ourselves (having being done by way of surrendering things that stunted our growth and evolvement-be it by way of people, certain situations, circumstances etc.)

I had completed the manuscript (which ended up being 600 pages). When I took a step back from it and evaluated it after some time, I started *hating* it-badly. I got discouraged. So I sat the manuscript down-for **years**.
In 2000, I picked it back up and started to "fine-tune" it. And that's when my feelings of *being* discouraged turn into courage. Because I began to re-write it **honestly** and from *my* voice-instead of trying to interject what the "new what's-happening" was (that self-help/spiritual market).
I'm already a spiritual person just-by nature. So I had a long talk with myself. I told myself to stop trying to write to please a whole world of people-so as to not offend, appall or isolate anyone. In short: BE YOURSELF ANGELA. The only way I could "be myself" was to write: introspectively, reflectively, and efficaciously. I had to tell myself to let the motivational/inspirational/self-help gurus (who define themselves as that) do their thing, and me-do mine. And in order for me to be myself and do my own thing; I had to come to realization that I was *indeed* going to offend, appall and isolate some people (in the world). I struggled with that. But I dealt with it.
I had to condition myself, to believe in myself by saying: *"so what, there is an audience out there that will appreciate you simply being yourself. And since you are naturally spiritual and a good storyteller; narrate your story as such that if there is any self-help, motivation and inspiration to be found within it; allow the reader to find it for themselves within the message in the story. Narrating and storytelling is your strength, so stick to that-even if you only have ten readers who*

love you. Do not try to please everybody. People who like you-will find their way to you and stick to you." That is the talk I **had** to have with myself. And after conditioning myself to write honestly and from the heart (introspectively, reflectively, and efficaciously); that 600-page manuscript looked a complete mess to me-how stupid and fake I sounded trying to be a little bit of myself plus tell a story, but at the same time, trying to be something that I wasn't-simply because sententious guruism was popular.

So in order to do it *my way*, I put out of my mind; having an audience of ten, one-hundred, one-thousand, ten-thousand or one-hundred thousand. I allowed myself to be my own audience. I then taped to the wall, these words when I began the re-write:
-Introspective
-Reflective
-Self-Efficacious
Although the concept and story was still in the crux of the manuscript; it required a complete literary overhaul. Page for page, and paragraph by paragraph; I was reading from the manuscript's (fakeness) and had to turn to the computer and say: *"Okay, now write it how you really wanted to write it. Say it how you really wanted to say it-and without fear of being judged and feeling the pressure to be apart of the guru market-share. Just do you-Boo."*
It was one of most the liberating but expensive, emotionally and creatively taxing experiences I had never gone through. Because the re-write had taken me more time to do-than it actually took for me to write the book itself. That experience (though it took years to discover) taught me a *big* lesson in being comfortable in my own writing skin: that even if my style or "way" wasn't the "new what's happening-" as long as I remained true to myself from start to finish; the task will be smooth and nothing but a total labor of love that will surely birth nothing but pretty little unique babies with their own look.
The lesson: be your own guru-your own way. Even if in the end, they have to create a genre around you…

2) Why the title? And how did it come about? The original title was called: "Keeping Secrets." I gave it that title because (as you know from reading the story) "Angie" (the main character) talks about many things that were kept secret, and how she had grown so accustomed to the "covert;" that almost by second nature, she was "pro-vert," (with all that was secret and covert). But then in the middle of my re-write, I discovered there were so many *situations* within the story surrounding, and within the main character: "Angie," that I felt compelled to change the title to: "Angie Situation."

3) Speaking of *"so many situations within the story, surrounding, and within the main character: 'Angie.'* " All that is packed in to her journey, life and experiences within this book; the reader learns a whole lot about: bullying, peer-pressure, molestation, sexuality, tween growing pangs, the mentor-mentee relationship, sexuality, sexual identity, bi-sexuality, teenage love and rebellion, teenage angst, the parent-child relationship (father-daughter/ mother-daughter), elitism, classicism and teenage-pregnancy. Did you have to do a lot of research in order to bring so many important, taboo, and heavy issues into the story? Scientific research-no. I went with and wrote on life as I know it, experienced it, heard tale of, supposed, witnessed and observed-period.

4) It is interesting to read this story from the voice of "Angie" (the story's main character) and her thoughts behind the goings on. Yet, we can clearly see all the other characters involved in the story as well. We know their personalities without you going in heavily on physically "describing" them and making your readers paint- by-number/page for page; trying to bring those characters to life through extensive physical description and excessive dialogue. It's like, you go right in to narrating your characters, and as we read on, we already know what they look like, what type of person they are, and how and why they do what they do within their role/ character without a lot of description and dialogue about them-in order to bring them to life. How did you manage to do that and why? When I write, I like to write how I like to read. And when I read, I want to read as though I am reading someone's diary. I want to read as though someone is telling me a story: uninterrupted-uninterrupted by my asking questions and uninterrupted by excessive quotations and dialogue. To me-a book is just like a diary. When we kept a diary, we didn't write a lot of dialogue and quotations in order to describe a conversation, secret, desire or happening. And when we talked about a *person* in our diary, we didn't go heavy in on describing them. We described them within the context of talking *about* them.
Don't "remind" me that I am reading a book. Make me *feel* like I am reading a diary (or watching a movie).
The "rule" in (fiction) writing is dialogue.
The "rule" of Angela Sherice fiction is "narration" and some dialogue (when absolutely necessary).

Because when you think about it, when a person buys a book and goes to tuck themselves away in the corner of a couch or an area to read it, they almost do it like it's a secret. (Take a look around at people at the bookstore-next time you go in). And when they go off to read a book, they tuck themselves away like they are hiding a secret. They want to be left alone to read [it]. When you catch someone staring at the book in your hand at the library or bookstore, what do you do? You draw back and frown, just like you would with a letter in your hand. Words are emotionally powerful (and personal). How often is it that two people get together and cuddle up in the corner of a couch and read out of the same book together? That visual is odd isn't it? That (to me), is because the reader wants to be a voyeur. And for me (in my opinion), I think it (subconsciously) forces the reader to *think* while reading (when there is too much quotation dialogue and description).

I feel that as a writer, if you are thorough enough in your storytelling; you can build the character's personality, their description and the scene right in your readers head through good narration and storytelling versus too much quotation-conversation (dialogue) and list-like description.

The five senses are *magical*. I'm an extreme "sensualist." And to me-reading is as personal as it is sensual, especially novel/fiction. Your words, your writing, and your storytelling can send your voice narrating to a reader's head like a movie in front of their eyes, and theme music in their ears. Too much dialogue (quotation-conversation) and description in order to build a scene makes a reader think and ascertain rather than see and voyeur. Readers tuck themselves away because they want to be a voyeur. I insist on allowing them to voyeur when they open up my book. I did all the thinking when I wrote it. None of the five senses require "thought." I just want the reader to voyeur and enjoy.
As a writer, I do not treat a book or novel any less different than a diary or a handwritten letter.

5) Speaking of characters. Some of your characters, you do give actual names to, while others-you give names like: "Ms. You Know Who," "Ms. Beautiful," "Painful Pam," "TGGF," "Basketball Lena," etc. That is very interesting, but why do you do that?
I do that almost for the same reason I elaborated on in the previous question. As a writer, I have the responsibility to take full control of how I deliver my story. And as I stated in the (previous) response,

narrating the story works best for me so that I can allow my readers to sit back and watch a movie in their head by the words that their eyes are seeing-line for line. In doing so (using names like: "Ms. You Know Who," "Ms. Beautiful," "Painful Pam," "TGGF," "Basketball Lena," etc.), challenges me to make sure I have done a thorough enough job in narrating my character's personalities, and what significance they play in a scene. And in having delivered that, what they *do* should be more memorable than what their name is.

It's just like watching a movie or television show. When we are telling someone about something that we watched once or for the first time, we may be talking about ten different people within that movie or television show. We may be able to recall two or three of ten of their names (definitely not all ten). But one thing we *will* remember about *all* ten of them is: what they did, what they wore and what their role was in the movie or television show. In recalling or re-enacting the movie to someone, when we don't recall the name-we will snap our fingers and say: "the one with the light-blue suit on-who showed up late to the meeting!" …(and recall the name after that-if at all).

Well, for me [if the moment hits me while writing, I feel that because of the role he may have played in my book] but that my reader may not recall his name; the fact that I know I was thorough enough in narrating the scene and the character, I leave myself with the *option* to call him: "Michael," or call him: "The Late Man in the Light Blue Suit"

As I stated before-two things: As a writer, I respect my reader enough to allow them to relax and voyeur. I don't want them to have to snap their fingers and "think" when trying to recall a character from any of my books. I've already done the thinking for them (in that regard). I just want then to "feel." It's no different than they saying: "people will not remember exactly what you said to them, but rather, how you made them feel."

That's what I mean when I say that I am an "extreme sensualist." An extreme sensualist doesn't just use their own eyes; they try to use someone else's eyes to see what they see, touch what they touch, smell what they smell, taste what they taste and hear what they hear, as well. An "extreme sensualist" will go the extra mile to *see* (and intermix): smell, taste, touch and sound, the same way a blind man has to go that extra mile to *hear* (and intermix): sight, touch and smell.

It may sound excessive and confusing to you, but I am the mother of a blind child so for years, my senses are like that of a blind person. I've

had to see, smell, touch, taste and hear for two people practically all my life, so for me-sensuality/the senses is second nature.
That being said, as a writer-I oversee my reader's senses like I've had to learn to oversee my child's senses-with him.

So in that regard, that's how the naming method fell into place for me. And in overseeing while writing, the task of remembering character's names takes me away from delivering a good story that my reader can experience. And as I said before, from a creative standpoint, I let go of trying keep up with the "new what's happening's." When I let go of trying to be that genre that hindered me from delivering good storytelling, I also stuck with all things (creatively) that worked for me-for my reader-as well.

So by my book "Michael" (the man in the light blue suit who showed up late for the meeting) might be: "The Late Man in the Light Blue Suit," so that my reader can move on. I'm not going to tie their brains up with trying to remember "Michael" by name when there may be nine other characters within the story with names as well. They're not necessarily going to remember all ten characters' names, but they will remember what all ten characters did, (and how those characters made them feel).

6) How has writing "Angie Situation" changed you, if at all, in any way? It humbled the hell out of me! Because (just like all novice writers feel) once that first manuscript is "completed," I thought I was ready for the literary world. In addition to that, you couldn't convince me that my manuscript wasn't blessed after the fact that in October '97, I had even gotten it to sit across of the desk at Oprah Winfrey's. And the fact that it was 600 pages of blood, sweat and tears, had me feeling like the rest of my literary career and process would be easy as pie. I felt like I had almost arrived after hearing all those voices in my head of the ghosts of millions of people chanting: "I always wanted to write a book." Well, I had done it. And to add homage to honor (after countless query letter mailings) a major New York publisher-Kensington Books did the proverbial rarity: wrote back and told me they were interested in reviewing some sample chapters of my manuscript after my writing and mailing to them-that winning query letter that piqued their interest.

"So step aside world-here I come!"

All up to that point was the high, stimulated by ups and downs at the fact that Kensington began asking for a few different sections of the manuscript versus simply asking for the entire manuscript. It annoyed me, and I couldn't understand why, until some time had passed and eating that humble pie: when I got the letter that they were going to pass on it. The only crumb I had left was the fact that I "almost" got picked up (maybe)-which still meant nothing, since "almost" never counted for anything. That shook my faith in the book, so I closed it for three years and went on to write and complete three other manuscripts (to feed my "I can write a whole book" ego). One book in which a smaller publisher was interested in publishing (my astrology book): "in about two years" from date. I was serious about writing, and two years was a lot of time to just hang around-happy, when I knew I still had the book ("Keeping Secrets"/"Angie Situation") lingering in my head.

By this time, it had become a handy-dandy footstool for all those years. I picked the book back up after three years, and dusted it off. As I began to look at it all over again, I could see it with a different set of eyes. I had done a lot of living, loving, thriving and growing (as a writer) and could now (finally) see what I suspect Kensington saw: The book's story was the "diamond," but the rest of it was fluff in the rough. The fluff was in the way-a distraction-and better suited for a whole other book (all the rhetoric and "lessons" of learning, earning, and surrendering-as mentioned in question number one).
 So I began to re-write it by being myself and writing in my own voice, versus trying to write so "safe" so as to not offend or appall any particular reader. In addition to that-I could clearly see what parts needed to be cut out, but it was interwoven so well with the storytelling that it was *very* hard to do-very hard to get to that diamond (buried) within the book. I suspected that editor knew if she asked for that entire manuscript-she would have turned me down immediately. Because after growing as a writer, I (myself) could tell that regardless what parts of a manuscript an editor asks for, the story should still flow and be able to be followed-regardless the break or interruption. Those certain sections, regardless which ones were asked to be sent via query, could tell a lot about the amount of editing that would have to be done to it in order to make it a marketable book that would resonate with readers and sell.
I had to do some creative and personal soul-searching and reminiscing. Over those few years, I would allow some of my close work-friends, associates, and friends read the manuscripts and I would end up having

conversations (and even handwritten letters) from them revealing to me-many things within the story they could relate to and had experienced. That's when I realized that the diamond was in the story and the storytelling, not the fluff (surrounding it).

I could clearly see it-but not until after all those years.

The diamond was interrupted with too much "teaching." The attractiveness and thick of the book was in the story. Inter-mixing both (the storytelling and the teaching) made the book run all over the place. I could finally see that Kensington sure as hell did not want to deal with all of that. It was a full-on, knock-down drag-out editing overhaul that even I (myself-the writer) did not want to tackle. So if I didn't want to do it, how could I expect them to?

My eyes and novice didn't know that, then. I was too busy being "impressed." I had to get rough and real with myself. First, by dropping and letting go of all that I had been "impressed" with:
-the fact that the manuscript lay across Oprah's desk once upon a time
-the fact that it got a second glance by a major New York publisher
-the fact that the manuscript was "600 pages" of a story
-the fact that I proved to my ego that I could write an entire book quicker than a person could write a love-letter

I had to slow down and get real with myself.

In getting real with myself, I had to have the same conversation with myself, and give myself the same advice that I would give to someone else who would ask me if they were in my shoes: *"you can remain impressed with those "impressionables" that really mean nothing anymore, other than the fact that you have a manuscript of "600 pages" that too, mean nothing. Because until those 600 pages are re-written right, you just have 600 pages of words on paper. Get over yourself and get over being impressed about something that amounted to and produced-nothing (for you or anyone else). Get to work on those 600 pages. Get to the crux and diamond that people are responding to and resonating with first: the story. Save the guru-ism and teaching for another book. Until then, those 600 pages will sit there and always serve no-body and no-thing until you do it right-by serving it like you (really) mean it. After that-then be 'impressed' ...with yourself. Because one thing is for sure: a good story-teller can still always 'teach' if he told a good story-the way it's supposed to be told. Whereas a good teacher can just- 'teach.' "*

7) "Angie Situation" was at one time, a stand-alone novel.
Now it is a trilogy. How'd that happen? I study the business and the

market as a publisher, an editor and a writer. It became a trilogy rather than a stand alone novel because in studying the market, you will eat even *more* humble pie and be forced to put your preconceived notations about how things are done-down. And in getting myself unimpressed with the fact that I had completed a "600 page manuscript, I had to remind myself that people aren't anymore impressed with a 600 paged book any more than they are with a novice bragging about having written any *number* of books. ONE good 100 paged book can vibrate, sell and resonate for twenty years. Times are getting tough, people are busy and attention spans are getting shorter. No one wants to read a 600 page book. However, a 200 paged book was more reasonable. Therefore, what was once 600 pages was eventually divided by 2 and made into a trilogy-broken down by its three main chapter titles: "Innocence," "Naivete,'" and "Sophistication." It made no sense to try and stuff an entire story that [in "Innocence"-alone] has a storyline built around issues dealing with: bullying, peer-pressure, molestation, sexuality, tween growing pangs, the mentor-mentee relationship, sexuality, sexual identity, bi-sexuality, teenage love and rebellion, teenage angst, the parent-child relationship (father-daughter/mother-daughter), elitism, classicism and teenage-pregnancy. So imagine what "Naivete,'" and "Sophistication's" storylines around *it* are going to contain? That's all too much for one book. Therefore, I made it a trilogy.

8) What (if anything) has surprised you the most about "Angie Situation" or since writing it? That so many people identified with some and most all parts of the main character and the storylines. And as a result, brought up a lot of old wounds and fond memories-alike, and as well; they still got those "lessons" that I wasted so much time trying to inter-weave into the story-anyway! Because the story provoked a lot of thought, consideration and proposed questions for many answers they thought they already had, while providing a resolve where there were once questions. I was surprised, humbled and inspired by that. That is what kept telling me that regardless how bad I ignored the book, there are people out in the world that needed it more than I ignored and suppressed it because my bruised ego wanted to battle it. I had to earn the right to write the book and eventually surrender to doing so, as well. To do anything else or start another book without finishing what I started was less than acceptable to my spirit-both creatively and personally. The book came back to bite at me one-too many times. Now, I know and have surrendered to the reasons-humbly so.

~READING GROUP GUIDE~

1) Although it happened some 20+ years prior, during a conversation with her mother, Angie revealed some of what had gone on in her life (with regard to her being molested) whereby, she (herself) was taken aback by her mother's "fresh like it had just happened yesterday" kind of response. In the book, Angie stated that because she was participating, enjoying [and in one particular case]: even "seducing" one of her offenders; she never regarded her being violated as "molestation," and always had a hard time seeing herself as a victim (although she was a child).
a. How did that reach you, or make you feel?
b. What or how did that make you think about cases like that?
c. Have you ever heard of such a reaction or misunderstanding/ misinterpretation coming from a victim of molestation?
d. Angie also stated that because she didn't go on to having deviate fetishes and thoughts and desires surrounding pedophilia, porn addiction, drugs, prostitution, bed-wetting, acting out, other behavioral problems etc; she just didn't think her being molested affected her in any way. In having read [book1/Innocence] of the trilogy; do you think that what happened to her manifested in any way and perhaps showed up in other ways? (Do not interject any thoughts or opinions about other excerpts or sneak peeks that you may have read off her website from book2/Naivete').

2) Do you think that Angie and her TGGF ever grow out of that situation they had going on?
a. Do you think it was a "phase" or something that will probably continue or re-surface in book2/Naivete' or book3/Sophistication?
b. Do you think the TGGF will end up being a mere BFF as Angie gets older in book2/Naivete' or book3/Sophistication?

3) How do you feel about "Ms. You Know Who?" Do you think that she dropped the ball too soon or do you think that (as woman herself-who too I am more than sure, experienced that teenage love and rebellion phase); felt that it was too much to contend with?
a. Do you think she could have handled it any more differently than she did? How would you have handled such as situation? (If you were "Ms. You Know Who").

b. Thus far, in having only read (and sticking strictly to this book1/ Innocence), how would you guess that Angie's life would have turned out had she followed through with Ms. You Know Who' "life plan" that she had mapped out for her-under her mentorship. (Think about and consider all situations that happened through to the end of this book1/Innocence).

4) How and what do you feel about Angie's mother? (Everything: what type of person she was, what she did, what she didn't do, what she should have done, what she could have done differently) etc.

5) How and what do you feel about Angie's father? (Everything: what type of person he was, what he did, what he didn't do, what he should have done, what he could have done differently) etc.

6) What do you feel about life in general, as compared to what Angie's situation and feelings were (with regard to the artsy-school she attended)?

7) What do you feel about Santana? Do you think they will break up and get back together and end up together throughout the 3-books/ trilogy and live that "happily ever after" in spite of all that had gone on thus far? (Do not interject any thoughts or opinions about other excerpts or sneak peeks that you may have read off her website from book2/Naivete'). What do you think will become of them (together)?

8) What is your interpretation of what was going on at the very end of the book-at "Day 7" through "Day 8" (the last 4 pages of the story)?

BONUS QUESTION
So, she (Angie) mentioned that thanks to Madonna's song "Papa Don't Preach" ringing in her head and playing on her heart; she could not term the pregnancy. Although we do not know what is going to become of that child throughout the trilogy, hypothetically speaking, if so-with Madonna having adopted all these kids, she's got another one out here she doesn't even know about huh?

In order to understand the joke, you would have to know that Madonna's adopted a few kids. :)

Find out what happens next, in Angie's life-in the sequel:
"Angie Situation (*NAIVETE')":

Chapter One

We had the time set-down to the literal minute that we would all need to finally spend time together.

Shana's mom would be leaving out for her club meeting at about 6:30p, but would be walking back into the building at exactly 9:25p. If all goes well, we all should be good and out by then.

We made plans to get together over at Shana's house on that cold November 4th day, where Shana would be cuddled up in her bedroom with his friend Wes. And he and I would be snuggled up on the comfy living room sofa by the door- you know: talking.

Shana and Wes tucked themselves back into her cozy bedroom-door closed, while he and I had the luxury of looking at the front door while we talked. My heart was beating fast. I was shaking like the last leaf on a tree.

"Come here and stand up, stand right here-right here in front of me," he said to me with a deep frown in his brow, strategically positioning me in front of him like a chess piece.

"Why?" I asked repeatedly all the while, allowing him to position me.

"I just want to look at you," he responded.

He began to run his hands down my arms, waist, hips and thighs without saying a word. It was weird to me: his touch, his way, the scene-everything. I couldn't tell if I was turned on, scared or both. I think it was both but I was so afraid to allow myself to be aroused enough to respond, so I stood there.

He then lifted my shirt up, grabbed me by the waist, and then turned me around so that he could now look at me from the back. I cooperated by still allowing him to turn me in circles like he was admiring something that he was about to buy, take home, and eat. When I made my way back around to standing in front of him, he moved closer to the edge of the couch while looking up at my face as if he was asking for permission, yet, nothing came out of his mouth. He placed his hands around my ass and something finally came out: "Why do you always wear things to cover your butt? You can still see it," he said-bluntly.

That caught me off guard and made the moment even more awkward for me. I reached to pull my shirt back down while quickly removing his hands from around me as if to convey the message: "*You blew it!*" to him.

He ignored the gesture. He then stood up to turn the kitchenette light on then turned off the living room light in the room where we were.

He sat back down and proceeded with more instructions: "Stand back right here," he asserted.

He was so awkward and technical. I was so nervous and nervous. When he reached underneath my shirt again, I jumped back a little bit- not wanting him to touch my stomach. He was going straight for my breasts anyway; grabbing them while letting out an awkwardly aroused sigh that sent chills through my body as he began to caress my breasts fervently.

Before I knew it, my pants had hit the floor along with my shirt and all the rest of my clothes. He scooted back on the couch for me to get on top of him. I grabbed his dick and thought hard about mounting him, and just going for it-only because I could tell that was what he was expecting and positioned himself for me to do.

I wasn't quite ready to do it though.

He had positioned himself about as blunt, awkward and assertive as he was in conversation that whole evening already. I was powerless the whole night: from the conversation, his touch and this very moment. I needed some time to think, even though my clothes were off of my body.

Although I knew he was laying there waiting for me to mount him, I could not do it. I froze. My mouth froze as well. I wanted to tell him that I needed him to enter me first-before I could mount him. At the point of intercourse and entry, I had a thing about being laid on my back, missionary or any way submissive and "in receipt-of," first- before the party could begin. It always seemed like that was they way it was supposed to go. It turned me on. I gestured to let him know how I wanted it without dripping a word from my frozen mouth. He cooperated. He laid me on the couch, folded my legs toward my chest and gently slid himself into to me. At that very moment, there were fireworks woven in between his moans, grunts and breathlessness. I had no idea this was going to be like this. I felt like a fucking virgin. It felt so good that I began to cry. I didn't know what was happening to me at this moment. I just couldn't process it at all. His shaking and deep breathing lead the whole moment as I followed his lead by slowly meeting his manly thrusts deep into me.

We were fucking as if each long stroke was something that we both wanted to last forever. We must have sound like two cats in heat.

He jumped, yelled out and pulled out of me as if he was trying to stop himself from cumming so soon: "Angie, please-please get on top of me, I want to talk to you," he pleaded. I could do it this time. By now, if he asked me to stand on my head I probably would have.

He lay on his back.

I got on top and mounted him. My legs were shaking nervously like a doe struggling for strength. I was afraid to grab him and put him inside of me, but rather-hoping he would take the lead again.

He did.

With his right hand, he grabbed his dick while holding my ass with his left hand and slid himself back into me, biting his bottom lip as if he was singing his favorite song; thrusting into me as if he was making moves to the beat of that very same song. It was awesome. All I could do was throw my head back and bite my own bottom lip.

He went from biting his bottom lip to puckering them and frowning with a kind of pleasure like he was in full concentration of the circumference of my warm vagina that gripped him so tightly. He nodded his head back and forth in total disbelief yelling "ah shit," repeatedly-as if after this night, it was going to be some trouble...

It was explosive.

It was weird because initially, I wasn't in the mood to fuck him and he hardly gave me the foreplay that I was so used to and I certainly didn't give him the foreplay that I loved to give. I wondered if my pussy would even get wet enough for him. But from the moment he lay me down and entered me-I exploded and it was on and popping from there.

His awkward lovemaking was slowly turning me on. I felt like I could get used to his way. His touch-every sound, every facial expression he made, turned me on. Every step of the way, he surpassed my arousal times ten. So much so that I could barely fuck him back. I remained frozen stiff throughout the entire fuck. I could hardly move-consistently. He dominated everything all the way down to the way he fucked and thrust me. It was as if he just wanted to take and scrape it all. I eventually allowed him to use me every which way he wanted to. I had no other choice.

This second, time felt like what my first time was supposed to be like. I didn't know the how-many-eth time it was for him and I didn't care. I just knew that from the moment I was with him this night, I felt like a virgin-all over again.

He more than busted my cherry (so it seemed), he also busted my fucking tear ducts because I cried silently while biting my own bottom lip as well, from the very moment he entered me throughout the entire fuck-the whole night. It felt unbelievable. I was a combination of: embarrassed, horny, virginal, sad, happy, worried, uptight and aroused. He didn't know what to think. All he could do was let all that he had inside of him-out, while he looked up at me wiping my tears:

"I wanted this so bad. I wanted you so bad. I thought about you for so long. You don't know how bad I wanted this moment. I'm so happy right now-girl, I'm so happy right now," he confessed.

I still could not say anything back-I was still frozen. He was still doing all the fucking and grinding deep up into me while my eyes continued to roll in my head and my tears rolled down my face. I believed what he said. He had been fucking me that night like he had been alone with me inside his mind and in his dreams he kissed my lips a thousand times, and sometimes saw me walk outside his door.

Hello…

I was stunned.

I placed my hands on top of one another, covering my lower stomach with my fingers and kneading my pussy-in an effort to keep his focus on and into my pussy only.

"Angie-you got some good pussy. This pus' is gooo-ed," he pronounced and grunted, with his lips puckered again-looking like he was some thug, yet he was far from one. He seemed to pucker his lips when it would get good to him. I liked that. It was especially exciting because I always had a thing for opening my legs for my lover. So the thought of mounting him with my legs spread apart while he looked right down into my world as he slurped through his lips, was exciting to me. He would grunt, pucker and stare at my crouch-while enjoying the rhythm he had going; thrusting himself upward and deep into me with that concentrating look on his face-listening to the sound of himself going in and out of me but puckering his lips and looking into my world as if he could see the circumference of it all in x-ray vision.

It was a mess between us. He was digging from inside of me-a wet rush down onto him that was making all kinds of sounds that he was enjoying like good music. Each thrust into me seemed to pop sparks inside of me, yet I still couldn't respond. He had a firm grip onto me and fucking me as if the top of me was not even there.

He kept grunting and stroking up and into me harder as if he was going to fuck a verbal response out of me. He grabbed me by my waist and held me stiff, then began to grind up into me like he was punishing me for not fucking him back or telling him how much I loved it. I refused to say a word and do anything more than bite down on my jowls and gasp and moan-out for mercy. He was working hard and enjoying it so much. It was almost like had I told him I loved it-the fuck wouldn't have been as good. I couldn't talk if I wanted to, I could only gasp and squeal into the air. I was too stunned and speechless.

The more I gasped and squealed with my head falling back, the harder, deeper and slower he grinded up into me. I dug my nails into his arms, biting down on my teeth until my jaws and ears wanted to pop out the sides of my head.

I couldn't take it anymore.

I fell into his chest and bawled myself up like a snail while he lifted his legs up-nearly folding me; thrusting even deeper, and harder up into me. In an instant, he grabbed my shoulders to look me in the face: "Angie-Angie! Say you'll have my lil' girl, say you'll have my baby. Say it-say you'll have my baby."

Little did he know, those were the magic words that snapped me out of the daze I was in: immediately. I wanted him out of me, and I wanted me having this lil' girl from out of his mind: immediately.

"No, no!" I finally spoke.

"Please!" he kept asking-desperately. "Please have my lil' girl."

I could hear him near gargling-so I quickly lifted off of him but held my face into his chest while holding his dick with my both my hands; covering it completely as if I did not want any air to get in and spoil his moment or change what it was his dick was feeling while being inside of me.

I was insulating. He was ejaculating. I was jerking him.

I made sure every ounce rested in my hands-not inside me.

I wanted off of him-but he kept holding me like he didn't want to let me go.

As we got dressed and after, I never responded to anything he said to me for the duration of his stay-at all. I just wouldn't talk to him. I froze up-all over again.

It was time for Shana to make he and Wes leave so that we could straighten up the house before her mom came back home.

I walked towards the kitchen away from him and he came following me, backing me into the wall. He kneeled and dropped down to his knees to look up at me almost apologetically and like he had a 70's Billy-Dee Williams moment. It was so manly and romantic-his way.

The way he frowned his brows and puckered his lips as if to say "ooh" when he would talk to me. It was a combination of lust and adoration; almost like my pussy was written all over his face. That's what turned me on more than anything about him. He looked at me the same way he did after we fucked, the way he did before we fucked. The same way he looked at me standing outside talking to me, in Wes' car and everywhere else. That look was there before and after.

He was so awkward, but sexy.

I was feeling just as awkward as I did before we fucked-standing there feeling just as awkward after. No less awkward while standing outside talking to him, in Wes' car and everywhere else.

I held my head downward but turned to the right some-not wanting him to look at me in the face. His placed his thick fingers to the sides of my face-trying to secure and center my face in his hands to look at him:

"Please talk to me. Tell me if I made you do something you didn't want to do?" he kept saying, over and over.

"No, I wanted it. I just have something on my mind, that's all," I responded.

To him, that must have sounded like this was goodbye forever:

"Angie, tell me. Is this the last time I'm going to see you again? Tell me," he demanded to know.

"No, no it's not." I responded.

"I'm going call you later tonight. Is that okay?" he asked.

He did.

We talked on the phone for a long time about the night we had and the days before it. All of a sudden, my other line rang. The male party asked: "Angie, what are you doing?"

I was confused because it didn't sound like Santana, but I knew that the only other guy who had my telephone number was Pucker (on the other line).

The male party opposite Pucker started laughing in my ear. I was really confused then. It was Pucker using his parent's line trying to confuse me. When we got back to our line he said to me: "Angie, I notice that you were nervous-real nervous, why? Why were you so nervous?"

I didn't have a clear answer for him, but I did not tell him that I thought he was Santana either. We talked for a while longer, and then got off the phone.

We ended up cozying up on the phone pretty much the same time everyday-routinely- until my schedule changed because I had gotten a job at the hamburger joint that I had applied for work at, the same night I *officially* met him.

You see, we had originally first saw one another once while shopping for sneakers for Santana one Saturday afternoon-back when I was pregnant and home on one of my weekends from the pregnant jail.

He and Wes were in the sneaker store following Santana and me around every section that we turned to walk through. Pucker would make his way across from me-forcing me into eye contact. I managed to ignore him for a long time, but it was obvious that he was not going to leave the store until I acknowledged his presence at some point. I decided to look back at him, and he looked at me like a baby deer caught in headlights. I kept Santana preoccupied with conversation representative of my being his personal shopper, slash fashion critic, slash buyer; so as to distract him away from this guy and his buddy who totally invaded my space.

I didn't think much of him at the time because he looked like an older guy. And by this time (and years into a relationship of normalcy with Santana); it was like my crushes on older guys and my flings with girls, was [what I thought it was]: a phase that would soon pass. So in that sneaker store, Pucker (in my eyes) was merely another cute older guy trying to get my attention. And I did not want to give Pucker the same opportunity that I gave the last older guy that sequestered me the last time I was in a store with Santana. It was a nightmare for me.

It happened quite some time before I was to report off to the pregnant jail. I was no where near showing-in the face or stomach.

Santana and I had walked around to the store to buy all the things to calm and satisfy my cravings I was having: vinegar, pickles, peppermints and plain potato chips. Out of nowhere appeared this older man (who invaded both of our spaces as well). He looked at Santana with his arm around me then looked at me as if he had a flashback and remembered his own daughter was once in love the way were. He had a few choice words for me:

"Don't let this young man ruin your life! Don't let him mess your life up before you get to live it! You bea-u-ti-ful girl you! Don't let him get you pregnant and make your life go down the drain! Don't do it!" yelled this stranger- sounding like the ghost of my estranged dad who would rather burn in hell than to know that I was in the condition that I was in.

It caught both Santana and me by surprise and ruined my day. I was already waning in and out and back and forth about what I was going to do about the pregnancy. This all was too much for me. I looked around for my dad in that store. Santana and I hurriedly walked out having bought nothing. My taste buds were even affected: my cravings were no longer. I just wanted to go home and finish off the cry that had begun the moment I turned away from that strange man and burst through the doors of that store to head home. Santana was so hurt. That scene both haunted and traumatized the both of us. Neither one of us said a word to each other about it-ever again. He just held me while I cried myself to sleep.

So when Santana and I were sequestered in that sneaker store as Pucker followed us around; I would be damned if this was going to be a repeat of what had happened just a short time right before. Uh uh-no how! No way! I insisted. So I broke Puckers forceful eye-contact then coached Santana into picking out the nearest sneaker, and we hauled ass out of that store.

But Pucker seemed to reappear what seemed like every other time Santana and me would go for a walk around the block and down to the (haunted) corner store.

From the moment we would make it to the left side of the street to begin our walk down on the long main street, like clockwork-this blue vehicle would be out in the distance blasting this classic jam by a group called "Cameo." As lyrics would play: "*Back-back-and-Fourth-and-Fourth. Our loves goes: Back-back-and-Fourth-Fourth. As we go...Back-back-and-Fourth-Fourth...*" I could tell when it would be moving closer to us, because they would sound clearer-back by a lot of base from his speakers. After about the third time this had happened, when I would hear it-my heart would begin to beat faster. Because just as disregarding to Santana's presence he was in the sneaker store-he was that same way when he would see us walking. It's just that when we were in the sneaker store, I had no idea that he was that *same* guy-all that time.

But this day in particular that he had come down the street blasting his music, it all came together-it was him, yet again. Each time we would see him, I would just lower my head and hold Santana's hand tightly, and he would grab mine even tighter. Even though Pucker was evasive, Santana knew I didn't know him-so we both just ignored him.Pucker refused to be ignored though. His face was becoming more common to me; popping up in strange places all over the city. This next time, from behind the kitchen of a chicken joint he was working at. He was peeking out at me looking like Tyrin Turner peeking from behind the fence in awe of Janet and her crew in that Rhythm Nation video. It was strange-he was strange.

This time however, I was not with Santana. I was with my oldest brother's girlfriend-out shopping. It was the same day that my mom and Dana's mom's had Santana sequestered in the house, torturing him by breaking the fake news to him that I was gone out on a date to explore my options. Ironically, I *was* out without Santana, but rather, *being* explored:

"Hi, how are you doing?" he asked, feeling like it was his lucky day.

"I've seen you before! I've seen you before! Can I talk to you for a second?" he said, excitedly and as if his double-confirming that he had seen me before was enough to have earned him the right to have my hand in conversation.

I didn't respond to him, but rather, acted as if I didn't hear him; fidgeting through my purse as if I was preoccupied and digging for something-do or die.

"Can I be your friend?" he asked-urgently. It was so awkward.

I thought he was weird-because he was so eager and excited. But he was simply trying to get in on this first open opportunity he had seen me without Santana-which was a rarity for anybody to see.

I looked up at him and snapped at him: "I have the same boyfriend!"

He kept on insisting:

"I can be your friend. Can I be your friend? I can be your friend," he kept insisting-impatiently and awkwardly as if he was bargaining at his last chance at life.

I scolded him with my eyes and gave him the look of death. Because although it wasn't visible to him, little did he know, I had a possibility growing inside of me and it felt gross to me-having him in my face way.

We made it out of the chicken joint without my being plucked.

Pucker refused to be ignored however.

He appeared again-the day Shana and me were up at the mall shopping and picking up job applications. We ended up, last, in Walgreens. At the end of the store aisle I saw a man staring down the isle as if he knew either Shana or me. I couldn't make out that I knew him and I was sure he didn't know me, so I moved out of his view and stood closer to Shana and whispered to her: "Girl, you didn't take nothing did you? 'Cause it's a man in here way down at the end of the isle-following us from isle to isle!"

I had to double-check on that with Shana because she was cunning as they come. She was a very sweet girl with a soft-spoken and delicate way about her, but you had to watch her. She could steal the clothes off your ass and have you walking around not knowing you were naked.

Once, she borrowed a pair of my sneakers and I called her up to get them back from her. She did me one better-she brought them to me. She allowed me (and went out of her way) to make me see that she was returning them by sliding them right back under my bed. But sometime during her visit, she stole them right back from me. She was sneaky like that-so, you had to watch Shana.

"Girl I didn't take anything! I swear-she insisted.

I responded: "Girl, he keeps looking down this isle at us like he knows one of us-or something."

She squinted and looked down the isle but he had walked away. Coast clear.

Another guy walked down the isle, and up on Shana:

"Hi Wes!" yelled Shana into the guys face, they hugged.

She introduced us.

"I'm in here with my dude-you guys hanging out longer? How are you getting home?" asked Wes.

From the other end of the isle, that *same* man walked towards us slowly.

He nodded and spoke to Shana as if he knew her. She spoke back to him. Wes was whispering in her ear.

Low and behold, it was that *same* guy who drives up and down my street, who works at the chicken joint and disregards my boyfriend.

This time, I was outnumbered-everyone knew each other except me. Confidently, patiently and like a gentleman, he gave me his hand, and introduced himself to me by name.

I replied: "Hi," I said quickly, throwing my hand up then down: quickly.

"Angie is it okay if Wes takes us home?" asked Shana-in front of everybody.

I pulled her to the end of the isle:

"That tall man always tries to talk to me girl! No! Not if he's with him!"

I laughed and gasped-thinking of how he seemed to show up

everywhere I seemed to be.

In her high pitched voice, Shana replied:

"Girl that aint no man! That's Wes' and n'em's boy. They all grew up together. They're all around the same age. He's only about a year or two older than you and me! He just looks older than us. He is **so** fine! All the girls chase him. He is fine! I don't know what you're talking about! You'd better get on with that one if he's chasing you like that!"

I laughed and said:

"He's so hairy and tall. Look at all that shadow hair on his face. He's got hair all on his arms and shit girl. What sixteen to eighteen year-old boy looks like that!" I cringed.

Shana thought that was the funniest things she had heard all day.

We walked out and over to Wes' car. Hairy got happy-thinking he was going to be able to sit next to me in that back seat that he stuffed himself into with space left for me. Before seating could take its course, I told Shana to switch places with me so that I could sit in the front with her friend Wes-who was driving. And she could sit stuffed in the back with happy Hairy. She agreed. We got situated and starting heading home.

From the back seat, Hairy's long arm kept reaching for my arm.

He kept begging for conversation in that same bargaining and impatient way he did at the chicken joint that day. I would short answer his constant questions with my head turned downward and to the left, then I'd turn quickly back to the right to look out of the window.

We pulled up to Shana's house and I hurriedly opened that car door to get away from that man.

"Could I PLEASE talk to you for a second, one second-PLEASE," he pleaded as if he could not take the chase anymore. I looked at him and squinted my eyes as if I was seeing if I could trust him:

"Yeah…" I replied.

He looked surprised, and looked me in the eyes as if he trying to trust that I would not yell: "Psyche!"

I didn't.

We stood outside the apartment talking small talk.

"May I switch phone numbers with you?" he asked.

"I keep telling you that I have a boyfriend. I can't call you. And you can't call me!" I said-firmly, desperately hoping that it was enough to make him go away and I would never see him again.

"Please, let me call you. Call me then-please, I just want to talk you soooo bad," he pleaded.

I paused. I was trying to think of a question to ask him that would be a perfect exit and way out for me. We went at it-and fast-like a game of talking tennis:

"Do you have a girlfriend?"

"No."

"Why?"

"We just broke up."

"What was her name?"

"Yolanda."

"Why did y'all break up?"

"It just wasn't working out."

He was ready. He *refused* to lose-knowing that he would never get another chance at me like this again. I paused for a second then mechanically gave him my phone number while still squinting my eyes, and looking him in his.

He called me that night and the next few nights.

I decided that I liked him after all. He was good-looking and it was something awkwardly sexy about him that I could not resist. And the way he would talk to me would be like he was pulling my arm-afraid that if he let go, he would never talk to me again. I could tell that he liked me a lot. During one of our conversations, it turned out that he lived in the next community over from me. We joked about him stalking me and clocking me down to the usual time of day I would be walking to the corner store-which typically would be the time Santana made it up to the house after work, and we would go on our daily walk and talk.

I would laugh-listening to his awkward methodology and things he was telling me he was doing trying to get to me and how he had narrowed down the proximity of where I lived. Little did he know, at that time, all those times that he would stalk me and Santana walking down to the corner store, I was craving something vinegary, salty, pepperminty and pickled in taste. My possibility would be sending me to the store almost the same time everyday with that craving (unbeknownst to him) but I did not tell him that part...

Day by day, however, I warmed up to him-letting him in on everything but that. We talked about everything and enjoying getting to know one another.

Although I enjoyed our talks and thoroughly enjoyed our first night over at Shana's house and every other time we would get together, all bets were off when it came down to actually discussing Santana and me.

Pucker had no idea that all those months he was stalking me; I was with-child. He had no idea about all the transitions, transformations and changes I had gone through in my life during all those *very* same times he was pursuing me. And as far as I was concerned, none of it was his business or a topic in our many lengthy conversations in getting to know one another. The fact still remained (and as he had already known) I still had that same boyfriend. And he had no idea that by the time we first got together over Shana's mom's house that day, I was no longer with-child.

But he had a secret too. All that time I was keeping a secret from him-he was keeping a secret from me too: a girl at the hamburger joint I had applied to and was working at. My new friend who too, worked there with me...

OTHER BOOKS BY ANGELA SHERICE:

Doing It! Mind-Blowing Sex Tips You Will Never Forget (The Fine Art of Intimate Sex)
ISBN 978 09709806 49
Sex Guide | Sex Instruction

Sequel to Angie Situation (INNOCENCE)

Angie Situation (NAIVETE')
ISBN: 978 09709806 56
Fiction Biographical | Drama

First Things First:
Discovering Your Karma Mission And Purpose in Life
ISBN: 978 09709806 32

Astrology | New Age| Personal Success | New Thought | Spirituality | Metaphysics

~ABOUT the AUTHOR~

Angela Sherice is a writer and expressionist of:
Erotic, Self-Efficacious, Introspective, Reflective and Metaphysical
Literature.

Ingest. Feel Empowered. Be Enlightened. Get Inspired.

Get acquainted with her by visiting:
http://WWW.ANGELASHERICE.COM

www.ingramcontent.com/pod-product-compliance
Lightning Source LLC
Chambersburg PA
CBHW031300170626
46807CB00001B/231